Dan'l was the first to glance up at the cliff, and what he saw confirmed his worst fears. The west summit was lined with war-painted Sioux.

"They're here," Dan'l shouted. "Get the long guns!" The words were barely out of his mouth when a rain of arrows came falling on them from above, plunging into the muddy ground, the wagons, and Gustav Dorf's chest.

They all heard the arrow whistle to its mark and thud into the German's torso. It passed almost entirely through him, and he stood, looking down at its feathered end, as if trying to grasp the significance of what had happened.

"Dorf!" Spencer shouted, but Dorf fell onto his face in the mud, the arrowhead protruding from his back.

"He's dead!" Dan'l said loudly. "Get your damn guns!"

The next moments were chaos, as they all ran for their rifles stacked nearby. Dan'l's Kentucky Rifle hung on the side of the wagon nearest to him, and he had it in hand in seconds, priming and readying it.

Another shower of arrows came down, several flaming. One caught the canvas of a wagon and set it ablaze.

"Jesus!" Padgett exclaimed. "They're everywhere up there!"

"That ain't the main force!" Dan'l called out. *"That's* the main force!" When they all looked where he pointed, they saw the mounted warriors at the mouth of the ravine, only fifty yards away. There were well over fifty of them.

Other Books in *Leisure's DAN'L BOONE: THE LOST WILDERNESS TALES* series:
A RIVER RUN RED
ALGONQUIN MASSACRE
DEATH AT SPANISH WELLS

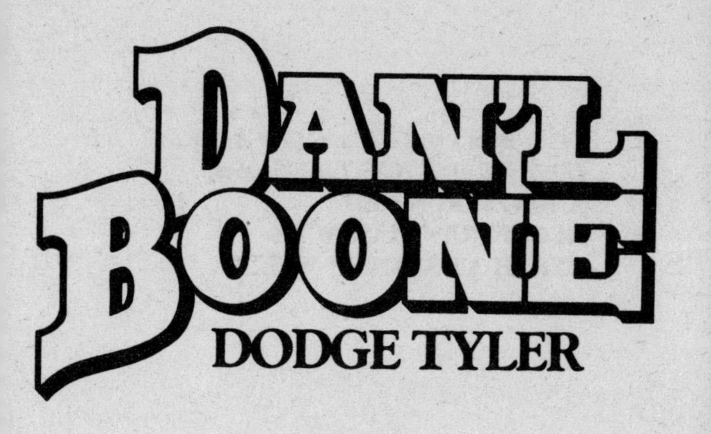

DODGE TYLER

WINTER KILL

LEISURE BOOKS NEW YORK CITY

A LEISURE BOOK®

October 1996

Published by

Dorchester Publishing Co., Inc.
276 Fifth Avenue
New York, NY 10001

Printed in the United States of America.

WINTER KILL

Prologue

The bearded frontiersman sat on the narrow stoop before his cabin and carefully cleaned the Kentucky rifle that lay across his knees. As he worked, he watched the approaching rider. Gradually the horseman loomed larger, coming through the corn, rocking in his saddle. Finally the rider stopped just a few yards away. He wore a bowler hat and wire spectacles; he gave the impression of being a preacher.

"They told me in town where to find you. Are you really the great Indian fighter and explorer Dan'l Boone?"

The old man set the rifle aside and squinted up at the mounted stranger through clear, penetrating eyes. Boone was bareheaded; his hair was thinning and almost white. He had a tooth missing at the corner of his mouth.

"What if I was?" he asked suspiciously.

The rider dismounted, retrieved a large notebook from a saddlebag, and came up onto the porch, where the old fellow sat on a willow chair. The musket leaned against the log wall of the cabin beside the frontiersman, but Boone saw no need for it.

"I'm Adam Hollis. I've come all the way from Boston to find you, Dan'l. I'm pleased and mighty proud to finally meet up with you."

"I don't talk to newspaper people." When Hollis smiled, Dan'l liked the eyes behind the glasses.

"I'm just a library clerk. Mind if I shake the riding cramps out on your porch?" Hollis asked.

When Dan'l motioned grudgingly to a second chair not far away, Hollis slumped onto it and stretched his legs. The aroma of cooking food came to him from inside. He looked out past the cornfield to the woods and admired the view.

"Thanks," he said wearily. "People have been coming to me for years, selling me bits and pieces of your life story because of my special interest."

Dan'l grunted. "Most of them is selling swamp fog."

Hollis grinned. "I figured as much. But all those stories got my curiosity up, sir, and I came to realize your own story could be one of the great untold legends of the frontier. So I spent my life savings to get out here, hoping you might talk to me some about yourself."

The old hunter regarded Hollis sidewise. "You want to write down all that stuff? Hell, ain't nobody'll want to read about them times. We're in a whole different century, by Jesus. Nobody gives a tinker's damn about that early stuff no more."

Hollis shook his head. "You'd be surprised, Dan'l. You're already something of a legend—even in Europe, I hear. But I think that's just the beginning. If you let me document your life while it's all still in your head, generations to come will know what wild adventures you had."

The great hunter rose from his chair. He no longer enjoyed the renowned robustness or grace of his youth, but he still looked as hard as sacked salt. Dan'l went to the far end of the porch and stared out into the green forest beyond the fields, the kind of country that had been his home for all of his life. He finally turned back to Hollis.

"What would you do with these stories once you got it all writ down on paper?"

Hollis shrugged. "Publish them, but only if you wanted me to. At least we'd have them all down. For safekeeping, you might say."

Dan'l shook his head. "I can't say I'd want them in no book. Not in my lifetime. Not the real stuff. Most of them are too damned private. There's too many people out there who might not want them told. Or they might be moved to correct them, so to speak. Come out with their own versions so they would look better."

A resolve settled over Hollis. "All right. It can all be hidden away till long after you're gone if that's what you'd like. Then if the stories don't get lost somewhere down the line, maybe they will all come out later, at a better time, and be given over to some book people. That's what I would hope for."

Dan'l thought for a long moment. "You'd promise that in writing?"

Hollis nodded. "I will."

A laugh rattled out of the old man's throat. "I guess you'd want even the bear mauling and the wolf eating and the nasty ways some redskins liked to treat a white man when they caught him?"

"Yes, everything," Hollis said.

"There's treks into the West, the far side of the Mississippi, that hardly a man alive now knows about," Dan'l said, reflecting. "And these eyes have seen things that nobody's going to believe."

Hollis was becoming excited. "I'd want it all."

Dan'l took a deep breath in and called, "Rebecca! You better put a big pot of coffee on! Looks like we got company for a spell!"

As Hollis relaxed and smiled, Dan'l heaved himself back onto the primitive chair and closed his eyes for a moment. Finally, he said, "I reckon we might as well get going on it then."

Hollis was caught off guard. He fumbled in a

pocket for a quill pen and a small ink pot, then opened up the thick but empty notebook. Hollis dipped his pen into the ink and waited.

"Most of it happened in about thirty years," Dan'l said quietly. "The important stuff. The stuff most folks don't know nothing about. That's when I got this raw hunger for the wild places, the far-off country where no settlers had been.

"I was just a stripling when I first started hearing about the land west of the Alleghenies," Dan'l said, his gaze wandering off toward the woods.

Hollis did not hesitate or interrupt with any questions. As the old man talked, he just began writing steadily in the thick book with an urgency he had never before experienced. He had to get every sentence down exactly as Dan'l said it. He could not miss a single word.

Chapter One

Dan'l Boone glanced past the other faces gathered around the buffalo-dung campfire, slowly rubbed the frost out of his hands, and once more squinted out across the vast expanse of grassland beyond the wagons. There was something out there. He had heard the almost inaudible wail of a distant coyote, and was trying to assess its meaning. Coyotes did not usually make any noise at breakfast time. He had learned that on an expedition to Santa Fe, over a year ago. He sniffed the air carefully, as a cougar might, and a slight frown crawled onto his square, weathered face with its graying full beard. He could make out a few turkey buzzards out there on the snowy-white horizon, seemingly painted against the sky, hovering as they would over a military column.

It was a quiet morning. The two-wagon party had encamped on this open, unprotected ground the night before with no thought of weather, but then a stiff wind had sprung up unexpectedly, and they had awakened to find a light carpet of snow had blown in on them, and covered their ground-sheets.

That early snow, though, was not the only thing bothering Dan'l as he stared past the other men at the fire.

"Everything all right, Dan'l?"

The man who spoke was Frank Davison, the leader of the small expedition. He was rather tall and lean, with silver in his hair and goatee, and everybody called him "Colonel." He had commanded the Carolina Militia at Salisbury, and had fought with Dan'l at Fort Duquesne as a lieutenant, and later in the Continental Army. He was a land investor now, and had brought this party west to find arable land, and to map a long stretch of the North Platte River. He had been guided to the area by Dan'l and a Lakota Sioux shaman turned scout.

Dan'l hunched his broad shoulders. Sleeping on the ground for thirty years had put a misery in his back, and he felt it on this cold morning. He had lines in his strong face, put there by years on the wilderness trail, but his physique was still hard and muscular, and he had more stamina than he'd had even as a fuzz-faced kid.

"I don't really know, Colonel," Dan'l said finally. Davison and the three other men at the fire eyed him soberly. Over by the wagons, several other men were attending to morning duties. "It's just a feeling I got, more than anything else. That wind might've blowed in something more than snow."

The trail boss, a tough-looking fellow named Wade Spencer, shook his head and spat into the melting snow at his feet. He was thickset and beefy, and had a flattened nose from a long-ago saloon fight. Also, most of his right ear was gone, lost in a knife fight with a Kiowa. He thought of himself as a great Indian fighter, and resented Dan'l's similar reputation. Davison had hired Dan'l personally in St. Louis, and Spencer had disliked him immediately. He was a couple of years younger than Dan'l, and twenty pounds heavier.

"You been having a lot of gut feelings," he said sourly to Dan'l. "Might be better if you depended on what your eyes and ears tell you. You talk a lot like that goddamn Indian."

Frank Davison cast a somber look at Spencer. He had known little about the man when he hired him in St. Louis, except that he had plenty of experience. "For Christ's sake, Spencer. Why don't you let it go?"

The fourth man at the fire, a German immigrant mapmaker named Gustav Dorf, laughed easily, which further irritated Davison. The fifth man, a very skilled surveyor named Henry Munro, looked over at Dan'l to see his reaction to all of this, but found Dan'l's face impassive.

Spencer was not finished, though. "I thought *you* was boss of this outfit," he said to Davison. "Not this Kentucky farmer. He don't know no more about this country than the rest of us, but he's all the time spouting his feelings and notions." He turned to Dan'l. "You been warning us about the Sioux for over a week now, and there ain't none come. You slowed us up considerable. And now you're worried about a goddamn inch of snow."

"By Jesus, Spencer—" Davison warned him.

But the German, Dorf, interrupted him. "Spencer is right, Colonel." He was quite tall, athletic-looking, and blond under a dark hat. If any member of the party was more arrogant than Spencer, it was Dorf. He had helped compile a good map of Tennessee, and had been on a previous trek with Spencer. He usually sided with him in any dispute. "We came here to map the North Platte, and we have not finished. We must ignore any risks from the Indians or the weather, and get on with our planned work."

Small, bespectacled Munro looked at Dorf. "Ignore the Indians?" he said doubtfully, in a rather high voice. In his fifties, he was a nondescript Easterner who knew George Washington personally, as Dan'l did, and had done most of his work in Virginia. He had watery eyes, a pale face, and coughed irregularly but persistently. "Couldn't that be rather dangerous?"

Spencer glared at him. "Why don't you just keep to looking through that glass of yours, and sticking sticks in the ground, and let the men worry over the Sioux."

The German laughed again.

Dan'l looked at his thick hands and then at Davison. "I ain't trying to tell nobody what to do. I'm just pointing out that the situation ain't the same as it was a week ago. It ain't just the inch of snow. It's how fast the leaves fell, and the furry look of the squirrels. And you notice the way the buffalo is moving away from open ground? I think the winter's coming on fast this year. If we get caught in it, we could've bought ourselfs a peck of trouble."

"Squirrels!" Spencer growled. He had learned little about nature's ways in his years on the trail. "You see what I'm talking about?" he asked Davison.

Davison sighed heavily. Spencer had not agreed with one thing Dan'l had said recently. But he had mixed feelings himself. "I would hate to quit early, of course," he said quietly, looking at the ground. "Some of the richest farmland on the river might lie to the west yet. If we let the weather stop us now, Dan'l, it would take a second expedition to find out."

"That's damn right," Spencer said firmly. He

took his crumpled, dark hat off, and ran a hand through thinning hair. "I say we take our chances on the snow."

He spoke directly to Dan'l, but Dan'l was no longer listening to them. He rose slowly from his camp stool and poured the last of a cup of chicory coffee onto the low fire, and it sizzled there. He set the cup on the stool and stared hard out over the prairie. He thought he had seen something out there, under the vultures. He let his gaze drift over the rest of their camp, to the two wagons, the tethered horses, the men putting saddlery on and loading equipment. Two professional hunters, handpicked by Dan'l. Four riflemen, ex-soldiers from the Continental Army. A black slave of Davison called Raven, and the Sioux guide hired by Dan'l, called Skin Walker.

He wondered if they would be enough.

If he was right.

"Now what, Boone?" Spencer asked with sarcasm.

"There's something out there," Dan'l said distractedly.

"Oh, hell," the German said.

Dan'l the Kentuckian paid no attention. He adjusted a black Quaker hat on unruly, thick hair and picked up his long rifle, which leaned against a dead aspen stump. He was dressed entirely in rawhides, with fringed sleeves and trousers. His boots came up to his knees, and the right one contained a sheath that held a skinning knife. On a heavy gunbelt, in an oiled holster, hung an Annely eight-shot revolver, which he had carried ever since the Santa Fe trip. Standing there with the rifle in hand now, he looked very dangerous.

While he stood there peering past them, they all rose, too, and turned toward the prairie.

"Something?" Davison said uneasily. "What do you see, Dan'l?"

"There!" Dan'l said, conviction in his voice now. "See them specks on the horizon? I reckon that's the Indians you said wouldn't come, Spencer."

They all squinted hard, and finally Davison whispered, "Holy God!"

"Sonofabitch," Spencer growled.

Over by the wagons, the ex-shaman, Skin Walker, dressed very much like Dan'l except for the eagle feather in a narrow-brim hat, pointed stoically toward the far horizon. "Sioux!" he said in a level, moderate tone.

"Oh, Jesus!" Henry Munro gasped.

Stopping in mid-stride, carrying several pots and pans, the husky-looking Raven stared, too. "Oh, Lord!"

"There must be thirty of them," Dan'l said, and began priming the rifle.

"Indians!" Davison called out. "Find your guns! Draw the wagons up together! Unload some crates for cover! Move!"

Suddenly the camp was in chaos. Dan'l helped

pull a wagon up near its mate, and in seconds the soldiers were busy stacking crates and boxes at their open ends. Skin Walker had the presence of mind to place a box of ammunition on the ground in the small enclosure formed by the wagons.

Dan'l was primed and cocked, and stood watching the riders approach. He had been right. There were over thirty of them, and they were Lakota Sioux, the same as Skin Walker, whom Dan'l had hired at a small trading post west of St. Louis. As the horses were led into the small compound, the mounted warriors halted about fifty yards from the camp.

One of the hunters, a tough-looking fellow named Cassidy, leaned the barrel of his Heinrich flintlock rifle on the end of a wagon, and watched the invaders. "Hey! They stopped!" he called out to the others.

The others were all lining up to defend, some kneeling, others standing. All four ex-soldiers, who had been hired primarily to guard the wagon party, had Charleville rifled muskets that had been used in the Revolution just a few years ago. They were all loaded and primed.

"Maybe they're friendly," a young man named Hawkins said nervously.

Dan'l turned to him. "No. They heard about us out here, and they're here for blood. They want our horses and our gear."

"You don't know that," Spencer said from nearby.

But Dan'l, whose eyes were like a hawk's, had already seen the war paint on their faces, red and black and yellow. And now a bold-looking young warrior in their fore raised his lance into the air above his head.

They had no way of knowing it, but the young warrior was Iron Knife, second son of Sitting Bear, one of the most powerful Sioux chiefs of that territory.

Iron Knife lowered the arm swiftly, and a war cry issued from his throat. It was echoed by his warriors as they started galloping toward the camp.

"Shit!" Spencer said in a low voice.

"They don't have guns," Dan'l said loudly. They had heard that these northern Indians did not have firearms yet. "That's to our advantage! Don't wait! Fire now!"

"Yes, fire now!" Davison repeated.

In the next second, a volley of explosions ripped the cold air in the encampment, white smoke lofting from the long guns, and a third of the galloping Sioux were punched off their ponies, hitting the ground in the shallow snow.

Horses reared and ran off, and some warriors reined in, shocked by what the guns had done. But then the whole party headed on in toward the camp.

The air was full of flying arrows that thudded into wagon boards, canvas tops, and the ground. One hit a camp horse in the flank, and another plunged into the chest of one of Davison's riflemen, the point exiting behind his right arm. The fellow dropped his gun and began walking around in circles in the compound, as if trying to find cover.

The Sioux had reached the wagons now, and were circling them, screaming and shooting at the Davison party. Two more warriors were knocked off their mounts when Dan'l and Cassidy hit their second targets after re-loading. An arrow hissed into the compound, just missed Dan'l, and thunked into Davison's side, missing his floating rib and almost passing all the way through him. He yelled out in pain and fell to the ground.

"Kill the bastards!" Spencer yelled. "Kill them all!"

Dan'l threw down the Kentucky rifle that he had been fighting with, drew the Annely, and primed it quickly. The long guns were no good for close-in fighting. They took too long to load. He, Davison, Spencer, and the German all wore side arms, and that was an advantage, but Davison was out of the fight for the moment. Both the others followed Dan'l's lead and were priming and firing the small guns. A warrior rode right into the camp, jumping his pony over a pile of crates, and hurled a long lance at one of the riflemen as he galloped through. The lance pierced the ex-soldier's chest just below his heart, tearing up inwards and breaking ribs, and then stuck in the ground behind him, leaving him impaled, hanging off the ground. Dan'l turned with the rider as he passed, fired the Annely, and hit the Indian in the back of the head, blowing his face off.

The Sioux were getting hit with regularity. The scene was a wild one, with the whooping and yelling of the attackers, the thunder of their hoofbeats, and the banging of rifle and pistol fire.

Davison was back on his feet, priming his side arm. His wound was not fatal. "Keep firing! Don't let them in here! Keep firing!"

But two more did come in. Iron Knife himself, looking primitive and deadly, full eagle-feather headdress fanning out behind him, rode right in among them and hurled a battle hatchet at Cassidy's sidekick, a hunter named Logan. Logan fired his Heinrich rifle at the same moment, and the hot ball of lead nicked Iron Knife's left arm. Then the tomahawk buried itself in Logan's chest.

Logan looked down at the handle of the hatchet curiously, but without any seeming concern in his square face. Then he toppled onto his face.

Iron Knife stopped for an instant. "Death to the white face!" he screamed. Then his pony jumped the barricade at the far end. Spencer fired after him, but missed.

Almost simultaneously another hard-looking

warrior came in, knocking Spencer down with his pony. But it was Dan'l he had targeted, because Dan'l was killing so many attackers. As Dan'l raised his Annely to fire, the Indian threw himself off his pony, and came down heavily onto Dan'l, knocking him to the ground.

Dan'l lost the Annely in the fall, and suddenly he had the Indian on top of him, a tomahawk raised over his head, ready to split Dan'l's skull wide open. Dan'l could smell the sweat of the Indian, and see the deadly look in his dark eyes, only inches away. But Dan'l grabbed at the arm that held the weapon and stopped it. Then he slid the skinning knife out of its boot sheath as the Indian strained to bring the hatchet down onto Dan'l's head. Dan'l got the knife up between them, and in a quick, fluid motion, shoved it up under the Indian's chin, into his brainpan.

The Sioux's eyes widened, an ugly sound issued from the depths of his throat, and he fell off Dan'l, then lay on the ground beside him, limbs flailing for a moment.

Iron knife gave a signal, with over half of his warriors dead or dying around the wagons, and the survivors all rode off in the direction they had come, just as abruptly as they'd arrived, kicking up dirt and snow as they galloped away.

Dan'l struggled to his feet and looked around. Two riflemen lay in awkward positions in pools of their own blood, as did the hunter called Logan.

Davison was leaning heavily against the side of a wagon, holding his side and looking very pale. Another rifleman, named Padgett, had received a shallow arm wound.

There were dead and dying Sioux everywhere, including the one at Dan'l's feet. The area looked like a slaughterhouse.

"We drove them off!" an excited Hawkins exclaimed. He was one of the two riflemen still standing. "We beat them, didn't we?"

Spencer gave him a sardonic look and heaved his thick frame against a wagon wheel.

"Goddamn it!" Davison said thickly.

Dan'l came over to him. "Are you okay, Colonel?"

Davison nodded. "I think so." He looked out over the prairie, to where the Sioux had disappeared, and his face showed his frustration and anger. He glanced over toward Spencer. "Don't worry about the Sioux. Huh, Spencer?"

Spencer made no reply.

"Let's get this mess cleaned up," Davison said.

It was only a few minutes later, when they were dragging bodies out of the enclosure, that rifleman Hawkins knelt over the Sioux Dan'l had killed with the knife, and stared at the Indian's left hand.

"Hey! Look at this!"

He pulled a gold ring off the Indian's finger and held it up for the others to see. Abe Cassidy came over carrying his Heinrich. Like Dan'l, he did not even look winded.

"What the hell you got there?" he said in his gruff voice. Even though Dan'l had recruited him and the dead Logan for this expedition because they were experienced hunters and could help find game for the party, Cassidy now seemed a cold fish to Dan'l, a hard fellow more like Spencer than Dan'l liked.

Hawkins rose and held the ring toward him. "Ain't that an emerald setting?"

Cassidy took it, and his eyes narrowed down on it. "I'll be damned."

Raven and Skin Walker had been dragging the corpse of a rifleman out of the wagon area. They came over to look, and Raven's eyes widened. "What is it?"

Skin Walker, a middle-aged but tough-looking Sioux, lean and sinewy, looked over Hawkins's shoulder. When he had been a shaman, he had cured and tanned the skin of tribal enemies killed in battle, donned the skin like a cloak, and danced in it for war ceremonies. That was how he had gotten his unusual name. The white men just called him Walker, which made him seem almost civilized. He helped Dan'l find the best routes to where they were going, and Dan'l liked him.

"Get back to your pots, nigger," Cassidy said to Raven. Then he turned to Spencer, who was just approaching. "Take a look at this."

Skin Walker saw clearly what it was, grunted sourly, and returned to the corpse with Raven. Walker liked the black man's company. He had never seen a black man until he hired on this expedition, and was endlessly fascinated by him.

Spencer took possession of the ring. "Is it an emerald?" he said to Cassidy.

"I think so."

"Son of a bitch," Spencer breathed. He looked down at the dead Indian. "Where would he get this?"

Padgett and Dan'l were beyond the perimeter of the wagons, making sure all the Sioux out there were dead. Davison was placing a bandage on his side, and the surveyor, Henry Munro, was helping him. But now Dorf came over to the small knot of men over the dead Indian.

"It's Spanish," Dorf said with finality.

The others all looked at him.

"It is well known that they were here first. Maybe not this far north, but they were here. That ring was taken off a Spaniard. Probably after they killed him."

Outside the wagons, they heard Padgett yell, "Hey, this one's alive!"

Dan'l, nearby, looked over at Padgett and began walking toward him. Davison and Spencer also looked up.

"Shoot him!" Spencer called out.

Padgett shrugged, raised the muzzle of his Charleville, and aimed it at the Indian's head.

"Hold it!" Dan'l barked.

Padgett looked over at him curiously.

"Get away from that man," Dan'l said, coming over to him.

The rifleman looked toward Spencer, who was already occupied again with the ring.

"What's going on?" Davison called out.

Dan'l came and stood over the Sioux. He was a young warrior, a nephew of Sitting Bear and cousin to Iron Fist. He had been shot in the thigh, but was otherwise unhurt. He had seen Dan'l save his life, and now regarded him quizzically as Dan'l looked down at him. Dan'l knew that some of these Sioux had learned some English from American trappers who had wandered into the area.

"You speak the white man's tongue?" Dan'l asked him.

The fellow hesitated, then nodded. "A few words."

"What's your name?"

"Pale Coyote," the Sioux responded. He grimaced in pain. His leg was bloody, and he lay in mud from the melting snow.

Dan'l nodded and turned to Padgett. "Take him into the campsite."

"What?" Padgett said. He was older than Hawkins, but a smaller man, slight and wiry-looking.

"You heard me," Dan'l said evenly.

Padgett stared down at the Indian for a moment, then followed orders. It was generally accepted that Dan'l outranked the hunters and riflemen escorts. Padgett helped the Sioux to his feet, and they went into camp with Dan'l following. The Indian limped badly. As he had gotten his feet under him, Dan'l had noticed a silver chain around his neck, with a pendant hanging from it.

Spencer saw them coming and frowned. "What the hell, Padgett! I told you to—"

"I stopped him," Dan'l said. "We don't execute prisoners where I come from."

When Padgett brought Pale Coyote over to them, Spencer saw the pendant hanging on the Indian's chest. "What's this redskin wearing?" He went up to Pale Coyote and yanked the chain off him. He held the pendant in his hand. "What's going on here?"

Pale Coyote had passed Skin Walker on the way in, and scowled deeply at him. There was no enemy more hated than a Sioux who had become a lackey of the paleface.

Davison and Munro came over, too. They all gathered around the dead Sioux on the ground, and the live one in Padgett's custody.

Dorf took the pendant from Spencer and examined it. "It looks like a Spanish coin."

"It's a piece of eight," Dan'l said. "I seen a couple of the old ones when I was in Santa Fe." He then looked at the emerald ring Spencer was still holding.

Davison was studying the two items, too. "What is all this?"

Spencer looked toward him. "Appears these Indians run onto some Spanish treasure, Colonel," he answered with a grin.

"Exactly so," Dorf agreed. "Does this one speak English?"

"A little," Dan'l told him.

Dorf grinned, too. "Then it is well we did not kill him, perhaps?" he said to Spencer.

Spencer rubbed at his stubbled chin, then scratched his half-ear. "Yeah. There could be more where this come from," he said thoughtfully.

Dan'l shook his head slowly. "Padgett, keep an eye on the Indian."

Padgett nodded and moved Pale Coyote off to the end of a wagon, still with the gun on him. Pale Coyote glanced back toward Dan'l, but Dan'l was taking Davison aside to discuss the Indian. The men around the dead Indian had lost interest in the live one now, and were examining the artifacts excitedly.

Dan'l had spoken briefly with Skin Walker, and now took Davison behind a wagon. "Let the Indian go. Walker says he's a nephew of Sitting Bear. It might buy us some goodwill till we get clear of this area."

Davison stroked his goatee. His light-colored, wide-brimmed hat almost hid his blue eyes. "You sure they won't take that as a sign of weakness?

Make them think of another attack?"

"You remember the Shawnee, Colonel. They respected a show of humanity."

Davison nodded. He had fought beside Dan'l in the second Fort Duquesne campaign, and knew the Shawnee well. Also, he respected Dan'l's judgment of the red man. It was one of the reasons he had asked Dan'l to guide this expedition, back in St. Louis.

"Well, I don't like the notion of executing prisoners, anyway, whether they're white or red."

Dan'l smiled. "Them was my thoughts."

"I'll speak to Spencer immediately. I figure on doing another couple days of mapping, and then head east, on your recommendation, Dan'l. We'll let the Indian know that. It could help."

There was a muffled scream from the other end of the compound, and they both turned toward it. Then they heard Spencer's angry voice.

"You tell us what you know, you dirty redskin!"

Davison exchanged a look with Dan'l.

"Oh, hell," Davison said.

Dan'l hurried to the other end of the wagons, and rounded the corner with Davison right behind him. Spencer and Dorf were standing before Pale Coyote, who was tied to the tailgate of a wagon. Padgett had been pushed to one side, and stood looking apologetically at Dan'l. Spencer had a knife in hand, and had sliced a large cross over the

Sioux's bare chest. Blood ran down his torso and onto his legs.

"What's going on here?" Davison said soberly.

The others stood off at a small distance, watching. Raven was wide-eyed, and Skin Walker looked very somber. Spencer looked at Davison.

"Don't pay us no mind, Colonel. We're questioning this goddamn Sioux."

Dorf grabbed the knife from Spencer. "You are going about it wrong, my friend. You must make him hurt. We will try his testicles. Savages put a high value on their sexual apparatus." He laughed, and lifted Pale Coyote's breechcloth.

Dan'l moved over to him, spun him around by the shoulder, and punched a thick fist into the taller man's face.

Dorf went down hard, with a look of absolute shock on his hard face. Then he stared up at Dan'l as if Dan'l had gone mad. "What the hell!"

"Damn you, Boone!" Spencer growled.

"We don't treat prisoners this way, by Jesus!" Dan'l said in a tight voice.

The German rose to his feet slowly, blood running from his nose. He was bigger and younger than Dan'l, and he had fire in his blue eyes. "I see I must teach you a lesson, Kentucky man."

"Dorf, stop it!" Davison said sharply.

But nobody was paying any attention to him. Dorf launched his big, athletic frame at Dan'l in a fury. Dan'l sidestepped with a fluidity that surprised all present, and then backhanded Dorf behind the left ear as he stumbled past, making an audible whacking sound. Dorf hurtled to the ground again, this time on his face.

But he was not finished. He had dropped the hunting knife when Dan'l hit him the first time, but now he found it on the ground. Bleeding and dizzy, he grabbed the weapon and rose unsteadily to his feet.

"I will cut your liver out!" he rasped hoarsely.

He came again, the knife out in front of him. Dan'l easily caught the knife hand, and bent it backwards as Dorf charged past. Dorf was thrown onto his back at Dan'l's feet, knocking the breath out of him, and suddenly the knife was in Dan'l's hand. He knelt over Dorf and shoved the point up against Dorf's cheek.

"You really want to die out here today?" Dan'l said softly into the German's face.

Spencer's eyes narrowed when he noted the ease with which the Kentuckian had dispatched the bigger, younger German.

Dorf hesitated, then shook his blond head.

Dan'l nodded. "Good," he said in a hard voice. He released his hold on Dorf, turned, and threw the knife toward the wagon. It impaled itself there, just beside the Sioux.

Dan'l got up and looked into Spencer's face. "We don't operate like this, Spencer!"

Dorf crawled off beside the wagon, shaken.

Spencer gave Dan'l a dark look. "What the hell do you mean, 'we'?" he said harshly. "You think you're running this outfit now?"

"No," Davison said coldly to Spencer. "But he knows I still do. And he's right. On this expedition, we don't torture prisoners. For any purpose."

Spencer came up very close to Davison. "You sure them is your words, Colonel? Or do they come from this Indian lover from Kentucky?"

Davison hesitated, showing his latent fear of this thug he had hired to run the expedition, and all present saw the hesitation.

"Untie that Indian," Davison finally said quietly.

Spencer turned and walked away, dark-visaged. "You do it, Colonel," he hurled over his shoulder.

Chapter Two

Chief Sitting Bear's village lay fifty miles to the west of the Davison encampment. It was a large collection of skin tipis and bark lodges, with a wide, circular lodge in its center, where the leader met for important palavers. Adjacent to the village was a pole corral that contained a couple hundred mustangs, broken from the wild but unshod, animals that would never reach the degree of tameness achieved by horses owned by the white man.

Yellow dogs ran free in the village, and ate scraps from meals cooked over open fires. Naked children played in the dirt compound, and women sat cross-legged before cooking pots and primitive looms.

They called themselves the Lakota, meaning "Allies." Since the early Spaniards had introduced the horse to the continent, they had become mounted warriors of the prairie, and other tribes kept out of their way. They were the undisputed rulers of the Great Plains.

Even though they had begun slash-and-burn farming, they still roamed about the grasslands, abandoning villages with every new season, seeking the best hunting. The buffalo was their lifeblood, and they considered the intrusion of the white man a threat to its existence.

On the gray afternoon of their attack on the Davison party, the tribe was celebrating. There was dancing and singing around a council fire, and feasting on buffalo steaks. Inside the big meeting lodge, Sitting Bear had called a formal meeting with his youngest son, Iron Knife. Also with him at that palaver were Eye of Hawk, his older son, and the head shaman of the village, a middle-aged man called Talking Sky.

Sitting Bear had put on a full, magnificent bald eagle headdress to talk to his people earlier, and still wore it at this meeting. He was in his forties, bronzed and muscular, with a long, bony face. His chest bore scars from great battles against Ojibwa and Crow as a young man. He wore beaded cloth trousers and skin moccasins, with rawhide leggings on his lower legs. Draped over his shoulders was an ermine skin, flawless in quality and combed out to exquisite softness.

Sitting Bear was the leader of all Sioux in that

area of the plains. He was powerful and much feared.

He sat at a low council fire in the center of the lodge, and the others shared the fire. On the dug-out floor where they sat, groundsheets of skins had been put down, which bore paintings of great hunts and bloody battles.

His two sons wore only breechcloths, leggings, and moccasins, and both had come bareheaded in deference to their father, except for headbands of beaded and worked rawhide. The young Iron Knife was flushed with the excitement of battle. His older brother, who was even bigger and more athletic-looking than Iron Knife, sat expressionless, showing no emotion, but wishing he had been with the war party when it came upon the white men. The tribe had tolerated earlier, single hunters in their territory, white men who had taught them English and Spanish. But they had warned earlier parties who came in numbers that they were not welcome. Now they treated all wagon expeditions with hostility.

The shaman, Talking Sky, sat near Sitting Bear, and looked very different from the others. He wore the flayed and tanned skin of a murdered mountain man over his shoulders and tied down along his arms. On top of his head he wore the light brown hair and scalp of the white face, and the man's skull hung from a rawhide thong on his chest.

It was the kind of thing Skin Walker had done as a younger man, when he was a shaman for this very tribe. The practice created powerful medicine, taking all the strong qualities of the deceased and concentrating them in a prayer to Siouan gods for good fortune. Skin walking had been brought from the southwest, and before that from the land of the Aztec. It was used with great reverence in dances and prayers, and extensively in the important Sun Dance, when they asked for success in hunting and in battle.

Talking Sky did not look bizarre to the others present. They knew he was making great magic for them, to help drive the white man from their buffalo ground, and they respected him for his ability to commune with the gods.

Talking Sky threw a powder into the fire. It sizzled, and white smoke rose and lofted to an opening in the bark-and-skin ceiling above them. He chanted in a singsong monotone, and they listened. Finally, he became silent.

Sitting Bear had been smoking a long brightly decorated pipe, with feathers and ribbons trailing from its stem. He put it down without offering it to his sons.

"You lost many warriors, Iron Knife," he said.

Iron Knife had expected this comment. He tried not to show his resentment of the criticism. "The white man had many guns, Father. Guns that spoke loudly and often. They killed many of us before we reached their camp."

Eye of Hawk grunted. "We have dealt with the barking sticks before. But our weapons matched them." He and Iron Knife were both members of the *akicita,* or warrior class. Their local society was labeled the Stronghearts, and they often went into battle wearing ermine-skin headdresses with antelope horns affixed. They were a proud group.

Iron Knife gave him a dark look. "My brave brother has not met this many guns, and such powerful ones. They had very long snouts, and could kill at a great distance. And there were small ones, like birds held in the hand, which could speak much more rapidly."

Sitting Bear clucked his tongue. "These whites have powerful medicine. Maybe they will not heed our warning."

"Do they hunt the Great Father Buffalo?" Talking Sky asked Iron Knife.

"We saw no skins in their camp," Iron Knife told him. "I believe if they hunt, it is only for meat. Like our own people."

"Last night under the full moon," Talking Sky said, "I shook the bones and smoked the pipe, and I had a vision."

They all looked toward him.

"I saw the white faces come like locusts upon the land. There were too many to fight, it was like a great plague. They slaughtered our buffalo and antelope by the millions, and laid the plains bare.

And there was great hunger and disease among our people. And our nation died."

Sitting Bear caught his gaze. "Is this true medicine?"

Talking Sky shook his head. "I do not know. It might be just a warning from the Yuwipi Night Gods. I saw a Winter Count painted on a buffalo robe, of the year's happenings in some future year, and the robe was empty of entries."

"It is an omen!" Eye of Hawk said excitedly. "If we do not heed it, we will perish as a nation. All white men must be driven from our land. No exceptions!"

Talking Sky reached into an antelope-udder pouch, and sprinkled some more powder onto the fire. He stared grimly at the white smoke. "These whites are not here for hunting. They want our land. It is in the smoke."

"The paleface has this strange notion," Sitting Bear said heavily, "that he can own the land. He does not understand that the land allows usage only by those who care for it."

"The white face is stupid!" Iron Knife said forcefully. "Even with his guns, he cannot beat the Lakota in open battle. We are his superior!"

"You mentioned that they have a devil man with them," Sitting Bear said to him.

Iron Knife nodded gravely. "His skin is black, like rich soil. And he has a face like a demon. He did not fight against us. He had no gun."

"That is because he does not need one to kill," Talking Sky said wisely. "He must have great medicine from the Nether World, to destroy with a look. Beware of him."

"There was also a brother there," Iron Knife added.

Sitting Bear regarded him curiously. "Yes?"

"You will remember the shaman Skin Walker. He left us in disgrace after taking a brother's woman to his bed without permission."

"That brother was my cousin," Talking Sky said grimly.

"He is with the white face now," Iron Knife went on. "I saw him clearly. He even used one of their guns against us."

"By the holy spirits!" Sitting Bear said.

"I hoped to kill him, but it was not possible."

"He is not important," Sitting Bear said. "He is a non-person."

"A non-person who leads the white face against us," Eye of Hawk said bitterly.

Before Sitting Bear could reply, a figure appeared in the doorway of the lodge, and a slim warrior entered, bending low to get through the doorway. "Excuse my presence, Great Chief."

Iron Knife turned. "Ah. It is Gray Wolf. I left him behind to spy on the white face camp from the river."

"Come in, my son," Sitting Bear said.

The warrior came and sat down, properly behind Sitting Bear's sons. He was slightly breathless, since he had just ridden into the village.

"Any news, brother?" Iron Knife asked him.

The warrior nodded. "I crept close in some small cottonwoods. They were torturing Pale Coyote."

"Aagh!" Iron Knife said bitterly. "I thought he was dead. Damn them!"

"They were looking at the Spanish relics they found. I think they were trying to find out where they were from."

Talking Sky made a hissing sound between his teeth. "You see? We have heard of this before. The white man has a sickness for gold and silver."

Sitting Bear sat there thinking. "This could make a difference to them."

"Yes," Eye of Hawk agreed. "The fever may make them ignore our warning."

"One of them stopped the mistreatment of Pale Coyote," Gray Wolf continued. "A man clothed in deerskin, like the hunters we have met before. He wears a beard and a black hat, and carries a very long gun."

Sitting Bear's face clouded over. "Are his eyes the color of the sky?"

The warrior shrugged. "I believe so."

Sitting Bear turned to Talking Sky. "It is Sheltowee!"

The shaman shook his head. "Aaiiy!"

"What?" Eye of Hawk said.

"He is the great enemy of the Shawnee," Talking Sky said gravely. "They believe he is unkillable. The Apaches hold him to be a god."

Gray Wolf and Eye of Hawk exchanged a dark look.

"I know that one!" Iron Knife said after a moment. "I fought with him, we exchanged fire. One of our brave warriors knocked him down and almost killed him."

"Almost?" Talking Sky said.

"The hunter . . . killed our man," Iron Knife admitted reluctantly.

"You see?" Talking Sky said, turning to Sitting Bear.

Iron Knife's young face showed anger. "The fight could have gone either way. I could have killed him, if I had known. He seemed very mortal to me!"

Sitting Bear sighed. "Well, if these men do not leave, we will have to give this Sheltowee our special attention. He could be very dangerous to us."

"He stopped the torture of Pale Coyote," Gray Wolf reminded them.

"Sheltowee may have dark powers," Talking Sky said. "He might have spared our cousin to look into his soul. For gold, or for conquest."

Sitting Bear nodded soberly.

Iron Knife frowned. "If the pale faces stay, I promise you I will personally kill this Sheltowee. With my own hands. I will blind and deafen him, then carefully remove his skin from his living body, for Talking Sky to wear in the next Sun Dance!" Iron Knife exclaimed.

Eye of Hawk smiled at the temerity of his younger brother, and swelled his muscular chest outward. "And if you fail, my brave brother, I will do it for you."

Iron Knife eyed him with a hard, fixed look. His older brother had always been regarded as stronger, wiser, and more deadly. But Iron Knife was ready to change all that.

"Don't concern yourself, brother. I will not fail."

At the Davison camp, Dan'l Boone was busy tending to Pale Coyote's wounds. The Indian sat on a camp stool, and Dan'l knelt beside him, applying bandages to the warrior's chest, where Spencer had slashed him, and to the wound from a musket ball on his thigh. Raven was standing nearby, holding a roll of gauze and watching. Pale Coyote could not take his eyes off the black man. Abe Cassidy walked past, shook his head slowly, and moved on. He had agreed with Spencer that the Indian should be interrogated in any way necessary. Hawkins and Padgett, the ex-soldiers, were busy re-loading the wagons.

Skin Walker came and stood near Dan'l, and Pale Coyote cast a diamond-hard look at him. "Why do we find you here with them, you traitor? Do you wish to be a white face?" All of this was said in Siouan, which Dan'l did not understand.

"I cannot be a Lakota," Walker replied. "Sitting Bear has judged me, and unfairly. The woman came to me, I did not go to her. But I am outcast. The white face treats me well."

"He uses you," Pale Coyote said. "He thinks you are an animal! He will slaughter you like a buffalo when he has finished with you, and eat your liver."

Dan'l caught Pale Coyote's eye. "You both talk English. Why not tell me what you're saying?"

Pale Coyote met his gaze. "Why are you kind to me?"

Dan'l smiled and applied a last bandage. "You got me wrong, I ain't no nice fellow. But I don't kill a man after he's disarmed and helpless neither. Well, not ordinarily."

Just at that moment, Spencer walked up to them, Davison close behind. Spencer stared down at Dan'l and Pale Coyote darkly. Skin Walker moved off.

"For Christ's sake, Boone, what's going on here? You going to bandage him up just to shoot him?"

"We aren't shooting anybody," Davison said from behind him.

Raven, seeing a conflict emerging, walked away, too. Spencer turned to Davison with his face screwed up in curiosity. "What?" he said. "You thinking of hauling him around with us? Like a goddamn prisoner of war?"

Davison shook his head as Dan'l rose from the

Indian. "No, of course not. I'm turning him loose."

Spencer could not believe his ears. "You're what?"

Dorf was down at the far end of the compound, still recovering from his fight with Dan'l. But Cassidy came up to them, and said to Davison, "That ain't really a good idea, Colonel."

Henry Munro came over to listen. He looked even paler than before the battle.

"A good idea!" Spencer said loudly. "It's goddamn craziness, is what it is! This damn ape was trying to kill all of us just a little while ago. You're going to reward him for that by letting him ride back and report to his chief? By God, Davison, you've lost your judgment."

"That was Iron Knife that led the attack. Walker told me all about him. He's already reported back to Sitting Bear," Davison said levelly, ignoring the insult. "Unless we intend to execute this man—and I'm not about to—we might as well let him go. It might buy us some trust with Sitting Bear."

"What the hell do I care if Sitting Bear trusts me!" Spencer yelled into Davison's face. "Him and all of them is goddamn subhuman devils!"

Pale Coyote understood most of that, and gave Spencer a cold look. Over beside a nearby wagon, Skin Walker narrowed his dark eyes on Spencer, and Raven, not far away, grunted in his throat. He had heard that kind of talk before.

"If you think that," Davison said slowly, "you

oughtn't to be out here among them."

Dan'l had kept quiet, but now he finally spoke up. "He's right, Spencer. The colonials had to learn that from the French, back in Kentucky. But you ain't learned it yet."

Spencer turned from him as if he had not spoken. "You release this redskin and they'll think they got a bunch of goddamn women out here! Then they'll be back!"

"That's a risk I intend to take," Davison said. He turned from Spencer. "Hawkins. There's still a couple of Indian ponies wandering around out there. Go round up one of them and give it over to this Indian. Then turn him loose."

"Yes, sir," Hawkins said from the nearby wagon.

Spencer turned and strode off stiff-backed, and Cassidy followed him. Dan'l turned to Davison. "It's a right decision, Colonel."

"I know," Davison said.

In the next twenty minutes or so, Hawkins went out and retrieved the Indian pony. Padgett, under Davison's orders, walked Pale Coyote to the end of the wagons, and Hawkins brought the retrieved horse there. Dan'l helped the Sioux mount the horse, with several of the others watching from a short distance.

"Tell Sitting Bear that we plan to leave this area right soon now," Dan'l said to the Indian. "We don't want no more trouble."

Pale Coyote studied Dan'l's face, then leaned

down close to him and spoke in confidential tones. "Your people will not go now. They have the fever."

Dan'l regarded him steadily. The Sioux knew the white man well. "You didn't tell them nothing about the gold," Dan'l observed.

Pale Coyote sighed. "They said you are from Kentucky. Are you Sheltowee?"

Dan'l shrugged. "You know that name clear out here?"

"It soars in the wind. Like the milkweed."

"It's something the Shawnee call me."

Pale Coyote nodded. "This is why I speak to you. Because your medicine is much respected. I told them nothing." He glanced toward Skin Walker, who was loading a wagon with Raven. "But you may find out by other means. If that happens, I tell you this because you free me, and because you are Sheltowee. To recover any gold, they must violate a battleground. And that would mean death for all of you. Especially you, Sheltowee. Because your medicine is much feared."

Dan'l nodded. "I understand."

"Return to the rising sun. And you will live to see many moons rise."

"Sounds like good advice."

Without further comment, Pale Coyote rode off. Dan'l watched him go for a moment, then turned back to the wagons. When he did, Spencer was there.

"Very interesting."

Dan'l frowned. "We was having a private talk, Spencer. You like to sneak around on people like this?"

"I don't sneak around," Spencer said easily. "But I heard the last part of that little talk. And now I realize why you wanted to spare that savage."

"Don't be a jackass, Spencer," Dan'l said.

Davison and Munro came over. "What's the trouble now, boys?" Davison said heavily.

Spencer said, "Boone here was talking to the Indian about them Spanish relics."

"That was the Sioux's idea," Dan'l said. "He was warning us off."

Dorf and Cassidy had now also joined the group, and stood listening to the conversation. Dorf's nose was still swollen where Dan'l had hit him a few hours ago, and his ego was still suffering under the embarrassment of his defeat at the hands of the Kentuckian.

"The Indian was worried we could find out about the Spanish stuff by talking to Skin Walker. I could see it in his eyes when he looked toward him," Spencer said. "Let's get Walker over here."

Davison was holding his right hand to his side, where the thick bandage protected his wound. "Is that right, Dan'l?"

Dan'l hunched his shoulders. "Maybe."

"Get Walker over here, Colonel," Cassidy said quickly. "This could be worth looking into."

"I agree, Colonel," Henry Munro said, pushing his glasses further up onto his narrow nose.

Davison saw the somber look on Dan'l's face, but knew he had to pursuse the matter. He turned to where Skin Walker and Raven were still getting some things back aboard a wagon. "Walker! Get over here!"

The Sioux scout gave Davison a long look, then reluctantly came over to the group. He showed no sign of having been through a battle.

"Yes, Colonel?"

"Spencer here would like to ask you a few questions. Right, Spencer?" he said caustically.

Spencer gave his boss an indifferent look and turned to the Sioux. "You know where that Spanish stuff came from, don't you?"

Skin Walker looked over at Dan'l. "I have never been there."

"That ain't what I asked you," Spencer said in a menacing voice.

The Sioux sighed shallowly. "I know it is a place where many Lakota have died, and it lies to the south. It could be one of several places."

"Why the hell didn't you say all that when we was questioning that other Indian?" Cassidy asked belligerently.

"He told you he don't know the exact place," Dan'l said.

"Yeah? Well, what's the most likely?" Spencer growled.

Skin Walker looked again at Dan'l. Dan'l hesitated, then nodded slightly.

"There is a place in a ravine, three days south, called the Place of Sleeping. Because of things I have heard, I have always thought that is where the Spanish things were found, many moons ago. But this is a guess, you understand. Only Sitting Bear and his close relatives know. Including Pale Coyote." He paused. "Also, the head shaman of each chief, like Talking Sky. I never reached that level of importance."

There was a long silence among them.

It was Spencer who spoke next. "Would you say your . . . guess is a good one?" he asked acidly.

Skin Walker looked around at the expectant faces. "Yes," he said heavily. "I would."

"Damn!" Cassidy exclaimed.

"Donnerwetter!" Dorf said under his breath.

"How much gold and silver is there at this . . . Place of Sleeping?" Munro asked.

Hawkins and Padgett and even Raven had come over now, curious.

"I know only what others have said over the years," Skin Walker told them. "But the rumor was that it was much."

"And it's still there?" Davison asked seriously.

The Sioux arched his dark brows. "These things have no value to my people, except as trinkets. I think most of it would be there still."

Another heavy silence.

"Did these rumors mention . . . gold?" Spencer said in a half-whisper.

The Sioux nodded. "Yes."

"Gold!" Cassidy muttered.

Then Spencer suddenly tore off his hat, and threw it into the air.

"By Jesus, Colonel! We're all going to be rich! To hell with mapping the North Platte! We'll go for the goddamn gold!"

Dan'l caught Davison's gaze, looked for reason there, and found none. Davison glanced down for a moment, avoiding Dan'l's eyes.

"Uh. We'll see, Spencer," he said quietly. "We'll see."

Chapter Three

The light snow had melted throughout the day, and the weather had warmed up again, but it was decided that they would not break camp until the following morning, because of all that had transpired over the last few hours.

After the revelations of Skin Walker, Frank Davison went off by himself while the others talked excitedly in small groups. He had a lot to think about. He had come to dislike the bully Spencer, and regretted hiring him to oversee daily routine on the expedition. But he had to admit that Spencer's interest in the reported gold was not entirely unreasonable. If there were riches within easy striking distance, and there would be plenty to split up, the booty could pay for another expedition, later. It was always difficult to find investment capital for this kind of enterprise.

Skin Walker had gone off to make sure all the horses were tethered properly, and after a short time, Dan'l came over to him to talk privately.

"They're all pretty excited about that gold story," Dan'l said as he patted the rump of the horse that Skin Walker was securing.

The Sioux gave Dan'l a serious look.

"You didn't have to tell them, Walker," Dan'l said.

The Sioux smiled wanly. "Yes, Sheltowee, I did. I walk in the world of the white man. Hated by many, feared by some, disliked by most. It is like trying to move slowly through a hostile camp, at night, hoping not to awaken the enemy."

Dan'l liked the comparison. He took a deep breath. "You're right. Don't pay no attention to me. Spencer guessed you know. He wouldn't've quit it."

Skin Walker tied a knot in a tether rope and adjusted the dark, narrow-brim hat he wore over braided, black hair. He owed his job to Dan'l. But he knew he had others to answer to. "He is a difficult man," he replied, refering to Spencer.

"He's a bastard," Dan'l said quietly. "And now, because of them damn trinkets, I'm going to have trouble with him."

"I am sorry, Sheltowee."

Dan'l eyed him. "What the hell was Spaniards doing way up here with all that gold and silver?"

Skin Walker shrugged eloquently. "There were outposts north of Santa Fe a hundred years ago. Maybe these men were thieves who robbed one of them, and brought the treasure north to hide it. Then our ancestors found them on the old battle site and killed all of them. But I don't really know."

"You ain't never been to this Place of Sleeping?"

"No. But I know where it is."

"They'll ask you to find it, maybe," Dan'l said.

"I know."

"Unless I can talk some sense into Davison," Dan'l added, looking off into the distance, where the sun was setting on a wide horizon. A coyote call came to them. A real one this time.

"When will it snow in earnest?" Dan'l asked seriously.

Skin Walker looked at the sky. "Soon. And there will be much, when it comes."

Dan'l nodded. "That was my guess."

Over by the campfire, Davison rose from a stool and called out to Dan'l. He was sitting there with Spencer, Dorf, and Munro. The hunter Cassidy was helping the two ex-soldiers with wagon repair, and Raven was cooking their supper in a large, black pot at a separate fire.

"Talk to you later," Dan'l told Skin Walker. Then he walked over to where the four men were sitting.

"Sit down, Dan'l," Davison said. "Spencer here has some ideas to discuss with us."

Dan'l hesitated, but sat on a stool near Davison.

Dorf, still recovering from the beating given to him by Dan'l, eyed Dan'l with hostility. He did not know why Davison showed the hunter such deference.

"Spencer has just been repeating what he suggested earlier," Davison began tentatively, watching Dan'l's face. "That we seriously consider abandoning our last few attcmpts at mapmaking, and make a small detour south to see if there's anything in this story about gold."

Dan'l grunted. "What a surprise."

Spencer, looking beefy and ugly across the fire, scowled fiercely at Dan'l. "What the hell is it with you, hunter?" he said in a hard voice. "You just natural-born contrary?"

Dan'l looked at him, but said nothing.

"Dorf here, and even Munro," Davison went on, "are thinking it's not a bad idea. But we want your opinion."

" 'We,' Colonel?" Dan'l said sourly.

Dorf laughed quietly, and Dan'l glanced at him. A hard grin slid off the German's face.

"I'd like to hear what you think," Henry Munro, the wan-looking surveyor, offered.

Dan'l saw Spencer eye Munro sideways. Dan'l took a deep breath, and folded his thick hands before him.

"I told you what I think before all this talk of gold come up. In another week or so, it's going to be winter out here. We ain't got proper shelter, and food will be hard to come by. Moving these wagons could become impossible. I think we ought to be well east when that happens."

"Oh, shit!" Spencer spat out.

Dan'l looked at him, and continued. "That opinion ain't been changed by all this that happened. In fact, now there's a lot more reason to leave while we can. You saw what just a small war party can do to us. We're down three men. Good men, with families waiting back home for them. But that ain't nothing to what the Sioux can do if they come in force. Look at what happened to them Spaniards that come here with their gold. The Sioux must be kind of touchy about that battleground. So now you got the Sioux to think about, and the winter. And the winter could be the worst of the two."

"Ha!" Gustav Dorf said. He was bareheaded at the moment, and his blond hair blew in a light breeze. "Boone is afraid! Of the Indians. Of the cold weather. Of what else?"

Munro coughed into a handkerchief several times. He had been told by a St. Louis physician that he had the beginnings of consumption, but he had sought a second opinion from a quack who had told him what he wanted to hear, that it was just chronic bronchitis.

"He is obviously not afraid of you, Herr Dorf," Munro said then, his eyes watery. He smiled a weak smile.

Dorf hurled a blistering look at him. "The rest of us are not so afraid of the Indians! Or the snow. If Boone wants to return to St. Louis, let him leave. We don't need him."

"I didn't say nothing about afraid," Dan'l said levelly. "But only a goddamn fool ignores the odds."

"I don't mind the odds," Spencer added, "when the stakes are sky-high." He paused for a moment. "Come on, Boone. Don't tell me you wouldn't like to be rich. Build your family a real house, right in St. Louis. Give your wife some fancy clothes, send the kids back east to school. If there's as much in that ravine as we're told, we might all be able to retire and live lives of luxury."

It was the most reasonable thing he had said to Dan'l in days. Dan'l smiled at the cajolery. "I don't hanker after none of that," he said slowly. "I just want to be able to keep on with this for a while. I got what I want, and no gold ain't going to make it no better. But even if I had the fever, I'd think it was damn foolhardy to take the time now to go to that ravine."

"Cassidy and Hawkins want to go, too," Davison told Dan'l. "Spencer says he'll share equally with everybody, except the Indian and my boy, Raven. And I would, too. Of course, they'd get something extra."

"Of course," Dan'l said sourly.

"If we went," Davison added, "I'd insist on leaving if it wasn't found immediately."

"It's at least three days down there," Dan'l reminded him. "Then you got to find the place. Then if you really found something, there's even more time involved. And you're farther from home. And what if Sitting Bear comes at us again? It all gets kind of complicated, don't it?"

Davison sighed. "Yes, I understand."

Spencer stood up angrily. "Look, Davison. You're the boss of this outfit, and you know that most of us want to go. You want to go, too. If he wasn't here," he said, jerking a thumb toward Dan'l, "you wouldn't be giving it a second thought. Let's just go, by Jesus!"

"Well, Dan'l does raise some interesting points," Davison said pensively. "I guess I'd better sleep on it tonight. I'll give you my decision in the morning."

"Oh, for God's sake!" Spencer exploded. He turned and walked away stiffly.

Dorf rose now, too. "It is foolish to listen to one man, Colonel. We should take a vote."

"This isn't the U.S. Congress, Dorf," Davison told him pointedly. "We don't vote on this expedition. We do what I say. I own everything here, and I pay your salaries."

Dorf gave him a long look, and then turned and left them.

"I didn't mean to cause you no trouble, Colonel," Dan'l said to Davison. "I just want you to make your decision with all the facts in front of you."

"Gold always causes trouble," Munro said quietly. "It's the curse of it."

Davison glanced at him. "I guess the trouble comes with the fever," he said. "Spencer has it, and so does Dorf."

"I heard the other men talking," Dan'l said. "They're pretty worked up, too. And I reckon Spencer will be talking to them. Whether you go or not, Colonel, you got to take charge here. You got to get Spencer under control."

"I'd agree with that," Munro said; then he coughed into his handkerchief. "I have a feeling about Spencer. He could be dangerous, I think."

"Really?" Davison said, laughing lightly. Then he sat there looking very serious. "Oh, I don't think so, Henry."

Dan'l poked up the fire with a stick, and sparks flew up into the air. It was almost dark now. The aroma of Raven's cooking came to them across the compound.

"Let's say there's a mountain of gold in that ravine," Dan'l finally said. "You heard what Skin Walker said. It's just trinkets and baubles to his people. It will all be there next spring, wouldn't you say?"

Davison nodded. "In all likelihood."

"So what's wrong with going home now, having Christmas with our families, and then planning a trek next spring for the gold? And exploration, too.

You'll have the weather on your side, and you can bring more men, to cope with the Sioux."

Davison smiled. "You sound so damn sensible, Dan'l. Trouble is, these men aren't in the mood to be sensible. And I do have to consider their feelings in this, to some extent. It's their expedition, too."

Dan'l rose and looked into Davison's eyes. "Just don't let their fever make you do something you know ain't right," he cautioned.

Then he, too, walked away, leaving Davison sitting there staring after him.

Later, after they ate Raven's stew in the dark, Spencer did not raise the issue of the gold again to Davison, but Dan'l saw him conferring with Dorf and Cassidy in low tones, as if they did not want to be overheard.

Davison, the only one of the party with a wound that was bothering him, changed the bandage that evening, with Padgett's help, and there was quite a bit of fever in the rib area. Padgett himself was nursing his arm wound, but it was already feeling better.

In those evening hours before they were all settled into covers for sleeping, there was an air of tension in the camp. Nobody wanted to talk about what they would do next, since Davison would not make his announcement until the following day, and he had the last word.

Dan'l and Skin Walker fed the animals while the rest of the camp prepared for sleep, except for Raven. He was still washing pots and pans in water from the nearby river, and humming odd little songs. Even though Raven was owned by Davison, he had always been treated well, and when Davison had offered to free him, when they'd moved from Tennessee to Missouri, Raven had pleaded to be kept on. So, technically, he was still Davison's slave, working for bed and board, but he was treated like an employee. He had been with Davison most of his life.

Before the Sioux had come, Raven had overheard a conversation between Abe Cassidy and the other hunter, Ben Logan, who had been killed in the Sioux attack along with the war veterans Tobias and Ingram. They had talked about Wade Spencer, and what they had said had made Raven want to go tell Frank Davison. But something Davison had said a long time ago had prevented him. Davison had made the offhand comment that he did not like men who told stories on other men.

So Raven had kept his silence and fretted about it. But on this dark, moonless evening, it was bothering him again. He liked Skin Walker and the hunter Boone. But he knew the Indian would not want to be involved, and he did not really know Dan'l very well. So he thought of Hawkins, the veteran soldier who had been kind to him on several occasions during this expedition. In late evening, when the others were getting their blankets down, he found Hawkins at the tailgate of a wagon, and stopped beside him.

"It gonna be warmer tonight, Boss," Raven said to Hawkins, flashing a white grin.

Hawkins had been counting rations in a crate. He turned and smiled back. He had light brown hair, and was slim and well built. He had scars under his clothing from the Battle of Yorktown, where he had fought under Davison. He and Padgett had been friends off and on since the war.

"All finished with your chores, Raven?" he said easily.

"Yessir, Boss. I be all ready for bed."

"I told you, Raven. You don't have to call me boss. Or anybody else except the colonel. You understand?"

"Yessir, Boss, I know what you saying." He stood there staring down toward the ground.

"What is it, Raven?" Hawkins asked him. "Something bothering you?"

Suddenly Raven had cold feet. "No, sir. Nothing bothering me."

Hawkins frowned and leaned against the tailgate. "You worried about what we're going to do tomorrow? Where we're going to go?"

"No, sir."

"Did the Indians scare you? I can talk the colonel into giving you a gun next time, maybe."

"No, sir. I don't want no gun. I just shoot my fool foot off."

Hawkins laughed lightly. "Okay. But something brought you over here. I can see it in your face."

Raven took in a deep breath. His round face was framed with graying, tight-cropped hair. He glanced into Hawkins's face, and then stared at a spot on the other man's tunic, just above his heart. It was his habit not to look directly into a white man's face when speaking with him.

"It about Mr. Spencer, Boss."

Hawkins frowned again. "Spencer? What about Spencer?"

Raven swallowed hard, looked furtively around him. But nobody was anywhere near them.

"A couple days ago. I heard Mr. Cassidy a-talking to Mr. Logan."

"Oh?"

Raven began sweating on his upper lip. "I ain't meaning to hear them. I knows no nigger ain't suspose to listen to no white mens talking."

"Go ahead, Raven."

"They was talking 'bout Mr. Spencer, Boss. Bad talk. Make you shiver in you spine. You know what I's saying?"

"Not really," Hawkins admitted.

Raven looked around again. "I don't knows if you is a-wanting to hear this, Boss."

"Yes, go on," Hawkins said with mild impatience.

"Well. Mr. Cassidy, he saying that Mr. Spencer . . . he wanted for murder."

"What!" Hawkins said.

"Yassir, that what he say. He say Mr. Spencer tole him that hisself. He kilt two mens in New Orleans. He taken their money. He wanted by the law all through the South."

"By Jesus," Hawkins said, looking toward Spencer, sitting by the low fire. "Does the colonel know this?"

"I don't think so, Mr. Hawkins. And I ain't gonna tell him. He don't want hear that from no nigger."

Hawkins sighed inaudibly. "I reckon that leaves it up to me."

"Yessir. Sorry, Boss."

"Did you talk to anybody else about this?"

"No, sir. Lord, I be in big trouble if'n I blab to the wrong white man."

Hawkins nodded. "Well, you just keep quiet about this, Raven. The colonel will have to be told, I suppose. But he's got a lot on his head right now. Let me think on it."

"Yessir, you do what you want," Raven assured him. "I be done with it, Mr. Hawkins."

"All right, Raven. I'll handle it."

Dawn came up like a stalking cougar the next day. Because of a heavy cloud cover, there was no real sunrise, just a dull light that crept into the sky, step by step, as if reluctant to disturb the night.

Dan'l and Raven were the first ones up, followed shortly by Skin Walker. After Dan'l gathered some firewood, the Indian built the fire up, while Raven set a pot over it on a portable spit.

Within a half hour of light, they were all up, moving about quietly, their heads filling with the tension of the previous evening. Waiting. Wondering what Frank Davison had inside his head.

Davison was up last, and dressed slowly, speaking to no one. Spencer and Cassidy eyed him covertly, trying to assess his mood. They expected him to be buoyant if he was going to the Place of Sleeping to look for the gold. But Davison looked rather somber as he moved over to the fire.

They were all sitting and standing around, eating a thick gruel and drinking chicory coffee. Davison glanced toward Spencer soberly, then spoke.

"I've been doing a lot of thinking about all this," he began. "I thought it was only fair to all of you to tell you as soon as possible."

Across the compound, leaning on a wagon and sipping hot coffee, Dan'l watched his face and wondered.

But before Davison could continue, Spencer interrupted. "Colonel, there ain't no reason to plunge into this before we got our vittles down. You and me was going to ride down to the river, remember, to look at that spring Walker reported there. Why don't you and me do that now, and you can make your talk to us when we're all awake, when we get back?"

Davison looked around at the men, half-dressed and bleary-eyed. "Maybe you're right, Spencer," he said tiredly. He poured the dregs of coffee onto the fire. "I'll go saddle up."

Hawkins, sitting on a stool at the fire, saw Spencer differently now, since his conversation with Raven. Dan'l walked over to Davison.

"Maybe you ought to take Walker with you. He knows right where that spring is, on that low cliff by the water."

Spencer said quickly to Dan'l, "The Indian told me where to find it, Boone. It won't be no problem for us."

"We'll be back in a half hour," Davison told them. "It's just back there around the river bend."

They saddled up quickly, and while the camp came further awake, Davison and Spencer set out along the river. Dan'l stared after them as they rode off, wondering why Spencer was more interested in drinking water than he was in the gold on that dark fall morning.

Hawkins had come out from a wagon, where he had gone for a spice jar, just as they were leaving, and called out to Davison to try to speak with him for a moment. But when he saw that Spencer would be within earshot, he changed his mind and said he would bring it up later, when they returned. He had decided to tell Davison what Raven had said about Spencer being a murderer.

When they were gone, Cassidy poured himself a second cup of coffee. He seemed particularly relaxed and self-satisfied to Dan'l, who knew how much Cassidy wanted to go south to find the ravine with the Spanish gold.

Down at the bank of the North Platte, Davison and Spencer rode along side by side, looking out over the river. It was rather wide at that point, and on that day it was a dark green. They had drunk its water, but felt obliged to boil it. If the spring offered pristine water for drinking, they would send some men out to gather some in water-tight containers.

They finally stopped and dismounted on a high escarpment overlooking the river. Spencer walked over to the precipice and peered over the edge.

"There it is. Right where the Indian said he saw it," Spencer said, pointing.

Davison looked down, and saw the spout of flowing water, coming from the side of the low cliff. It looked clear and pure. "Yes," Davison said. "It looks good, Spencer."

They had spoken very little on the way there. Spencer had commented briefly on the fact that they had seen no more Indians since the attack, and how that was probably a good sign. But he had avoided raising the issue of the gold.

Now he turned to face Davison, very close to him.

"I reckon you guessed why I really wanted to get you out here," he said slowly to Davison.

Davison furrowed his brow.

"I'm your trail boss, Davison. I think you owe me something in this. I'd like to know your decision. Ahead of your announcement."

"Oh," Davison said. "Why, if you'd come to me this morning at camp, I'd have told you." He turned and looked out toward the river. "I've given this matter a lot of thought, Spencer. Like I said earlier, I didn't get much sleep, frankly."

"And?" Spencer urged him.

Davison caught his eye. "And I agree with Dan'l. I think we ought to head home, then tackle this next spring. We really don't have the time now. It's too damned dangerous."

Spencer let out a long breath. "I thought that goddamn buffalo hunter would turn your head around."

Davison frowned. "Don't blame Dan'l. I knew it myself, I just didn't want to face up to it. I don't want to be out here when winter comes. I hear it can be fierce. If we couldn't get back, we'd never last the winter out here. No, we have to turn back, Spencer. And I'm relying on you to do your duty and follow my wishes. I don't want any trouble."

Spencer grinned tightly. "Oh, there won't be no trouble, Colonel. No trouble at all." He drew the

Annely revolver on his hip, and showed it to Davison.

"What the hell are you doing?" Davison said, staring hard at the gun. "Are you threatening me, damn it? The others won't let you get away with anything, you know."

"The others won't know what happened," Spencer told him.

Davison was suddenly scared. "Have you gone mad? You'd shoot me down in cold blood, a mile from camp?"

"No, there won't be no shooting," Spencer said. Then, in a sudden movement, he swung the barrel of the gun against Davison's head.

The gunmetal cracked hard onto Davison's skull, smashing and cracking bone. Davison yelled under the impact, then fell to the ground right at the edge of the escarpment.

He lay there bleeding, partially conscious, his jaw working. Blood seeped from his head and dampened the ground beside him, turning it a dark color. Spencer re-holstered the gun and turned and picked up a large stone about the size of a man's head. He lifted it high above his head, then hurled it onto Davison's face. The stone hit with a sickening thud, caving Davison's face and head in.

Blood and gray matter spattered onto the ground, making more of a mess. While Davison was still bleeding, Spencer dragged him to the edge of the cliff, and threw his body over.

It plunged down the cliffside, and hit on boulders down below, at the river's edge.

Spencer stared down at it, all twisted and broken down there. Davison was dead.

Spencer slapped Davison's horse on the rump, and it ran off along the river. Then he spent the next ten minutes kicking dirt and gravel over the edge that contained Davison's blood, cleaning up the place where he had fallen.

After that, he rode quickly back to camp, dusting to a stop right in the middle of the wagons, waving his hat and looking scared.

"Quick, I need some help!" he called out wildly. "Back there at the spring! Something awful just happened!"

Chapter Four

Dan'l jumped on his mount bareback, not taking time to saddle the animal, and Skin Walker did likewise.

"Cassidy, you come, too," Spencer told him. Cassidy already had his mount saddled. "The rest of you stay put."

The four of them rode back out to the spring site, and dismounted where Spencer directed them.

"He's down there!" Spencer said. "His horse reared and threw him, and he went over. I wasn't close enough to stop it. He hit bottom hard. I don't know if he's dead or alive, but I knew I couldn't get him up here alone."

They looked over the edge of the cliff, and there was Davison's body, motionless. He looked very dead. Dan'l and Skin Walker exchanged a sober look. Cassidy shook his head.

"Well, I'll be damned," he said.

Dan'l thought Cassidy's reaction was rather mild. "Let's get down there," he said heavily.

It took them most of an hour to haul the corpse back up to the top of the escarpment, and when they got it up there, they just stared hard at the mess that was Davison's head. All but Spencer were dumbstruck.

They all started back, with few words among them, Davison's corpse slung over the back of the Indian's mount. Dan'l said to go ahead without him, he would follow right behind. Spencer eyed him for a long moment, then rode off with the others.

Alone at the cliffside, Dan'l walked over to its edge again, and looked down at the rocks below. It did not seem possible to him that Davison could have suffered such severe injury from hitting those rocks. Also, when Dan'l had been down below, he'd noted that a particular rock, the size of a man's head, had had a small amount of blood on it even though it was ten feet from the corpse.

Dan'l studied the ground at the cliff's edge, and noted some of the dirt there had been scraped, as if by a foot. He knelt and took some dirt between his thumb and finger, as he had done so many times on the trail when tracking an enemy or game. The sand was slightly darker in color than that surrounding it, and it had an odor. Maybe of blood.

Maybe not.

He was about to rise when he spotted the dull glint of metal in the dirt at his feet. He moved the sand and uncovered a brass button. It was off Davison's tunic.

Dan'l frowned. "If he just fell off his horse, why would he lose a button up here?" he muttered to himself.

It could be evidence of a struggle. Between Davison and Spencer.

Or it could have caught on something and pulled off when he fell.

It could even have come off when they were bringing the body back up to the cliff edge.

It was all very inconclusive.

But it made Dan'l wonder.

He pocketed the button, and decided to keep his concerns to himself. They were, after all, only concerns.

When he arrived back at their camp, Hawkins and Padgett were already digging a grave for Davison. Dan'l dismounted and walked over to where Spencer was talking to the others. Spencer saw Dan'l and studied his face as he approached them. Dan'l met his look and said nothing.

"Glad you got back here, Boone," Spencer said to him. "I was just telling the boys what the colonel was talking to me about just before he died out there."

Dan'l glanced over toward the covered body of Davison on the ground near a half-dug grave. "Yeah?"

"Davison said he'd leave it up to a vote," Spencer went on blandly.

Dan'l eyed him suspiciously. "Is that what he said, Spencer?"

Spencer studied Dan'l's square face. "You saying it ain't?"

"I ain't saying nothing about it."

"Well, that's a smart decision," Spencer said tonelessly. "Since you wasn't there."

Dorf laughed quietly from nearby.

"While you was gone, we been talking it over," Spencer went on. "It looks like we got a majority, hunter. Us that wants to go for the gold."

"Oh?" Dan'l said. He looked around at the faces. He already knew that Dorf and Cassidy would side with Spencer. He met Hawkins's gaze, and Hawkins averted his eyes. Dan'l turned to Padgett. "You, too, Padgett?"

Padgett rubbed his wounded arm. He had shown little interest in going to the Place of Sleeping.

"Well, if the others want to go, why should I stand in the way?"

Dan'l looked over at the diminutive Henry Munro.

"I voted against it," Munro said to him.

Dan'l turned back to Spencer. "What about Walker? And Raven?"

Skin Walker stood off to one side, arms folded, his face expressionless. Raven busied himself at the side of a wagon nearby, casting furtive glances at the group.

Spencer burst out into hard laughter. "A redskin and a nigger? Hey, you got a real sense of humor, Kentucky man!"

"I wasn't joking," Dan'l told him.

Dorf made a sound in his throat. "I told you he was stupid."

Dan'l hurled a look at Dorf that Munro, standing beside him, thought could have blistered the paint off the face of a warpath Sioux.

"You want some more, Dorf?" Dan'l growled at the German.

It was Cassidy that broke the tension.

"Hell, Boone. Cool it down. There ain't no place back east where no Injun or no black's got any vote. You know that."

"This ain't back east," Dan'l reminded him.

"It wouldn't matter if they both voted with you and Munro, against going," Spencer said. "We'd still have the majority."

Dan'l took a step closer to Spencer, and they all saw Spencer flinch slightly. "You got it all figured out, ain't you?"

Spencer frowned. "What the hell do you mean by that?"

Dan'l's gaze burned through Spencer's eyes clear to the back of his head, trying to see the truth. "What happened out there, Spencer? Out by the river?"

Spencer's face darkened. "Are you accusing me of something, hunter? If you are, spit it out."

Over at the grave site, Hawkins and Padgett had stopped digging. They had made the hole deep enough to receive Davison's corpse. Hawkins listened to the exchange with doubt twisting in his gut, remembering what Raven had confided to him.

"I just think it's real nice for you," Dan'l said evenly, "since you want to go to the ravine for the gold, that Davison talked all this over with you. And that it come out just the way you wanted."

"Why, you son of a bitch!" Spencer said loudly.

Tension crackled like sheet lightning around them.

"You would think you might've been talking about that springwater," Dan'l pressed on, ignoring Spencer's outburst. "Instead of the gold, I mean. 'Specially since Davison had said he was going to wait to tell us his decision."

"I'm his trail master, goddamn it!" Spencer roared. "He always told me ahead of the others. Even your thick head ought to understand that."

Dan'l fished in a pocket and came up with the

brass button he had found at the site of the struggle. "I found this on top of that cliff, Spencer."

Spencer took the button and looked at it.

"It's off Davison's tunic," Dan'l said.

Spencer seemed a bit more subdued. "So?"

"So I just have to wonder how it would come off up there," Dan'l said, "if he just fell off his mount."

Hawkins and Padgett came over, and both stared hard at the button. Dorf and Cassidy exchanged a subtle look. They had both been told by Spencer that he was going to make things right for them. But not how. Henry Munro came closer, wide-eyed.

"Well, how the hell would I know?" Spencer said innocently. "Maybe he caught it on the reins when the horse reared. Maybe the goddamn thing was loose to begin with. That don't mean nothing."

Dan'l grunted. "I also found a rock down there where we got his body. It was several yards from the body, and it had blood on it. But since you was there, I reckon you can explain that, too, Spencer."

Now Spencer's anger overcame his fear of Dan'l and he leaned in toward him menacingly. "Listen, you bastard. All I know is what I saw with my own eyes. Maybe he bounced down there and rolled. Yeah, I remember now, he did. I saw blood spatter when he hit, too. But I don't have to explain any of this to you. You understand?"

Hawkins, standing nearby, swallowed hard. Suddenly he knew in his heart that Davison had been murdered by Spencer. But he did not want to be the one to say so.

Raven, over by the wagon, was just as sure. "Oh, Lord," he whispered to himself.

Dan'l and Spencer were still standing nose to nose, with neither speaking. It was Cassidy who interrupted the crisis for the second time.

"Come on, Boone. He give you a reasonable explanation for all of that. Let's quit this bickering and get the colonel buried."

"A very good idea," Dorf put in quickly.

Spencer moved off a bit, but still kept his eyes glued on Dan'l. "Get him in the ground," he said to the diggers without looking at them.

Soon Davison was underground, a mound of rocky dirt on top of him. Then everybody except Skin Walker went and stood over the grave, while Munro took a small book from his belt.

"We were buried with Jesus through our baptism into His death, in order that we should walk in a newness of life. For if we have become united with Him in the likeness of His death, so shall we certainly be united with Him in the likeness of His resurrection. For the first part of man is out of the earth and made of dust, but the second man is out of heaven."

"Amen," several of them said in unison.

"All right, that's enough of that," Spencer said impatiently. "Let's all gather around the fire over here for a few minutes."

Dan'l was the last to leave the grave site. He stood there staring down at it as the others walked away, his Quaker hat held in both hands before him, his wild-looking hair blowing in a small breeze. Davison had fought with Dan'l against the French, and they each had a mutual respect for the other's soldiering. Davison had already planned further trips west, and had told Dan'l he hoped Dan'l would be with him again, maybe as wagon master. Dan'l was going to miss the colonel.

After a few moments he returned to the circle of men at the fire. Spencer had called Skin Walker and Raven over, too, to hear what he had to say. Dan'l stood across the fire from Spencer. Munro and Cassidy were seated on stools, but the rest of them were standing.

"When the leader of an expedition dies," Spencer began slowly, "or gets disabled so he can't do his duties anymore, his leadership falls on the wagon master, and that's me. Anybody have any problem with that?"

He looked directly at Dan'l.

Dan'l made no response.

"So I'm running this show from here on out," Spencer went on. "And Cassidy here will be my second in command."

Complete silence.

"Cassidy is an experienced man," Spencer added.

"What about Boone?" Munro said in a small voice from a place near Dan'l. "He's the senior guide and hunter."

Spencer's look made him start coughing again. The coughing went on for quite a bit, while everybody waited.

"I think," Spencer said then, "that Cassidy's judgment is better than Boone's. Does that answer it?"

He looked at Dan'l, who said nothing.

"Now. We already voted on whether to go to this Sioux ravine, and most of us want to go. So we'll start off as soon as this meeting is finished."

"Good," Dorf commented. "We are wasting time."

"I agree," Spencer said. "Anybody that don't want in on this can go his own way." He looked at Dan'l again. "I ain't going to try to force nobody to do nothing he don't want to."

How nice, Dan'l thought.

"You obviously think this is a bad decision," Spencer said directly to Dan'l. "You and our map-maker here with the bad lungs."

"My lungs are all right," Munro said forcefully.

Dorf gave that irritating, quiet laugh again.

"What I'm saying is, you two can do what you want," Spencer said to Dan'l. "We'll even give you some supplies, if you want to head east right now. And two saddle horses." As much as Spencer disliked and feared Dan'l, though, he preferred that he go with them. Dan'l was good at finding the best terrain to follow, and locating well-worn animal trails. He was also the best shot among them, and that skill would come in handy, both in hunting game for the party and if the Sioux came again.

"What about Skin Walker?" Dan'l said. "Can he go, too, if he wants?"

Dan'l knew that they needed the Indian, so the question was a facetious one. Only Skin Walker knew exactly where the ravine was located, even though he had never been there. The party could wander around in the wrong place for days if he was not with them.

"Walker is part of this expedition," Spencer said firmly. "He hired on to do a job, and that job ain't finished till I say it is."

"I reckon he's got the right to go or not, just like any of us," Dan'l said to Spencer.

"He ain't got no rights at all," Spencer growled. "Except what his hire contract gives him. He's going."

"I ain't heard what Walker thinks about that," Dan'l said.

Everybody turned to the Indian, and over by a wagon, Raven held his breath.

"I will go if Boone goes," the Sioux finally said.

"You'll go, anyway!" Spencer yelled at him.

"If he won't talk to you about the Place of Sleeping, what will you do about it?" Dan'l asked in a low voice.

Spencer regarded Dan'l darkly. "I think he'll honor his contract, with a little encouragement from you. If not, well, I got ways of making Indians talk."

"Oh, really!" Henry Munro objected.

"I wouldn't let that happen, Spencer," Dan'l said matter-of-factly.

Spencer grunted a laugh. "I don't think you'll have much to say about it, if you ain't here."

Dan'l was becoming angry, and Hawkins saw it in his eyes. Before the quarrel could escalate, he stepped forward. "The Indian will go if you go, Boone. If Spencer won't ask you, I will. Come along with us. We're going to need you. All of us." He did not want to go off on that detour with Spencer free to do things just any way he pleased. That seemed much too dangerous to him.

"That's true, Boone," Padgett said.

Even Henry Munro joined in. "We might as well go with them, Dan'l. I'd be too big a burden on you, if we headed east together."

Dan'l knew Munro was right. Munro did not look good. If he really got sick, he might need the comfort of the wagons, and the extra care he could receive. Also, if Walker insisted on leaving with him and Munro, there could be gunplay, and that could end in killing.

"If you go," Dan'l said slowly, "you'd have to restrict your search to just a few days. Or you'll never beat the winter."

Spencer thought for a moment. "We could do that."

"You couldn't have the last word on everything neither," Dan'l said. "You'd have to listen to people what know more about some things than you."

"Like you?" Spencer said acidly.

"Maybe," Dan'l said.

Spencer shrugged. "I'm a reasonable man. I'll listen to any good advice that comes my way."

Dan'l took a deep breath. "Then I'll go with you. If it's all right with Walker."

Over at the perimeter of the camp, Skin Walker nodded his assent. "I will go with you, Sheltowee."

Raven sighed a long sigh of relief. He was scared to death of Spencer now. And of his partners, Dorf and Cassidy.

"Now you're being smart, Boone," Spencer said with a grin. He stuck a big hand out. "Welcome to the treasure hunt."

Dan'l just looked at his hand and turned away. "I'll go get the animals into harness," he said stiffly, then walked off toward the horses.

Spencer lowered his hand, and stared hard after the Kentucky hunter. He and Dorf exchanged a somber look, as the others prepared to break camp.

The wagons made good time through the rest of that day. Instead of heading east, which Dan'l was still certain was the safest thing to do, they were headed southwest now, toward the South Platte and Spanish Peaks.

The terrain was still flat, and that made the going easy. The weather was warming up, and there were still some green leaves mixed in with the yellow on the cottonwoods, and Spencer could be heard joking with Dorf about Dan'l's concern about encroaching winter. On that fall day, it seemed that winter was a long way off.

It got so warm that the men sweated whenever they had to exert themselves to get a wagon past a rut, or to pull a wagon team around an obstacle.

Because of the good miles made, Spencer called a halt to the wagons a couple of hours before dark, with the hope that they would all get a good rest that night, and that maybe Dan'l and Cassidy might go find them some table meat.

Skin Walker and Dan'l had ridden out in front of the wagons all day, following the Indian's general directions, and diverting their trail whenever Dan'l advised it because of terrain. The Sioux was worried about the whole expedition now, and was sorry he had somehow involved Dan'l in this new enterprise, which he considered deadly dangerous.

After they had set up camp beside a small creek, where golden aspens decorated its banks, Spencer came over to Dan'l with a false show of amiability.

"We made good time. I'm glad you came with

us," he said. "Maybe you will be, too, when we find that gold."

Dan'l turned from unbuckling the harness on a wagon team. "Let's get something straight, Spencer. I don't like what we're doing, and I don't like you. As soon as we get this foolishness over with, I want to get away from here as fast as these animals will take us. And when we get back to St. Louis, I never want to see your face again."

Spencer's eyes went flat. "I knew you was stupid, Boone. But I thought you had enough sense to try to get along till this is over. If this is the way you want it, this is the way you'll get it, by Jesus."

"I ain't much good at pretending, Spencer. You and me was at cross-grain long before what happened out there this morning, whatever it was. Let's just try to keep out of each other's way as much as possible. I think that'll be better for both of us."

"That suits me right down to the ground," Spencer said.

After they were encamped, Dan'l and Cassidy saddled up their mounts to go out hunting, and were just about ready to leave when Raven came over to them.

"Mr. Boone, Mr. Cassidy. I cain't do no cooking till you-all gets back with some meat. You-all minds if I rides out with you-all, just to watch you track them critters?"

Dan'l stared solemnly at him. Raven had never

made such a request before on the expedition. He had hardly ever spoken to Dan'l at all.

"Well . . ." Dan'l said.

"Just get back to your pots," Cassidy said curtly.

Just as Gustav Dorf walked past, Raven spoke again. "I wouldn't be no problem, Mr. Cassidy. Just tag along behind you-all."

"You black ape!" Dorf said loudly. He swung a rifle butt at Raven, and it cracked him alongside the head. Raven fell backwards to the ground, bleeding at the left ear. "Don't you hear right with those lumps of coal you call ears? You get a fire built!"

Dan'l could not believe it. "You son of a bitch! You're just out hunting for trouble, ain't you?" He dropped his mount's reins and headed for Dorf.

But Dorf raised the muzzle of the rifle and pointed it at Dan'l's chest, breathing hard.

Dan'l stopped just a few feet from him.

Dorf had the gun primed already, and now he cocked it. He had heard part of the exchange between Dan'l and Spencer, and figured Spencer would not complain too loudly if he took this chance to kill this hunter he hated so profoundly.

"Now, you backwoods piece of buffalo dung!" he spat at Dan'l. "I will shoot your liver out through your backbone."

His finger whitened over the trigger.

"Hold it, Dorf!" Spencer called from across the area.

Dorf turned just slightly. "Everything is fine. I am going to rid us of this scum now. We don't need him."

"I said stop!" Spencer said, coming up to him. "Put that goddamn gun down!"

"Don't be a jackass, Dorf," Cassidy said easily.

The others were all looking on, watching the small drama. Skin Walker had drawn a war knife from its sheath, and intended to kill Dorf with it if he shot Dan'l.

"Mother of Jesus!" Hawkins whispered from nearby.

"Let him shoot," Dan'l said, his blue eyes flashing hot anger. "I'll come through the lead and kill him." He slid his skinning knife out of its boot sheath, and held it out in front of him.

Spencer took the gun away from Dorf in a single motion. Dorf met his look defiantly.

"We don't need this, goddamn it," Spencer said.

Raven had crawled away from them, and got to his feet, leaning against a nearby wagon. "I's sorry, Boss," he said to Spencer. "I didn't want to cause no trouble."

"Get over there and make a fire," Spencer told him without looking at him.

Raven walked away, and Skin Walker slid his knife back into place. Dan'l held onto his. A short distance away, the surveyor Munro was shaking his head, looking pale. The wiry Padgett was just staring hard at them.

"He wouldn't've asked," Spencer said to Dan'l, "if you and Hawkins over there wasn't all the time treating him like he was white."

Dan'l ignored the criticism and met Dorf's eyes. "You pull a gun on me again, you're a dead man," he said quietly.

"Cool off," Spencer told him. He was disgusted that of Dorf, Cassidy, and himself, he was the only one who seemed to understand the importance of having Dan'l with them. Until they were out of the territory.

"You keep that damn fool away from me," Dan'l said hotly to Spencer. He slid the knife back where it belonged, and turned and mounted his appaloosa. "Come on, Cassidy. If you're going."

Raven, a few yards away, cast a quick glance toward Dan'l. He had hoped to be able to talk privately with the Kentuckian about Spencer, since Hawkins obviously had not. But his plan had only caused trouble.

Skin Walker came over to the group as Cassidy mounted his horse. "I think I will go also," he said to Dan'l. Then he looked at Cassidy.

"Hell, you got duties too, Walker," Spencer said. "It don't take three to find a rabbit or two out there."

"I am going," the Indian said to Spencer.

Spencer saw the resolve in the Sioux's face. "Oh, all right. Jesus. Let's just get some work done around here."

Dorf walked away without looking at Dan'l. Skin Walker mounted up quickly, and the three of them rode out.

Dan'l and Cassidy crossed the small creek immediately, riding side by side, and the Sioux rode behind them. They headed south because Dan'l and the Indian had spotted a small antelope herd in that direction during their scouting. Cassidy rode along quietly. He wore rawhides too, and looked something like Dan'l, except he was a little taller. He wore a full beard, like Dan'l, and had gray, lined eyes. He was a deadly shot, and had been hired by Davison for that reason. He had never killed another white man, but he had been a brawler, like Spencer, and a hard drinker. Spencer had hinted to him and Dorf that he intended to make this side trip happen, no matter what it took, so they had rightly guessed what had happened to Davison. Spencer was a cautious, if ruthless, man.

Skin Walker rode along stiffly erect under his dark, narrow-brim hat. He had thrown a sarape-type Lakota blanket over his rawhide shirt, and rode with a rifle over his saddle.

Dan'l, as usual, rode like a man very much in charge. If they had met up with strangers, it would have been Dan'l that they spoke to first, because of his manner.

The antelope herd had disappeared onto the plain, and Dan'l was disappointed. Cassidy shot a large rabbit, so they knew they would not go back empty-handed. But then they received a big surprise.

They crested a small slope, and suddenly before them was a herd of magnificent buffalo.

They covered a wide, grassy area like a dark blanket, standing almost shoulder to shoulder, looking massive and beautiful. They could not quite see the far side of the herd, it was so big.

"Holy Christ!" Cassidy breathed. They had not come upon such a herd on the entire expedition.

Skin Walker just sat his mount and smiled. It was a wonderful sight, one he had seen many times as a younger man. It was why the Sioux did not want the white man in the territory. They did not want their herds disturbed.

"That's a damn fine bunch of animals," Dan'l said. "This is the way they was in Kentucky in the early days."

Dan'l had taken a couple of hunting parties into Kentucky after the first explorations. Europeans were coming over to hunt the shaggies for sport. Quite a ritual had developed among them, with "tossing the feather" to test the wind, and then stripping all unnecessary weight and paraphernalia off the hunter and his fleet-footed horse. Frenchmen would often tie a kerchief around their heads, and roll their sleeves up to be unencombered. Pockets and pouches would be chock full of cartridges, and maybe even several would be held in the hunter's mouth. Then they would ride through the herd, shooting and killing. When the herd began running, the noise would be so great that the hunters could not hear their guns go off. Bulls would gore the horses and knock some down.

Dan'l had known it could not last.

Not in Kentucky, and not here.

"There are some fine robes," Skin Walker told them.

Dan'l nodded. This was the part of his work he liked the best. Only, he would have liked it better if it had been just him and the Indian.

"You want to go in," Cassidy asked him, sliding a long Heinrich out of its saddle scabbard, "or try to get a few from out here?"

Dan'l thought about that. The Indian way was to ride in among the animals when weather permitted, and shoot as they rode. The buffalo would usually run away in all directions, but not until the hunter had made several kills. But some hunters preferred to sit out away from the herd, with powerful rifles, and pick the buffalo off from long range. Sometimes the animals did not realize they were under attack that way until a number of them had fallen.

"We could probably ride right in among them," Dan'l said. "But there's so damn many. It could be real dangerous."

"It's the way to get the most animals," Cassidy

said. "And we need meat."

"I seen a man trampled back in Kentucky," Dan'l said. He sat there, remembering. "It wasn't just that they killed him. There wasn't hardly nothing left to look at. You couldn't really tell he had ever been no human being."

Cassidy looked at him with narrowed eyes.

Skin Walker came up beside Dan'l. "It is dangerous, with so big a herd. But it is the honorable way. Our brother the buffalo does not understand if he is shot from a distance."

Dan'l looked into the Sioux's face. "All right, Walker. I guess I'm outvoted."

All three of them loaded and primed their long guns without dismounting from their horses. Cassidy's mount whinnied nervously, and all three animals were acting tense.

The herd had not spotted them, although one very large bull turned and looked right at them, nostrils glistening, and then went back to feeding. Finally the men were ready.

"If anybody gets unseated, we go after him," Dan'l said to them. "The hunt is over."

Cassidy nodded. "Right."

The buffalo were acting a little spooked now, moving about, even though the hunters were downwind from them. At a hand signal from Dan'l, the trio walked their mounts right into the herd.

The animals did not run. A few bucked and trotted away from them, making a path for them to ride through. But there was no general panic. Soon the hunters were well in the midst of the herd.

"Now!" Dan'l called.

Dan'l's big gun ripped the silence when he fired at a big, dark bull nearby. The animal just collapsed onto its side, puffing up some dust. Cassidy followed suit, and then the Indian, and suddenly three buffalo were down.

Now there was complete chaos in the herd, as they all began stampeding in all directions. The hunters started their mounts into a gallop, into the bulk of the herd, re-loading and priming as they went. Skin Walker gave up on the long gun, slid it into its sheath, and grabbed a bow he had brought with him. Reaching for a quiver on his back, he drew an iron-point arrow out.

Dan'l fired again, on the gallop, and brought another buffalo down. His mount leapt over it, and then was slammed in the rump by a charging bull. The appaloosa almost lost its footing, but righted itself. Cassidy, not far away, also got a second shot in, but did not hit a vital spot, and the buffalo kept running.

Just as Skin Walker was about to unleash an arrow at a cow just a few feet ahead of him, another enormous bull charged him from the side, blindsiding him, and the horse went down.

Suddenly the Sioux was on the ground, with

hooves all around him, making the earth tremble. Dan'l saw his predicament immediately, but was thirty yards away. Cassidy was very close to the Indian.

"Cassidy! Get Walker!" Dan'l yelled at the top of his lungs.

Cassidy had seen Skin Walker go down, too, and even though he could not hear what Dan'l yelled, he knew what Dan'l was telling him. But he just looked away from the Indian, who was fighting to avoid flailing hooves, and continued re-priming his Heinrich.

"Goddamn it!" Dan'l grated out. He wheeled his mount, and another bull ran past and almost knocked the horse off its feet a second time. Dan'l spurred the horse forward into the melee, and rode over to the Indian.

Skin Walker's horse had run off, and buffalo were stampeding past him on all sides. As Dan'l approached, the Sioux was kicked in the side and the thigh by hooves. Dan'l could hardly see him because of all the dust. Then he was right over the Sioux. He reached down, Skin Walker reached up, and Dan'l swung him off the ground and onto the rump of the appaloosa.

Now even more buffalo were rampaging past them, right where the Indian had been lying on the ground. Dan'l held the reins tightly, guiding the horse through the running animals, fighting to keep the mount under control. Out of the corner of his eye, he could see that Cassidy had fired again, and was now trying to make his way toward them.

Several moments later, it was over. All the buffalo had run off, disappearing in a black cloud over a hill nearby, and leaving the two mounts alone and snorting, with several dead buffalo littering the ground around them.

Dan'l guided his horse over to Cassidy, who looked winded and tired.

"I guess you got the Indian just in time," Cassidy said, giving a small grin.

"You should have got him!" Dan'l shouted into his face. "What the hell is the matter with you, Cassidy? He could've been killed!"

Cassidy narrowed his hard eyes. Sitting on the rump of the appaloosa, a bruised and bleeding Skin Walker eyed Cassidy dourly.

"We needed another buff. I took a last shot, that's all. You got the Indian, didn't you?"

"You was closer to him, damn it!" Dan'l growled. "It was your move!"

"I didn't see it that way," Cassidy said impassively.

"It is all right, Dan'l," Skin Walker said weakly. "I am not hurt badly."

"I would expect that of Spencer," Dan'l said more quietly. "But I thought you knowed better."

"Maybe you ought to get it in your head," Cassidy said deliberately. "Me and Spencer ain't that far different."

It was a warning to Dan'l, and he knew it. "I'm right sorry to hear that," he replied. He looked at the sky; dusk was settling over them. "Now let's get back to camp for Walker. We can skin them shaggies at first light tomorrow."

Cassidy smirked slightly. "I wouldn't have it any other way."

Chapter Five

It was even warmer the following morning, and the light snowfall had been completely forgotten. It was almost like late summer again, with a moderate breeze blowing up from the south, from the direction of Santa Fe.

In Chief Sitting Bear's village, though, preparations were already being made for winter. Buffalo robes were being cut and fitted, and bearskins were being made into coats. Leggings of fur and fur hats were coming out of storage, all for the colder weather that was sure to come. The medicine dances through the summer had produced rich gardens, and the hunting had been particularly good. The Buffalo Dreamers, among whom Talking Sky enjoyed a high rank, had predicted a hard winter would come early, and a great stockpile of dried meat and grains had been stored up for the duration. A beautiful buffalo robe had been prepared as a canvas for the Winter Count, the pictograph that would record the year's happenings, and which would be painted by the tribe's skilled artists.

Many buffalo hides were being tanned by the women of the village. They were concocting a soupy mixture from the livers and brains of the skinned animals, and rubbing it into the hides, which were staked to the ground. Later the hides would be "grained" by scraping them with a rough stone, and then with elk-horn knives.

It was important to be prepared for the change of seasons.

Winter, they knew, could be dangerous.

Sitting Bear had welcomed Pale Coyote back with affection when he returned from the white man's camp. Actually, both he and his sons were rather surprised to see the chief's nephew back, alive and reasonably well. They had thought he would surely be killed by his captors, despite the fact that their courier had seen Dan'l stop the others from harming him.

Sitting Bear had not pressed Pale Coyote about details of his capture. He did not consider it polite to press his nephew until his wounds were dressed with a mud poultice and wrappings of cloth and aspen leaves. But now, on this summer-like morning, Sitting Bear visited Pale Coyote in his bark lodge, taking his eldest son, Eye of Hawk, with him.

A couple of women who were tending Pale Coyote were asked to leave. Then Sitting Bear and his son seated themselves on a blanket near where Pale Coyote propped himself against a cottonwood-bark support. Sitting Bear had not brought Talking Sky because he wanted this meeting to be informal.

Eye of Hawk was not so pleased to see Pale Coyote back, nor was his younger brother, Iron Knife. First of all, Pale Coyote had always vied for the affection of Sitting Bear, because he was of the chief's blood, and Sitting Bear had always treated him like a third son. But also, Eye of Hawk was suspicious that Pale Coyote had been set free, and he wondered why.

All three men wore rawhide trousers and dark-cloth shirts, and headbands with no decorations. Eye of Hawk was by far the biggest of the three, very muscular and hard-looking.

"Are you feeling better, my nephew?" Sitting Bear inquired of the wounded man.

Pale Coyote had started to rise to greet his chief, but Sitting Bear had waved him down.

"Yes, my lord. I am being well tended."

"The chest cut looked very deep."

"They would have done much worse, except for the bearded man named Boone."

"Gray Wolf thought this man might be Sheltowee, the white Shawnee."

Pale Coyote nodded. "He admitted such to me."

Eye of Hawk muttered an obscenity, and Sitting Bear stared past his nephew for a long moment. "It is said he comes like the thunder and lightning, sweeping all obstacles from his path."

But Eye of Hawk shared his brother's disdain for the Kentuckian. "They are less than a dozen. We are hundreds. If Iron Knife does not fulfill his vow to kill this Sheltowee, the next time he shows his white face to us, I will do it for him."

Pale Coyote eyed him doubtfully. "The Shawnee say he will live forever."

Eye of Hawk gave him a hard look.

"Anyway, he behaves like the Lakota. He has honor. He stopped them from killing me. He set me free."

"And to what purpose?" Eye of Hawk demanded. "To send you here to say he is an honorable man? To lure us into sleep? Did you not hear? He is just now leading them toward the Place of Sleeping!"

Pale Coyote turned to Sitting Bear.

"It is true, my nephew," the chief said. "Our scouts report they began their march yesterday. They are going for the Spanish trinkets."

"And they will defile our honored dead!" Eye of Hawk said angrily.

"The older man, their leader, is dead," Sitting Bear said. "They were seen burying him. Perhaps from his battle wounds, or maybe one of them killed him."

"The whites often fight among themselves," Eye of Hawk offered.

"I am surprised that Sheltowee rides to the battleground," Pale Coyote said. "He told me that their plan was to return to the east."

"You damn fool!" Eye of Hawk barked, his patience gone. "He was lying to you. While you report his lies to us, he leads the whites to the Place of Sleeping, hoping we will not know."

Eye of Hawk had always treated Pale Coyote like a dumb younger brother, and Pale Coyote had resented it. "I do not think Sheltowee lied," he said quietly. "I think he was told that they would return east by their leader."

"Sheltowee is their real leader," Eye of Hawk said. "How could it be otherwise?"

"The white man has strange ways," Pale Coyote said with a shrug.

"Maybe that is why the older man is dead," Sitting Bear conjectured. "Because he wanted to return to the Father River."

"And maybe it is Sheltowee who killed him," Eye of Hawk added.

Pale Coyote shook his head, which irritated Eye of Hawk. He leaned toward him. "Why is it that they know how to go to the Place of Sleeping? Did you tell this Sheltowee where it is?"

Now Pale Coyote was angry. His eyes blazed. "I

would not do that! When they cut me, or when he stopped them! I told him that the Lakota would not allow them to vandalize the site, that it might mean death for them."

Suddenly Eye of Hawk was up on his knees, and had drawn a war knife from his belt. He stuck it up under Pale Coyote's chin, his eyes wild. "They would not know where to go if you did not tell them, damn you."

"My son!" Sitting Bear protested.

Pale Coyote stared past the knife blade into his cousin's hard eyes. "The Lakota they have with them, Skin Walker. You remember him. He knows."

Eye of Hawk stared hard at him. "He would not know! Only high-ranking Buffalo Dreamers and the noble class had knowledge of the exact site! Including you, cousin!"

"He knows enough, I am sure," Pale Coyote said heavily. "It is he who leads them to the ravine."

"Put the knife away, my son," Sitting Bear said.

Eye of Hawk paused, then took the blade away from his cousin's throat. He sat back down reluctantly. "You are fortunate that Iron Knife is not present," he said. "Our father would not let him come, because of his temper. He thinks you told them to save your skin. I am still not so sure he is wrong."

"Believe what you will," Pale Coyote said. "But know this. The palefaces have long guns and short guns. They also know defensive tactics. If we attack them, there will be a heavy loss of life."

"Do you doubt the bravery of the Lakota, their ability to defend their sacred honor?" Eye of Hawk fumed.

"Silence!" Sitting Bear ordered loudly.

They both looked toward him.

"I agree with our cousin. Even though their party is small, they have great medicine in their fire-sticks. If we do battle, it will be bloody."

Eye of Hawk turned away in frustration.

"But we must respond to any invasion of the Place of Sleeping," Sitting Bear went on.

Eye of Hawk turned back to his father, and Pale Coyote regarded the older man solemnly.

"They may not defile this ancient battleground to hunt for gold," Sitting Bear continued. "We would lose our honor if we allowed this."

"It is true," his son agreed.

"We will watch their progress. Maybe they will not find the place, even with Skin Walker's help."

"You should have killed him!" Eye of Hawk said harshly to his cousin. "Even if it meant your own life!"

Pale Coyote sighed heavily. "There was no opportunity, cousin. None at all."

"What is done is done," Sitting Bear declared. "And it is my judgment that no blame attaches to our dear nephew in this matter."

Eye of Hawk stared at the ground gloomily.

"If the white faces enter the ravine where the ancient battle took place, all must die. No exceptions. No one must leave to tell others of this place."

"Agreed," Eye of Hawk said fiercely.

"Yes," Pale Coyote said almost inaudibly. "That is what I told them."

"Then it is settled," Sitting Bear said.

He and his son rose and left the lodge.

At the same time, many miles to the south and east, the Davison expedition made its way across rolling prairie, again making good time, with Skin Walker and Dan'l well out in front of the wagons, leading the party directly to a long, wide ravine in steep hills that the Spaniards had called the *Barranca Perdida,* the Lost Gorge. But that name had not survived the bearded thieves who had stumbled onto it, and no other white men had ever been there.

Spencer had been a changed man since this detour. Under Davison, looking for farmland and making maps, he had been rather surly, not very much interested in the goals of the expedition. But now there was a glitter in his dark eyes, and his face did not have quite the same ugly look, even with the missing right ear. He was very excited about the prospect of being a rich man after all of these years, and he had a gut feeling that they would be successful in their quest for the Spanish gold.

He had told the group that there would be equal sharing, except for Skin Walker and Raven, but it was very well settled in his head now that there was no point in giving anything to anybody but Dorf and Cassidy. It just did not make sense.

Dan'l guided thc party around some steep hills in the afternoon, finding routes that even Skin Walker would have missed. There were a lot of birds around as they headed south, particularly hawks and vultures, and some antelope carrion in the long grass. In the afternoon, Dan'l found the spoor of a cougar at the remains of an antelope kill.

The land was obviously good for grazing, and they saw two small herds of buffalo at a distance, but they had plenty of meat now, from the buffalo that had been shot on the preceding day. Dan'l had also stripped some hides off the animals. He had slit the skins down the bellies from the throat to the root of the tail, and down the inside of each leg to the knees. Then he had staked the head of each animal to the ground with wagon rods, hitched a rope to the hide on the back of the neck, and let his mount rip the skin off the animals' backs. He had done it many times back in Kentucky.

"Now we must turn more toward the setting sun," Skin Walker told him in late afternoon.

Dan'l, riding beside him, nodded. "I think I see a buffalo trail through them breaks. We'll go that way."

And so it went all that day. When they camped that evening, they figured they had covered most of the distance to the site.

Raven had given up on telling Dan'l what he had heard about Spencer, and decided if Hawkins did not, it would not be told. He was a black man in a white man's world, and he could not afford to cause trouble. As for Hawkins, who rode back behind the wagons as a lookout, he wanted the Spanish gold almost as much as Spencer, and had decided to keep quiet about what Raven had told him. His comrade-at-arms, Padgett, believed Spencer's story about Davison falling from his horse, and Hawkins had told him himself that there was no way to prove otherwise. After all, the Kentuckian had admitted as much.

Padgett and Cassidy rode out in front of the wagons a few hundred yards, keeping a watch out for Indians and game, but were still out of sight of Dan'l and the Sioux, who rode out ahead by a half mile or more. Padgett was healing well, and now kept talking about the gold. Cassidy just listened silently, for the most part. Padgett was not part of the inner circle, and Cassidy was.

Henry Munro drove a wagon, as did Dorf. Munro was looking worse and worse. Something had gotten into his lungs when the light snow had come down, and his coughing was terrible. Dan'l wondered how long he would last if they were caught in the real winter of the Great Plains.

They encamped beside a stand of poplars just before dusk, and soon the odors of Raven's cooking filled the site. It had been another warm, sunny day, and Dorf did not let Dan'l forget it.

"Is this the cold weather you were predicting so darkly, Boone?" he said as he passed Dan'l near the picketed horses. He laughed easily. "You see, there was no basis for your fears."

"That's right," Spencer agreed, over by a low-built fire. "Your concerns seem to have been for nothing, hunter." He was very full of himself. Everything was going just as he had hoped, and now they were one day away from their planned destination.

Skin Walker was squatting by the fire. He was very somber about this whole venture, and sorry he had ever joined up with Davison. The only saving grace was having Dan'l along. "I saw the gray coyote today," he said to Spencer. "He was wearing a thick coat for protection."

"Oh, for God's sake!" Dorf complained.

Cassidy stood nearby, sharpening a skinning knife on a stone. "I don't put no credence in none of that," he said.

Dan'l gave him a look, but said nothing. He knew that Cassidy was an excellent shot. But he was not much of an outdoorsman. He had not seemed to learn much from being exposed to the wilderness.

Munro, sitting on a camp stool, began coughing a raking cough, and could not seem to stop. Dan'l saw Spencer look over at him with a long, disdainful glare.

"Can't you take something for that?" Spencer finally said.

"I had some medicine," Munro gasped. "But it ran out."

"Shit," Spencer muttered, walking away toward a wagon.

"Keep something over your mouth when you do that," Dorf said to Munro.

Munro's rheumy eyes were even more watery now. "I'm feeling better," he lied. "I'll be all right."

The smell of buffalo steaks came to them from the spit Raven had put up over a cooking fire. It smelled good and whetted their appetites.

"It smells better than venison to me," Padgett said, securing utensils to the side of a wagon. "Don't that smell better than deer, Hawkins?"

"You have not eaten meat until you have had Black Forest beef," Dorf said, sitting down at the campfire. "None of you here knows what real meat tastes like. I could make you *Wiener schnitzel* that would make you drool onto your chin."

"Well, maybe we all ought to move to Germany," Padgett said, grinning. Neither he nor Hawkins liked Dorf.

Dorf ignored the sarcasm. "You might all live longer if you did. German food is good for the belly. And the beer also."

"I don't like that German food," Padgett said. "You got to lay right down and rest after you eat it." He and Hawkins had fought against mercenary Hessians in the Revolution.

Hawkins stood beside Dan'l at the fire. "Those hides you took off the buffalo. They was plenty thick, too, wasn't they?"

Dan'l nodded. "The fur is almost twice as thick as I seen back east."

"But look at the weather we're having," Hawkins said. His blondish hair was slightly damp under his slouch hat. He and Dorf were the most apparently athletic men of the party, both trim and military-looking. "It's almost like summer out here."

"That can change in a hurry," Dan'l told him. "Even back in St. Louis. I went to bed one night there, a couple of years past, and it was summer when I turned the lanterns down and hit the pillow. Next morning there was a foot of snow."

"Here we go again," Dorf said sourly.

"From what I hear, you ain't never seen winter till you get caught in it out here," Dan'l said slowly. "Indians been found froze into blocks of ice, huddled in a blanket, sitting up against a tree."

"That is true, Sheltowee," Skin Walker said, looking into the fire. "I found a cousin once. He was caught in a strong storm, out in the open, on his horse. When I came upon him, he and the horse were frozen in place, the horse still standing, my cousin still holding the reins. They were both dead."

Dorf laughed loudly. "The Indian has you beat, Boone. He outdid you."

Dan'l rose without comment, and walked over to see how Raven was coming with the meal. Cassidy had joined Spencer at the rear of a wagon, and when Dorf turned toward them, Spencer motioned for him to join them.

Dan'l saw them together back there as he watched Raven turn the spit, and gave them a long, serious look.

"Quit trying to irritate that Kentucky man," Spencer said sharply to Dorf. "There ain't no point in it. Whether or not we like the bastard, he's valuable to us. For now."

Dorf grinned. "What about later?" he said.

"Later will be different," Spencer said meaningfully.

Cassidy watched Spencer's face, with its broken nose and deep-set eyes, and was uncomfortable with what he saw in it. "You ain't told us, Spencer," he said. "Dorf and me. What did you do to Davison out there on the river bank?"

Spencer grinned slightly. "Do I got to spell it out for you?"

Cassidy was grim-faced. He was skittery about

murder, even out in the middle of nowhere. But Dorf was very relaxed.

"You don't have to say anything," he said. "I know exactly how it happened. I would have helped you do it, if you had asked."

Spencer saw Cassidy's doubt. "Look," he said. "This might be the biggest thing that will ever happen to us. Would you want us to throw it away because of some goddamn weak-kneed son of a bitch like Davison?"

Cassidy hesitated. "No," he said.

Spencer looked toward the others and lowered his voice. "There ain't nobody going to share in that gold, whatever there is, excepting us three."

Cassidy stared at him. Dorf grinned broadly. That was just what he wanted to hear.

"I hoped you would see it that way," Dorf said.

"I'll make them think it's equal shares, right up to the last minute. Then we'll just leave them flat, and take the gold with us."

"Won't they come after us?" Cassidy suggested.

"Them two soldier boys ain't got the guts to shoot it out with us. And you can forget Munro."

"What about Boone?" Cassidy said.

Spencer arched his thick brows. "Boone? Why, I'll let Dorf take care of Boone."

Dorf grinned again and chuckled softly. "It will be my great pleasure."

Cassidy rubbed a hand through his beard. He did not like all this talk of killing. And he figured

Dan'l might not be all that easy to kill.

"Well," he said.

"Don't worry, my friend," Dorf said to him. "It will all work out perfectly."

Spencer looked toward the cooking fire, and saw Dan'l staring toward them. "Come on, boys," he said. "I think supper is about ready."

The following morning, they all woke up cold. The temperature had dropped thirty degrees.

Hawkins and Padgett broke out military capes they had brought from St. Louis, and the others, except for Dan'l and Skin Walker, dug thick coats out of their belongings. The Sioux just put on a heavier sarape, and Dan'l did absolutely nothing. He was accustomed to extreme temperature, and hardly noticed the new chill in the air.

There was a lot of grumbling about the sudden change of weather as they ate a light breakfast and got under way. Nobody was joking about Dan'l's predictions now. It was clear that the good weather was gone.

They moved out an hour after sunrise, and the temperature rose as they moved across the prairie again, but not much. Fortunately, there was no real wind. The sky was partly cloudy, and there was a different feeling in the air.

Dan'l made no comment about the change. But he and Skin Walker exchanged knowing looks as the others threw on their extra clothing to try to keep warm.

For the third day in a row, the going was good. They were getting into higher country now, though, and the wagon teams struggled more to make the same time. There were also buttes they had to guide themselves around, and in early afternoon there was a river to cross. By the time they got to the far side, they were all tired, wet, and out of sorts.

Skin Walker and Dan'l had doubled back to help with the river crossing, and now joined the others beside the wagons on the muddy riverbank.

"You sure we're still going the right way?" Spencer said to the Indian as they all stood around getting their breath back. "We're heading more west now."

Spencer had thought they would be there by this time.

"I am sure," Skin Walker said.

"If you are leading us away from it, you will answer to this," Dorf said to him, touching the Annely on his hip. Cassidy had taken Frank Davison's side arm, and now it hung on his belt, too. Munro had never carried a firearm.

"Easy, Dorf," Spencer told him pleasantly. "I'm certain the Indian would not lie to us about something so important. Right, Walker?"

"He wouldn't lie to you about anything," Dan'l said clearly from nearby. "He ain't like us. He thinks it's dishonorable to lie."

Spencer disliked this Kentuckian more and more as the days wore on. Maybe he would have to do the job on him himself. "You're probably right, Boone," he forced himself to say. "But how sure is he that we're headed right?"

"He said he ain't never been there," Cassidy reminded Dan'l.

"The way I heard it said," Skin Walker answered quietly, "the ravine is just over that range of hills ahead of us. We should be there with three hours of riding."

Spencer's face brightened. "Three hours! Why, hell, that ain't nothing. We can camp here and still get there tomorrow morning."

"I like that idea," Padgett said. He looked very tired.

Raven stood to one side, keeping quiet, as usual. He was shivering with the wet and cold. Munro broke into a fit of coughing, and Dan'l thought he was sounding worse. If Munro was caught out in a real winter, Dan'l did not know how he would make it. He probably would not.

"We better get off this riverbank and the mud," Cassidy suggested.

"I'll get the lead wagon," Hawkins told them. Young-looking and pink-cheeked, he seemed healthier than most of them.

Dan'l was looking at the western sky, where the lowering sun was hiding behind a dark cloud bank. Skin Walker saw him studying the sky, and stared at it, too.

"I think we got to do better than that," Dan'l said, stopping Hawkins.

"What?" Dorf asked arrogantly.

"Look at the sky," Dan'l told them. "We maybe got a storm brewing off to the west there."

They all looked, but most were not impressed.

"Hell," Spencer said. "We had dark skies before. No need wearing ourselves out by trying to make that hill cover tonight. We'll camp by that stand of poplars, up on high ground."

"Boone is right," Skin Walker offered. "There will be snow."

"Did anybody ask you?" Dorf said hostilely.

"Look, damn it," Dan'l snapped at Spencer. "Let's not make this personal. I'm telling you for your own good. We don't want to be out in the open tonight. This could be the start of it. The beginning of winter."

Before Spencer could respond, though, Dorf came and stood between him and Dan'l.

"More interference, Boone? More timidity about the weather?"

Dan'l frowned at him. Looking into Dorf's square face, he spoke to Spencer. "I thought I made it clear, Spencer. Keep this goddamn fool away from me!"

Spencer did not want a premature confrontation. He figured Dan'l still had value to them. "It's all right, Dorf."

But Dorf had a vicious gleam in his cold blue eyes. He threw a hat off, and his blond hair was mussed. He looked big and dangerous. "You do not speak to me in this way! You will apologize!"

"Oh, Lord," Raven exclaimed in a hushed tone, from the far end of a wagon.

"Why don't you go threaten somebody else, Dorf?" Dan'l growled at him in a low voice. "That's about all you been good for since we got out here, anyway."

The German was livid. He had convinced himself that Dan'l had been lucky with him when they fought before, and that he was the older man's physical superior. But he did not intend to prove the point. Suddenly his Annely revolver was in his hand, loaded and primed.

"What the hell," Hawkins muttered.

Everybody was surprised, even Spencer. Spencer backed off a couple of steps, and just stared at Dorf.

"Dorf, put the damn thing away," Cassidy said.

"Oh, God!" Munro said weakly, and coughed into a cloth.

"I am going to blow your heart out of your goddamn chest!" Dorf snarled at Dan'l, hearing nobody. "No goddamn backwoods farmer insults Gustav Dorf!"

Padgett, who disliked Dorf almost as much as

Dan'l did, actually started forward to intervene.

But he would have been much too late. As Dorf's finger tightened over the trigger, Dan'l reacted. His right hand flashed out at the same time the gun exploded in the cold air. The slug tore at his rawhide shirt, cutting a shallow bite out of his flesh near his neck, on his right shoulder.

Dan'l grabbed Dorf's gun hand with both of his, and squeezed it in an iron grip. Dorf screamed as his fingers fractured in the human vise, and the gun went flying to the ground. Then Dan'l released the injured hand and threw a hard fist into Dorf's face, breaking bone in his nose and fracturing his jaw.

Dorf went down, thunking into the mud at their feet. Dan'l, wild-eyed, thick hair flying in a cold breeze, stood over the fallen man like a grizzly bear, growling in his throat.

Dorf lay there inert, as if he were dead.

Dan'l stood over him, looking primordial and deadly with the thick beard and wild hair, eyes flashing hellfire.

The rest of them just stood there, staring at him and at the unconscious Dorf.

Cassidy narrowed his eyes on Dan'l. He had never seen anything like that in his life. He suspected it would have been about the same even if Dorf had put a bullet in the Kentuckian's chest.

"Damn!" Hawkins whispered.

Spencer had a new look in his eyes as he saw

what Dan'l had done to the big, strong German. Dan'l was even more dangerous to them than he had thought. He found himself wishing Dorf had managed to shoot him through the heart.

"For Christ's sake, Boone!" he finally managed.

Over near the closest wagon, Skin Walker had a slight smile on his stolid face. He had enjoyed the show very much.

Dan'l stepped away from Dorf finally. Blood trickled down his shirt front from where Dorf had shot him. He walked over to Spencer, and Spencer unconsciously tightened inside at his approach.

"Well?" Dan'l said thickly. "You want to move up into them hills tonight, or what?"

Spencer looked into Dan'l's eyes and did not feel like making an issue of it. Not at that moment.

"Hell, if you think it's important, Boone."

Dan'l nodded. "You better get that German into one of the wagons. He'll need tending to."

Henry Munro, huddled a few yards away, figured that might be the understatement of the whole trip.

Chapter Six

Chief Sitting Bear stood on the raised platform in the middle of the village. He was dressed in brightly worked cloth shirt and trousers and a warm ermine cape. On his head was a full-spread eagle headdress, and his leggings were of beaver fur.

On his face were painted markings of war.

Bright red, black, yellow.

Beside him stood Eye of Hawk, on one side, and Iron Knife, on the other. They wore buffalo robe capes, and high leggings decorated with ribbons. Each wore a wolf's-head headdress, the open mouth of the animal fitted above their faces. They, too, wore the war paint.

Behind them on the platform stood their mother, Birdsong, in a full-length dress of blue cloth and a mantle of reed-and-bead design. Talking Sky stood beside her.

"We have just received word from our brave scouts!" Sitting Bear announced loudly. Surrounding the platform on the ground were hundreds of villagers, mostly warriors. "The white face prepares to enter the Place of Sleeping!"

There were cries of anger and dismay, and Sitting Bear waited for the noise to subside.

"When they do so, we will be at war!" he finally added.

There was a lot of yelling and whooping, with warriors waving lances in the air, and calling for blood.

"They have been warned by our cousin Pale Coyote. They chose not to heed that warning."

At every pause, there was more wild yelling. The two warrior sons stood impassive at Sitting Bear's side, and behind them, Birdsong seemed slightly scared.

"It is the time of the *akicita!*" the chief went on. "The time of our Stronghearts, our warriors!"

A few of them broke into a brief war dance.

"It is time to defend our land, and our sacred honor," Sitting Bear shouted.

The din around him was deafening. Eye of Hawk shouted, "Yes! Yes!" Iron Knife made the war cry, and waved his lance above his head.

"When they enter the Place of Sleeping, we will engage them in battle," the chief promised. "They will all perish. None will leave the site."

"Their hearts will be cut out and brought back!" Iron Knife called out. "They will be prepared as a victory feast!"

More wild yelling.

"Their bones will rot in the ravine!" Eye of Hawk yelled.

In the ensuing tumult, Sitting Bear roared out a fierce prophecy to the darkened autumn sky, the same cold, threatening sky that had caused Dan'l Boone such concern just an hour earlier.

"A special buffalo robe will be prepared," he cried to the heavens. "And a record of this battle will be preserved for all future Lakota to know and take pride in! It will be painted in the blood of triumphant warriors!"

The shouting and whooping were deafening.

As in the historic buffalo hunts of the past, the Place of Sleeping would become the slaughter ground for a bloody winter kill.

The Davison party, meanwhile, had moved on up from the river, and by dusk the wagons rested snugly between two low hills, which gave some relief from the rising and very frigid wind. With the sun's absence now, it was difficult to see just how angry-looking the clouds overhead had become, but Dan'l felt in his bones there was snow in them.

When darkness fell, they were well settled in,

the wagons drawn up tight together, the horses picketed close to them, under a stand of bare cottonwoods.

Dorf had been laid on a makeshift bed inside one of the wagons, and was tended by Raven and Hawkins.

He was a mess. He looked like a wagon had run over him.

He came around just as they encamped, but he was seeing double, and bleeding from the right ear and the nose. His nose was swollen across his face, and Raven had splinted two fingers together on his right hand. His jaw had a hairline fracture that hurt when he talked, but was not serious.

"What happened?" he said thickly when he came around. "Where am I?"

Hawkins was sitting in the wagon beside him. "You run into a brick wall, Dorf," he said pleasantly. "You'll be all right."

"Brick wall?"

"Well, more like a gone-wild bull buffalo," Hawkins amended.

Spencer and Cassidy both climbed into the wagon after a brief evening meal to see how Dorf was doing. Spencer was unnerved by the whole incident. He had lost a valuable ally in Dorf, at least for the time being. It would take him a while to heal. And it had all happened so fast. He had always had respect for the woodsman Boone, but had had no idea he was quite so dangerous.

Raven did not cook that evening. They ate dried meat and hardtack, and swigged a lot of hot coffee. They had to secure the camp against the weather.

"Well, Boone?" Spencer said as they all stood around the fire in the rising wind. "You're the one that got us up here away from the river. What now?"

Dan'l saw a small snowflake land on his sleeve, and looked up at the black sky. "It's coming tonight, I'd reckon. We ought to cut some wood and pile brush up at the end of the wagons to make a closed perimeter, then bring the animals into it before we go to sleep. We'll all have to sleep in the covered wagons, so it'll be mighty crowded."

"What?" Cassidy said.

Munro was coughing heavily. "Sounds right to me."

"Hell, we already got Dorf trying to rest in one of them," Spencer reminded Dan'l.

"Well," Padgett said, "that's four in one wagon. I guess we could do it."

"It's five in one of them," Dan'l said.

Cassidy eyed him in surprise. "You think any of us is going to sleep under the same canvas with a black man? Or a goddamn renegade Sioux?"

Dan'l regarded him seriously. "Maybe you think they ain't entitled to protection?"

Skin Walker, standing nearby, shook his head

slowly. Raven walked away, not wanting to be a part of it.

"They aren't entitled to anything we don't give them," Padgett spat. Unlike his friend Hawkins, who'd befriended both Raven and Skin Walker, Padgett had always steered clear of both of them.

Dan'l turned to Padgett. "I'm not talking about a permanent arrangement here. I'm talking survival for one night."

"It ain't one of your better ideas, Boone," Spencer said with a light grin, enjoying the opposition to Dan'l's suggestion.

The Sioux came forward. "It is all right, Sheltowee. I, too, would prefer something else. I will sleep under a wagon. The black man may sleep with me."

"It could get bad out here," Dan'l said, bracing against the frigid wind as it whipped through the camp, carrying light snow.

"Hell, a little snow ain't going to hurt nobody," Spencer said. "I might sleep out here myself."

Dan'l gave him a look, then asked Skin Walker, "Are you sure?"

"Yes, very sure," he replied.

From a short distance away, Raven nodded quickly. "I sleeps under the wagon. No trouble."

"Then it's settled," Cassidy proclaimed.

In the next hour or so, the wind rose slowly, and more and more snow was in it. By the time they had cut some brush and piled it around the perimeter, it was getting fierce and very cold, and they were all glad to follow Dan'l's suggestions. The horses, all very nervous, were brought into the enclosure and picketed to the wagons.

The men had all donned heavy coats, including Dan'l, who had finally gotten his bearskin coat out of his belongings and put it on. Cassidy took a long look at him once he had buttoned it up, and thought that Dan'l was the wildest-looking human he had ever set eyes on. He was glad it was Dorf who had challenged him, and not himself.

After the campsite was secured, they went about making beds for themselves inside the wagons, out of the wind and snow. Spencer and Cassidy went in the wagon already occupied by the ailing Dorf, and Dan'l put his bedding down in the other one, with Hawkins, Padgett, and Munro. Munro was coughing frequently, and that irritated Padgett.

"For God's sake, do you have to do that?" he complained when he, Hawkins, and Munro had bedded down. Dan'l was still outside.

"I think he probably does," Hawkins told him quietly.

Hawkins had almost told Dan'l what Raven had heard about Spencer on two separate occasions, but had felt either the timing was wrong, or that it was too dangerous at the moment. So he'd kept it inside him, hoping there would be no more trouble from Spencer. Anyway, he reasoned, there was little Dan'l could do about it. There was no hard evidence that Spencer had killed Davison.

Outside in the mounting storm, Dan'l quieted the horses, then went to where Skin Walker and Raven had both found some minimal shelter under the wagon where Dan'l was to sleep. Skin Walker had built up some blankets around them, and had allowed Raven to bed down within a few feet of him.

Dan'l knelt and peered at them as they were just getting settled in. The wind was coming hard now, and snow was driven in it.

"Are you both all right?" he asked.

"Yessir," Raven said quickly. "We be jus fine, Mr. Boone. No trouble."

The Sioux caught Dan'l's eye. "Maybe it will stop soon." He looked at the bundle under Dan'l's arm. "What is that, Sheltowee?"

"Just a couple minutes ago, I went and got my bedding. I'm sleeping under the other wagon."

Skin Walker's brow furrowed.

"Oh, no, Mr. Boone," Raven protested. He was shivering. "They's lots of room for you inside. We be fine out here."

"I know." Dan'l smiled at him. "But it can't hurt to have another hand out here if the horses panic in this. I'll be right over here."

The Sioux returned the smile. "I understand, Sheltowee."

Dan'l crawled under the other wagon, gathered

some blankets around him, and hunkered down. The horses huddled against the wagons and snorted out their fear and discomfort occasionally.

Inside the wagons, oil lanterns kept the temperature up somewhat, and very little wind came in. Outside, a blizzard was mounting, and the temperature had fallen to almost zero. Wind-driven snow was so heavy that visibility was cut to a few feet, and the icy flakes pelted the wagons like tiny lead bullets.

Dan'l lay awake for a short time, and resolved that if it got too bad, he would take Raven and Skin Walker into the nearest wagon in his place, and to hell with whether the others liked it.

Then he fell asleep under the cover of bearskin and blankets.

Under the other wagon, Skin Walker also hunkered into his thick cover and finally dozed, despite the numbing cold. But just a few feet away, Raven shook and shivered and rolled around. He fell into a troubled sleep, and dreamed he was at the North Pole, naked, surrounded by polar bears. He fussed and kicked in his light sleep, and ended up kicking most of the covers off him. The cold bit into him, deeper and deeper, and very soon it numbed him so that it was no longer uncomfortable. He fell into a deeper sleep.

Dan'l woke three times that night, and each time looked over toward the other wagon. But through the snow, all he could see were two sleeping figures. They both looked all right.

Skin Walker woke, too, and turned toward Raven. But the blankets had piled up on the near side of Raven, giving the impression he was covered.

The storm crested in the wee hours of morning, and deposited several inches of snow over the landscape. It had drifted to heights of two feet in places around the wagons. By the time the men began waking up, it was over. But the temperature was still bitter cold.

Dan'l and Skin Walker woke about the same time, ahead of the rest of the camp. Dan'l brushed six inches of snow off his bedding, and crawled stiffly out from under the wagon. The horses were shuffling about, trying to keep warm. He peered under the other wagon, where Skin Walker and Raven lay. Moving a couple of horses out of the way, he walked over and knelt down just as Skin Walker was propping himself up.

"Well, I see you fared all right," Dan'l said to him. "How's Raven?"

The Sioux realized in that moment that he had not checked on Raven recently. He turned quickly and pulled the snow-covered mound of blankets down, so they could get a look at him.

The Sioux uttered a low obscenity.

"Oh, damn," Dan'l said.

Raven lay out in the open, unprotected, even his

coat separated in the front. He lay on the windward side of the wagon, and he was covered with light snow.

The Indian touched him, and he was frozen solid.

"He is dead, Sheltowee," Skin Walker said.

"Son of a bitch!" Dan'l swore.

They pulled the stiffened corpse out into the compound, and Dan'l leaned down and listened for a heartbeat. There was none.

Spencer was just climbing down out of the wagon under which Raven had died. He was rubbing his hands and complaining about the cold.

"Well, Boone. It looks like you called it right. We are going to have some winter before we get out of here."

Dan'l rose and glared at him.

"It is my fault, Sheltowee," the Sioux said. "I did not see he was in trouble."

"The hell it was your fault," Dan'l said grimly. He walked over to Spencer. "Raven is dead, Spencer. And it's your doing."

"What?" Spencer said, focusing on the stiff figure on the ground.

"Raven froze to death out here last night because he didn't know how to protect himself. You killed him, Spencer."

Spencer frowned heavily at Dan'l. Cassidy and Hawkins were climbing out of the wagons now, and staring at Raven.

"Are you out of your head?" Spencer said. "How the hell did I kill him?"

"You're in charge of this party now, damn you!" Dan'l said ferociously. "You should have arranged for everybody to sleep inside the wagons!"

Spencer came over and stared down at the dead black man. "This ain't my fault, by God. The others wouldn't put up with him inside. You know that."

"They would if you told them to," Dan'l insisted.

"You're pretty good at throwing accusations around, ain't you, hunter? You was out here. Why didn't you do something to keep him out of it?"

Dan'l had no quick answer for that, and it touched a chord of guilt in his gut. "Hell!" he spat. "Let's get some shovels and get him buried."

"Good God!" Cassidy said under his breath when he looked down at Raven.

Padgett came stumbling over, too, kicking up light snow, moving a horse out of the way. "I'll be damned. He's dead, huh?"

"What happened?" Henry Munro said, coughing into his hand. "Oh, my God! Is it the black man?"

Hawkins and Padgett took the animals out of the enclosure, and knocked some of the brush down. Dan'l and Skin Walker came over to Raven with picks and shovels.

"Come on, Cassidy. Spencer. You can help, too," Dan'l said to them.

Spencer blew onto his hands to warm them.

"You can't get him under the ground. It's frozen stiff as concrete."

"We'll use picks first, then," Dan'l said.

"Hell, leave him," Cassidy said. "What's the difference?"

Dan'l's face remained impassive. He gave Cassidy a withering look. "We ain't moving out till this man gets a proper burial," he said in a hard voice.

"He ought to be buried, Spencer," Munro coughed out.

Nobody paid any attention to him.

"Are you giving the orders here now, Boone?" Spencer said menacingly.

Dan'l glued his look onto Spencer's face. "We ain't leaving till this man's under the ground," he repeated slowly.

Dorf broke the tension. He climbed down out of the far wagon and peered into the compound. He looked awful.

"What is it?" he said in his German accent. "Is the *schwarze* dead?" He looked from the corpse to Dan'l, then quickly away.

Spencer took one look at Dorf and was reminded how dangerous the Kentuckian could be when aroused.

"Hell," he said in a quiet voice. "All right, we'll try to bury him. But don't try to blame his death on me, hunter. You understand?"

The last part allowed him to save face. Dan'l did not bother to reply. He started picking at the hard ground, to make a grave right in the enclosure.

"Cassidy, give them a hand," Spencer added, walking away. "I'll get Padgett to start a fire."

After Raven was buried in the snowy campground, they all had coffee around a fire. The mood was somber, despite the fact they were so near the ravine.

"I regret the death of the nigger as much as anybody here," Spencer said to them as they stood around quietly. He cast a quick look toward Dan'l, who was leaning pensively against a wagon wheel. "But we didn't know it was going to go below zero last night. That was just the luck of the draw. We can all forget that now, and remember why we're down here. We got a ravine to explore, and I say we start out immediately. We could all be rich men tomorrow."

"Yeah, let's get in there and get to hunting for the gold!" Padgett said loudly.

Everybody looked at him, and he shrugged. "I'm just saying what's on everybody's mind."

Munro coughed raggedly, and he seemed worse after the night he had spent. Dan'l saw Spencer give him a diamond-hard glare.

"I'll get the teams hitched," Cassidy volunteered.

"I'll help," Padgett said quickly.

Dan'l said, "If we spend much time on this, Spencer, we could all be dead men. This come on faster even than I thought. Last night was just a warning."

Spencer nodded. "We'll just be in there long enough to scoop up that gold," he said evenly. "Then we'll be gone."

The temperature rose above freezing later that morning, and the snow began melting off under a clear sky. Actually, it was one of most beautiful winter mornings Dan'l could recall seeing. The trees they passed were covered with ice, and when the sun started melting it, it became transparent and glistening, like crystal chandeliers. The snow had crusted over, and reflected a hard sheen back to their eyes. The red buttes were white-capped, and narrow striations of rock held the snow, striping the surfaces of cliffs like bright chalk marks. Undergrowth hung heavy with snow, drooping to the ground.

It was tough going for the horses, trying to pull the wagons through drifts of the white, wet stuff. By mid-morning their flanks were frothy from the hard exertion.

Skin Walker took them around a couple of low hills, and turned them west and then south. He paused to look over the terrain often. Finally, with the wagons and mounted riders pulling up behind him and Dan'l, he made his announcement.

"It is here," he said simply.

He pointed to a wide opening between two steep cliffs, rocky but not really buttes, that lay directly ahead of them.

"This is the Place of Sleeping?" Dan'l asked.

Spencer and Cassidy rode up beside them. "What did he say? This is the place?" Spencer said excitedly.

"Yes, this is the place," the Sioux said. "This is our ancient battlefield."

"Are you sure?" Cassidy wondered.

Skin Walker looked over at the bearded man. "I am sure. Look."

He pointed this time toward the ground just within the ravine. Dan'l could not make out what he was looking at for a moment. There were white objects sticking up out of the shallow snow. Long, thin objects, and a roundish one now and then.

They were bones.

Human bones.

"I'll be damned," Dan'l finally said.

"In the summer, the ravine floor is littered with their shapes. The remains of our ancestors," Skin Walker said. "In the winter, they are barely visible."

"Damn!" Spencer exclaimed. "Damn!"

"I have not seen it before," Skin Walker added. His voice sounded sad. Under his narrow-brim hat he wore a cloth that covered his ears, and tied it under his chin. But he wore no gloves. He took the hat off, pulled the cloth off his head, and replaced the hat. He wanted to hear the eerie silence.

"Well, let's get in there!" Cassidy said.

They drove the wagons into the wide ravine, and

after about a half hour Spencer called them to a halt. They were right between high cliffs, with a ravine floor under them fifty yards wide. The Sioux had guided them in, so that they missed riding over most of the ancient bones. Now Spencer looked around.

"Well?" he said, turning to Skin Walker. "You got any ideas where we should start looking?"

Skin Walker had been sitting on his mount quietly, looking at the rubble that showed through the snow and symbolized an ancient battle with traditional enemies.

"From what I have heard, I believe the Spaniards were in a cave, and probably on the west side of the ravine."

Everybody within earshot turned toward the west cliff. Adrenaline was pumping through Spencer and Cassidy now.

"Damn!" Spencer murmured. "I can see several places over there that could be caves. Let's get a camp made, and get to work!"

"Better draw the wagons up tight again," Dan'l suggested to him. "In case we have trouble."

"Trouble?" Cassidy said. "Hell, the storm is gone, Boone."

"On the way in, we spotted two lone Sioux," Dan'l told them. "Up on the west cliff. Just watching us."

"They were warriors of Sitting Bear," Skin Walker said.

"They know we're here now," Dan'l went on. "That could mean big trouble for us in the next day or two. If we're still here."

"Well, we drove them off the first time," Cassidy said.

Dan'l gave him a sour look. "We drove off a small war party. The next time, there could be a hundred or more."

Spencer intervened. "In that case, we better get at this as fast as possible. Let's move!"

It took most of another hour to set up camp, and now that Raven was gone, there was nobody to build a fire or boil coffee. Skin Walker had made it clear that he would not do menial work that was ordinarily allotted to women, and Spencer did not want to offend him at this point, so he did not ask. He finally decided on Munro. "You ain't good for much of anything else, anyway," he said.

Munro accepted the tasks assigned, surprisingly, without complaint, but he was hacking and coughing regularly now. Dan'l also noticed that he was sweating with the slightest effort, despite the cold.

Spencer was obviously irritated by all the coughing and Munro's apparent lack of value to the new project.

After the men and animals had moved about the camp for a while, all snow was melted within the area, and they were left with muddy ground. Whenever they ran onto a human bone from the ancient battlefield, most of the men would just pick it up and throw it out of camp nonchalantly, and Dan'l saw the pain in Skin Walker's face when that happened. This was all sacred to him, and he did not like any of it. Also, Dan'l knew, if the Indian were caught alive in here by Sitting Bear's warriors, he would suffer a death that was best not thought about.

Dan'l insisted on picketing the horses down to the far end of the ravine so they would have no place to run if they were spooked. He also got Padgett to help him tie thick rope from one wagon to the other at both ends to form an enclosure, and then they stacked barrels and boxes to the level of the ropes, to further seal off the camp area. Spencer had no objection to any of that, but made it clear he thought it was all wasted time that could be put to use looking for the Spanish cave.

It was late morning when they began surveying the western cliff base. They were all involved in the search except for Munro, who was left to guard the camp and to start some food cooking. Even Dorf helped, even though his right hand was almost useless, and he grimaced in pain with every movement.

Dorf had made up his mind after the severe beating at Dan'l's hands. He was going to kill Dan'l at the earliest opportunity. Spencer could not say they needed him any more. And there would be no hand-to-hand struggle this time around. When

Dan'l least expected it, he would just shoot him in the back of the head. It would all be over in moments, and they would be rid of him. And Dorf could feel like a man again.

Spencer, Cassidy, and Dorf searched down at the far end of the ravine. Dan'l, Skin Walker, and Hawkins looked over the cliff face nearer the campsite, and Padgett wandered out near the mouth of the ravine by himself.

There were several places where overhangs of rock looked like caves at a distance, but which were very shallow at closer look. It was tough going, too, with deep snow in some places, and snow-covered underbrush in others. Dan'l had shed the bear coat, and still felt warm, even though the temperature was still under forty.

At just before high noon, it was Hawkins that called out, "Hey! Look at this!"

Dan'l and Skin Walker hurried over to where he stood, looking into a hole in the cliff wall. It was only chest-high, and partly obscured by a snowy shrub, but it was obviously a cave.

Skin Walker settled into himself heavily, and muttered something in Siouan.

"That's probably it," Dan'l said soberly.

Hawkins turned and called out again. "Spencer! Over here!"

It took only moments for them to all gather at the hole in the rock. Spencer took one look at it, and a glaze came over his eyes. "By Jesus! This could be it, boys!"

Dan'l chopped the brush away from the mouth of the cave with a small shovel; then they filed into the dark interior, with Hawkins and Cassidy lighting oil lanterns and holding them aloft.

Dan'l was in second, after Spencer, and then it was Cassidy with the first lantern. In moments they were all inside.

Just inside the entrance, the cave widened dramatically, and they found themselves in a sizeable room, ten feet high and fifteen across. The lanterns were held high so they could get a good look around. A smaller passage opened at the back end of the room, and led directly away from the cliff face.

At their feet lay the bones and breastplate of a Spaniard, covered with dust. Spencer bent down to study them. "He's been here a long time," he said. He recalled that the date on the Spanish coin they had found earlier had been 1648. He looked around at the floor of the room. There was nothing else there.

"It's not here," Cassidy said tensely. "It must be farther in. Through that tunnel."

"They wanted the stuff out of sight!" Dorf said.

The seven of them ducked down into the low passageway, the lanterns making kaleidoscopic patterns on the walls and ceiling of the cave. Something fluttered past their heads, and Padgett leaped back sharply and fell against the cave wall.

"A bat," Spencer told them.

After a lengthy walk of several hundred yards, with moisture dripping on them from the low ceiling, and long-legged insects skittering away from them on its surface, they came into another room, this one even larger than the first.

Hawkins held the first lantern high, and as they filed in, they just stared for a long moment in silence.

Finally, Spencer spoke. "My God!" he breathed.

The rotting bones of five more Spaniards decorated the sandy floor of the room, in various positions of death. A couple of Sioux arrows stuck out of the bones, and a decorated lance. Just beyond the remains of the men was what they were now all staring at wide-eyed.

There were two small chests, made of wood and iron. One contained stacked pieces of eight, several hundred of them, with some spilled onto the sand around the box. Not far away was the other chest, and that one was filled with gold coins, and on top of the coins lay emerald rings, gold and emerald crosses, and several multi-stone brooches of gold and emeralds.

Hawkins crossed himself and spoke for all of them. "Mother of God in heaven!" he croaked out hoarsely.

"We're all rich!"

Chapter Seven

Padgett issued a whooping scream from his throat just after Hawkins's hushed remarks, and did a little dance on the sandy cave floor. "We did it, by Jesus!" He threw his hat into the air. *"We did it!"*

His loud outcry alarmed Skin Walker, who now looked at Padgett as if he had gone insane. This was what his people called the white man's gold fever. It was not pretty to watch.

They were all at the chests now, on their hands and knees, except for the Sioux and Dan'l. Skin Walker hung back, watching solemnly. Dan'l came up behind the others, staring down unbelieving at all the gold and silver and gems. He had not really believed there would be much there. But this was a fortune, and a large one.

Spencer held the jewelry up to the light, and

gazed spellbound at a particularly beautiful cross on a gold chain. The cross was gold, too, and each arm of it was set in glowing, breathtaking green stones, stones that reflected the cool beauty of mountain rivers to the viewer's eye.

At the other chest, Padgett let pieces of silver fall between his fingers, and both Cassidy and Dorf were kneeling beside Spencer, examining gold coins and emerald rings. Dorf worked a large ring onto his good hand, and held it up to the light.

"The quality is incredible!" he said excitedly. "I have never seen better stones!"

"These gold coins are dated, too, most of them," Cassidy said hoarsely. "Each of these is worth a damn fortune back east."

"Did I tell you?" Spencer said with a broad grin. "This is it, boys! None of you won't never have to work again! We hit a goddamn mother lode!"

Dan'l knelt and picked up a small, intricately carved ring with three perfect stones set in it. He shook his head slowly. It must have been some robbery. They must have been chased and hunted for weeks or months. They came all the way up here, and thought they were safe. Then the Sioux found them.

Justice had a way of taking improbable turns.

Spencer stood up, wearing the gold cross on his chest and two rings on his thick fingers. He looked at Dan'l, who had now risen, too.

"Now what do you think, Kentucky boy?" he

gloated. "You think it was worth it to come in here?"

Dan'l sighed. "I'll tell you that when we're gone," he said quietly. He suddenly realized that if Spencer had been a dangerous man before, he was much more so now.

Spencer said to all of them, "I want every piece of jewelry and every coin back in them chests. We'll carry them out of here and get them aboard the wagons. Then we'll divide it up later."

Dan'l had never seen Spencer quite so animated. The gold had turned him into a different man. Dan'l wondered if he really intended to share the treasure with the others.

The artifacts were all returned to the chests, and the men laboriously carried the heavy boxes out of the cave. Spencer then put Hawkins and Padgett in charge of searching through the sandy floor for further treasure. All of that took time, and by the time they had packed the stuff aboard the wagons, and had a light meal, it was mid-afternoon. They were all sitting around a campfire, with Munro pouring coffee, when Spencer turned to Dan'l.

"Well, you was right about the winter a-coming at us, Boone. But I don't see hide nor hair of them Sioux you was so all-fired worried over."

"It'll take them a while to get here," Dan'l said. "But my guess is, they'll come. This place is important to them. They can't just ignore us."

Spencer looked at Skin Walker. "What do you say, Walker?"

The Sioux regarded him without expression. "They will come."

Munro came and poured Hawkins some more coffee, and Hawkins smiled happily at him. Munro had been shocked at the sight of all the treasure when they carried it out, but his excitement was quickly dissipated in his growing discomfort. He coughed all the time now, and he was irritating Spencer more and more.

"So I suppose you want us to get all our gear together and light out of here today?" Spencer said to Dan'l. Now that they had the treasure secured inside the wagons, Spencer did not really care what Dan'l thought. The Kentuckian would be dead at the earliest opportunity, anyway. But not until after Spencer was sure they had gotten clear of the Sioux.

Dan'l's answer surprised Spencer. "I think we already been here much too long. I say we stay put tonight. At least we got a good defensive position here, the way we set up the camp, the cliffs on either side. If we head out, we'll be easier to pick apart."

Hawkins nodded. "That's sound military strategy," he said, swigging his chicory coffee. When several of them looked over at him, he seemed embarrassed. "That's just my opinion, of course."

"Hell, if them Indians was coming, they'd be

here," Padgett told the group. They were all on camp stools, sitting in the mud. Around them, heavy snow still clung to the ground.

Dorf was holding his injured hand at chest level. He had switched his Annely revolver over to his left hip, and Dan'l had not missed the change. "I don't see any military experts here," Dorf said, giving Dan'l a strange, fierce look.

Skin Walker saw the look, and in that moment, knew that Dorf intended to kill Dan'l.

Munro reached over to pour Spencer some more coffee, but in the middle of it, he had a coughing fit. Suddenly the coffee was spilling everywhere—on the ground, on himself, and on Spencer.

Spencer leapt up from the stool, hot coffee burning through a heavy shirt he was wearing. He threw the cup down furiously.

"You stupid goddamn nitwit!" he thundered at Munro, and threw a thick fist into Munro's face.

Munro was caught entirely by surprise. The blow hit him like a thunderbolt, cracking bone in his nose, breaking a lens in his spectacles, and throwing him heavily to the muddy ground. The coffeepot went flying, and Munro lay there dazed, his glasses hanging on the side of his face.

The coughing stopped momentarily. Everybody just stared down at Munro wordlessly. Finally, he was able to speak. "I couldn't help it!" he gritted out. Blood ran from his nose and mouth. He took hold of his glasses, and the frame came apart in his hand.

Dan'l rose to his feet. "What the hell is the matter with you, Spencer? It was an accident!"

Spencer started to speak, but did not. He sat back down, took Hawkins's cup from him, and swigged the coffee from it. Hawkins made no protest.

"Get back over to the fire and boil some more coffee!" Spencer hurled over his shoulder at Munro.

Dan'l helped the surveyor to his feet. Munro looked down at his broken spectacles. "I can't see to make coffee. You broke my glasses!" He wiped blood off his lower face with his sleeve. "You busted my goddamn glasses!"

"I just made you a rich man, Mr. Surveyor," Spencer said in a grating voice. "You can afford to buy yourself a new pair of glasses."

"He didn't mean anything," Hawkins said quietly to Spencer.

"Go take a rest, Munro," Dan'l told him.

Munro nodded, then coughed. "All right, Dan'l."

"Don't make no big thing out of this, Boone," Spencer said, watching Munro walk toward a wagon. "That little bastard ain't pulled his weight for a long time around here."

"He was hired to do surveying," Dan'l said, coming back to the circle of stools. "He ain't cut out for heavy work."

"He ain't cut out for much of anything," Spencer said.

Cassidy laughed softly, and Dorf grinned at Dan'l.

Dan'l ignored them and sat back down. He looked over at Spencer. "How much you think is there, Spencer?"

"Huh?"

"The gold and silver. What do you think it adds up to?"

Suddenly everybody was listening intently. Even Skin Walker, who had come to know the value of the white man's dollars.

"Why, I don't know," Spencer said. "With the jewelry throwed in, maybe close to a million."

"Maybe even more," Dan'l suggested.

Both Spencer and Cassidy eyed him curiously.

"I thought you wasn't all that interested, hunter," Spencer noted with a grin. "It kind of gets to a man, don't it?"

"How was you thinking of dividing it?" Dan'l asked him, ignoring his commentary.

It was a question everybody had in the back of their heads, except for Cassidy and Dorf, who figured they knew Spencer's intentions.

"Well, well," Spencer purred. "Now it comes out. The Kentuckian is just as greedy as the rest of us poor mortals. Kind of exciting to get the fever, ain't it?"

Dan'l sighed. "You ain't answered the question, Spencer."

Spencer shrugged. "Why, share and share alike," he said innocently. "How else?"

Dan'l knew, by that reply, that Spencer did not intend to share it at all. Not with the whole group.

"Of course, I'm talking about white folks," Spencer added. "The Indian wouldn't know what to do with it."

Dan'l caught Skin Walker's solemn look. "Seems like he's got as much right as any of us," Dan'l said. "Maybe more."

Spencer shrugged again. "I suppose we can work something out. Hell, don't worry your head none. We're all rich, by God."

Dan'l had been asking for the others, rather than himself, but he could never explain that to a man like Spencer. "I think that would be nice," he said. "For Skin Walker to get a share."

"It'll all work out," Spencer assured him.

That's for damn sure, Cassidy thought.

"So," Spencer added. "Are we agreed to staying the night, then?"

"Hell, it's fine with me," Cassidy said.

"Sounds like a good idea," Padgett put in. "Maybe we can get a better look at that gold." He grinned.

Spencer scowled. "Nobody's to touch them chests. Is that understood?"

Nobody responded. Padgett finally shrugged his

shoulders. His hawkish nose looked particularly large when he did not have a hat on, as now. But he still wore a coat over his shirt. "Hell. It was just an idea."

By the time they made further arrangements for camp security that night, and chose who the sentries would be, it was time to eat a light meal and start thinking about bedding down. Dan'l helped Munro cook up some leftover stew, and they all ate by firelight and talked quietly about what they would do with their sudden riches. All except Spencer and Dan'l. Spencer just stared into the fire, thinking how his whole life had been changed by his wealth. And how he would find a way to keep it to himself, except to maybe give some to Cassidy. But they had to get out of Sioux territory first.

The temperature was dropping again as they prepared to turn in for the night. This time, though, Spencer assented to the Sioux's sleeping in a wagon, if it was with men who agreed. Skin Walker declined. He preferred to sleep outside. Dan'l made the same decision. So the two ex-soldiers and Dorf bedded down in one wagon, while Spencer and Cassidy took Munro in with them. That surprised Dan'l, since Munro was a constant irritant to Spencer.

Before they all got settled in, Spencer took Cassidy aside at the front end of their wagon, and for the first time discussed his plans in detail with the professional hunter.

Spencer glanced over at Dan'l, who was checking the animals picketed just outside the camp perimeter, at the far end of the closed ravine.

"Boone says if we don't see the Sioux tomorrow morning, we might as well leave and make as much time as we can to get away from Sitting Bear's territory. I agree."

Cassidy eyed him. "You beginning to take stock in that hunter's notions?"

Spencer grunted. "He ain't stupid, you know. But we need him till we get clear of Sitting Bear. He can kill Sioux, he showed us that."

"And then what?" Cassidy said.

Spencer looked into Cassidy's steely eyes. "Then I'm going to shoot him in his sleep."

Cassidy nodded doubtfully. He would not want to be the one to try that.

"What about the others?" he said.

"The way I see it, it's only Boone that we have to worry about. Maybe we'll shoot the Indian, too. The others will take what we give them. Or nothing."

"You promised Dorf a split."

Spencer made a sound in his throat. "That was when he was some use to us. We'll see."

"Why did you invite that goddamn Munro into our wagon tonight?" Cassidy wondered.

"'Cause you're going to kill him."

"What?"

"That little son of a bitch is driving me crazy with that hacking every minute of the day and night. And he's got some lawyer cousin in Boston. That could cause us trouble. I hate that little bastard. It's tonight."

"Hell. Why don't you do it?" Cassidy said.

"'Cause Boone would suspect me right away," Spencer told him. "I'll make a point of leaving the wagon late in the night. Say I can't take his coughing. Either Boone or the Indian will see me out there, putting down a bedroll. They'll know he's alive at that point. A little later, you'll smother him with his goddamn pillow. They'll think he died in the night. Of pneumonia or consumption or some damn thing."

Cassidy rubbed a hand through his beard. "I don't know."

Spencer peered up into his face. "You ain't got no choice in this. You follow me?"

Cassidy held his dark look. "Yeah."

"It'll be easy. Just don't wake up anybody outside. You'll be alone in there with him."

"Which means I'll be the only goddamn suspect," Cassidy complained.

"They'll believe you. They won't have no choice. You'll play it innocent, and there won't be no witnesses."

"Shit," Cassidy said.

"Don't let me down on this," Spencer warned him.

Cassidy let out a long breath. "Right."

It was still frosty the following morning, and Dan'l was stiff when he woke up just before dawn. He had seen Spencer come out in the night, complaining to himself about Munro. What surprised Dan'l now, as he awoke, was that he had not heard Munro coughing the rest of the night.

Dan'l was already up and throwing sticks on a guttering fire, and Skin Walker and Spencer were getting some cooking utensils out, when Cassidy climbed off the wagon and called out to them.

"Hey! There's something wrong with Munro!"

Dan'l and Skin Walker looked at each other, and Spencer furrowed his brow. Hawkins was just climbing down from the other wagon. "Huh? What happened?" he asked.

"Did he say Munro?" Spencer asked Dan'l innocently.

Dan'l and Skin Walker had volunteered to keep informal sentry duty through the night, and Spencer had taken a turn when he came outside, which rather surprised Dan'l. Dan'l now hurried to the back end of the Cassidy wagon, with Skin Walker following. Spencer came more slowly, and now Padgett and Dorf were also outside and wondering what was happening.

"He don't seem to be breathing," Cassidy said to

Dan'l. He tried not to sound too concerned. That would be out of character.

Dan'l went inside, and could find no pulse in Munro. He and the Sioux carried the inert form out onto the muddy ground, and inspected it more closely.

"He's dead," Dan'l finally announced, with everybody standing around. He looked right at Spencer, but knew that Spencer had been outside for most of the night.

"Well, I'll be damned," Spencer said in a quiet voice. "I guess that lung thing finally took him. Not too surprising, in this cold."

"I woke up, and didn't hear no breathing," Cassidy said easily. "I sleep like a log. He could've been dead for quite a while."

Dan'l was studying Cassidy's face, and Cassidy knew it. He held Dan'l's look. Munro had been sick, all right. But not sick enough to die in the night.

"What the hell really happened here, Spencer?" Dan'l said in a hard voice.

Spencer put a look of surprise on his thick, broken-nose face. "What do you mean, damn you?"

"You hated that little surveyor," Dan'l said. "What did you and this hunter do to him?"

"Hey, that's a goddamn accusation!" Cassidy blustered.

"Have you gone out of your head, Boone?" Spencer laughed harshly. "I wasn't nowhere near

Munro last night. And Cassidy here liked the little guy. You better watch who you're accusing, mister."

"You ain't got no call to get on Spencer," Padgett said from nearby. "The surveyor was dying, anybody could see that. It was just a matter of time."

Spencer made a mental note that Padgett had defended him.

Hawkins, though, who knew what Raven had told him about Spencer, also suspected the two men.

"Boone is having one of his delusions again," Dorf said, jumping in quickly on the side of Spencer. He wanted to say more, but was afraid of Dan'l now.

"I know there ain't no proof of nothing," Dan'l said in a low growl. "But it just seems that people tend to kick off very conveniently around you, Spencer." He had rather liked Henry Munro.

"You better find something to occupy your mind, hunter," Spencer said. "You're beginning to imagine things."

"Why don't we just drop it?" Hawkins suggested. "We got other things to think about. Like getting Munro buried, for one."

"There won't be time for that," Skin Walker said.

They all looked at him, and he pointed toward the nearest cliff-top. Dan'l was the first to glance upward, and what he saw confirmed his worst fears.

The west summit was lined with war-painted Sioux.

"Son of a bitch!" Spencer muttered.

"My God!" Hawkins managed.

"They're here," Dan'l announced. "Get the long guns!"

The words were barely out of his mouth when a rain of arrows came falling down around them from above, plunging into the muddy ground, the wagons, and Gustav Dorf's chest.

They all heard the arrow whistle to its mark, and thud into the German's torso. It passed almost entirely through him, and then he stood looking down at its feathered end, as if trying to grasp what had happened.

"Dorf!" Spencer said to him.

But Dorf fell onto his face in the mud, the arrow protruding from his back.

Hawkins bent over him. "Dorf!"

"He's dead!" Dan'l said loudly. "Get your damn guns!"

The next moments were chaos, as they all ran for their rifles, stacked nearby. Dan'l's Kentucky rifle hung on the side of the nearest wagon and he had it in hand in seconds, and was priming and readying it.

Another shower of arrows came down, several of them flaming, and one set fire to the canvas of a wagon. Dan'l was glad, though, that these plains Indians had not adopted the white man's guns yet.

Even though they would be badly outnumbered by the Sioux, they would have the only firepower.

"Jesus!" Padgett exclaimed. "They're everywhere up there!"

"That ain't the main force!" Dan'l called out. "*That's* the main force!"

Now it was he who was pointing, and when they looked, they saw the mounted warriors at the mouth of the ravine, only fifty yards away. There were well over fifty of them.

"Shit!" Cassidy said.

The wagons had been parked so that they were parallel to the ravine's entrance, and to each other. Now all seven men, including Skin Walker, took cover behind the outermost wagon, and cocked the long guns, just as Sitting Bear, in the midst of his warriors, gave his hand signal to attack.

Suddenly there was raucous yelling from the Sioux, and then they thundered into the ravine, like devils from Hades.

"Don't fire till they're right on us!" Dan'l called out. "Wait till you can see the paint on their faces!"

"Get your rifles ready for re-loading!" Spencer yelled. "Pick out a single target and hit it!"

As the Sioux charged from the open end of the ravine, a third shower of arrows rained down, sounding like hornets all around them as they hit willy-nilly in the camp area. One thudded into the wagon beside Dan'l's head, missing him by an inch, and another hit Skin Walker in the thigh. He cried out dully, but kept his rifle aimed at the attackers.

Then they were there.

Sitting Bear had remained behind to direct the attack. But Eye of Hawk and Iron Knife both rode in with the first wave of riders, yelling fiercely and brandishing lances. At twenty yards, the defenders all fired almost simultaneously, and several warriors were knocked off their mounts. Then, while the Indians rode right up to the wagons, into the teeth of the guns, Dan'l, Spencer, and Cassidy drew their primed Annely revolvers and fired again, killing three more Sioux. Hawkins was at the side of the fallen Dorf, wresting Dorf's pistol from its holster.

The Sioux unleashed another shower of arrows at the wagons, and now were circling the compound, but could not find an easy way in because of Dan'l's defensive redoubts of barrels, crates, and rope at the ends of the wagons.

Skin Walker had described Iron Knife after the previous attack, and now Dan'l saw him in the midst of the attackers, yelling loudly and urging his fighters on.

The four men with side arms had only to re-prime quickly, cock, and fire, and were getting more and more shots in as the Indians circled. Skin Walker and Padgett, who had only long guns, had re-loaded now and each knocked another Sioux off his mount.

Arrows were thudding into the two wagons regularly, and just as Hawkins was about to fire his confiscated Annely a second time, an arrow struck him hard in the left arm, knocking him against the wagon he used as cover. He yelled loudly, but nobody heard him. Then he tried to cock and aim with his good arm.

Dan'l was priming and firing fast, and hitting a Sioux with every shot. He fired again and blew the side of a warrior's face away as he rode on past, dead on his mount.

Then two bold and skillful riders leapt an end barrier at the same time, coming right into the defensive compound. One of them was shot immediately by Cassidy. The other came right at Dan'l.

It was Iron Knife.

The son of Sitting Bear who had pledged to kill the feared Kentuckian.

"Sheltowee!" he cried out as he came. "You are dead!"

He spurred his horse directly at Dan'l, not caring whether he himself survived the attack. He looked wild and deadly.

"Look out, Boone!" Padgett yelled.

Iron Knife did not hurl the lance. He carried it right to the wagon, intending to impale Dan'l to its side.

Dan'l cocked the revolver and aimed it at the onrushing rider, but he did not have time to get off a shot. The lance came at his chest almost as fast as if it had been thrown, and Dan'l turned awkwardly to his left to present a smaller target. The lance grazed his stomach, slicing into flesh and ripping through his rawhides, then thudding into the sideboard of the wagon, pinning Dan'l there by his clothing.

Dust flew up in front of him, and the pony reared and almost kicked him in the face. Then Iron Knife hurled himself off the mount onto Dan'l, a long knife now in his grasp.

On his way down, Dan'l spun back to face the new assault, and finally managed to fire the revolver. The explosion was hardly audible in the melee, but the ball hit Iron Knife in the throat, ripping through his jugular.

He was slamming hard against Dan'l, the wild look still on his war-painted, handsome face. He struck with the knife, and managed a shallow stab into Dan'l's shoulder, a crimson fountain spurting from his throat. Then he went slack and slid down Dan'l's body, dying as he hit the ground at Dan'l's feet.

"Goddamn," Dan'l muttered.

The chief's son had been a magnificent soldier.

There had been no joy in killing him.

The wounded Indian who had jumped the barricade threw a tomahawk and narrowly missed splitting Spencer's head wide open. Spencer fired and hit the warrior in the side. The Indian wheeled the horse, drawing a war knife, and spied Skin Walker, leaning against the wagon, firing and killing Sioux.

"The traitor!" he grated out.

Hawkins fired and hit him again, this time in the low chest. The Indian reeled under the impact, but before he fell from his mount, he hurled the knife into Skin Walker's back.

Skin Walker felt the blade penetrate his back, and then his heart. His eyes widened slightly as he reached for the knife, but he could not get to it. He slid to the ground not far from Dan'l, his eyes glazing over.

He looked up at Dan'l. "Sheltowee!" he hissed out.

Then he was dead.

"Son of a bitch," Dan'l said to himself.

More Sioux were hitting the ground around the wagons, and now the wagon set afire was burning brightly behind the defenders. Dan'l turned and spotted Sitting Bear only fifty yards away. The chief had seen his son go into the compound and not come back out. He raised his war lance and let out a long yell, and suddenly the circling warriors were riding away, leaving the ravine.

Spencer could not believe it. There had been a lot of Indians left. It had seemed to him that all of them in the compound would be killed. And now the attackers were riding off.

As the Sioux rode toward the mouth of the ravine, Dan'l saw a young Sioux attired like Iron Knife, and looking like a bigger version of him, and knew it was Eye of Hawk, the other son, whom Skin Walker had told him about. Eye of Hawk now raised his arm in a threatening gesture, with a look of deadly rage in his young face.

Then they all rode out of the ravine and disappeared.

The ones on the cliff were gone, too.

Chapter Eight

The defenders could not believe it was over.

"What happened?" Spencer said tiredly. He had a cut on the side of his head, where a Sioux arrow had grazed him. "I was sure they had us beat, and then they was running. What happened?"

Dan'l was kneeling over the fallen Skin Walker, feeling for a pulse. There was none. The knife still protruded from the Indian's back, and the arrow was still sticking out of his right thigh.

"They didn't run," Dan'l said, rising. "Sitting Bear lost his son, and that took the fight out of him. For now. He'll go back and mourn."

Cassidy grunted. "A crazy people," he said.

Dan'l regarded him silently.

"Will they come back?" Spencer said.

Dan'l looked from him to the dead Iron Knife.

Dan'l had also gotten a glimpse of Pale Coyote in the battle. The one whose life he had saved previously. He thought Pale Coyote had survived this fight, too. Maybe the Indian had a charmed life.

Dan'l cast a dour look at Spencer. "Not now, I reckon. Not here. They lost too many warriors because of this defensive position. I think they'll wait till we're out on the prairie. Heading home."

"Look!" Cassidy said. "The wagon bed is on fire!"

The rearward wagon was burning fast now, and its bed had caught, too, the wood sending black smoke into the sky.

"Damn it!" Spencer said loudly. He had not noticed, in the excitement. "The silver's in there!"

The five men that were still standing all ran for the water casks at the same time. But in the next few minutes it became clear that there was no stopping the fire. It was consuming the wagon, and everything in it. The pieces of eight, some extra guns, some camp equipment, a little food. Fortunately, most of their food and water and all the spare ammunition was on the other wagon.

After a few halfhearted efforts to stop it, they just all stood around and watched it burn. Then Spencer walked over to Dorf.

"Well. They got two of us. But that ain't bad, considering. I reckon we can take them on again."

Dan'l looked over at the corpse of Iron Knife, and realized what a frenzy that would put Sitting Bear in.

"You don't get it, do you, Spencer?" Dan'l said. "The next time they come, they'll kill us to the man. They might even keep a couple of us alive for special kinds of death."

The fire was burning itself out at the other wagon, but they could still feel the heat of it on their faces. Listening to Dan'l words, they stood silently.

"Our only chance now is to outrun them," Dan'l added. "To go so far so fast they won't bother chasing us. But I think that ain't likely. Not with this man dead at our feet." He gestured toward the dead Iron Knife.

"Maybe we better get ready to get out of here," Padgett said in a hollow voice. He saw the horses were still at the far end of the ravine. The Sioux had not bothered with them.

"I'd vote for that," Hawkins said with a wry grin. He had fought well, despite the wound in his left arm. Dan'l rather liked him. He was very different from Padgett, who had joined the expedition with him.

"Then let's get going," Spencer said. "Padgett, Hawkins, see if there's any salvage in that mess. And haul that pile of silver out of there, I don't care if it's all melted down, it's worth something." He paused. "At least they didn't get the gold and jewels."

Dan'l shook his head. "If we got any spare room in this one wagon, Spencer, it ain't going to no melted lump of silver. And don't have these men wasting our time going through them remains. We got to move. Now."

Spencer was taken aback slightly. Dan'l was usurping his authority, and in front of all of them. But he did not want an open confrontation with the Kentuckian.

He rubbed at his chin. "Oh, hell. All right, forget the other wagon. Get the team hitched up and let's get to hell out of here. I seen enough of this place to last me a goddamn lifetime."

With those words, they all began preparing to move out.

Following Dan'l's directions, they spent no time going through the smoldering rubble of the second wagon. But young Padgett made a mental note that there was a lot of silver bullion waiting for somebody to just pick up sometime, and maybe some unmelted pieces of eight, too.

Spencer forced himself to put the lost silver out of his mind. The important treasure, the stuff that would bring him a fortune, was still intact. And he mentally resolved that he was not about to turn it back over to the Sioux.

Within an hour the party was under way, heading out of the ravine, and turning due east. Back toward Missouri. They had not buried the dead, not even their own, and Dan'l did not argue about it. He did not care whether the German went underground. And he knew that Skin Walker would have been pleased to have his bones lie among the ancient ones on the surface of the ravine.

The Place of Sleeping had become his resting place, too.

As well as that of Iron Knife.

For additional speed in their race out of Sioux territory, they hitched up all four wagon horses as a single team. Dan'l was their only guide now, and rode up ahead of the wagon a half mile, looking for the easiest and fastest route through the low hills. Hawkins drove the wagon, with his left arm in a sling. Spencer and Cassidy flanked the wagon, watching for trouble, and Padgett brought up the rear on Skin Walker's mount. Logan's mount had been lost in the original attack.

Since they did not get started until mid-morning, they made no stops and did not eat a midday meal. They all knew their very lives depended on making the fastest time possible. The wagon, with extra animals pulling it, rumbled along the rough prairie at a fast pace, bouncing Hawkins around quite a bit, but the miles passed quickly.

By mid-afternoon, they were well away from the *Barranca Perdida*, where the thieving Spaniards and so many Sioux had lost their lives in battle.

Finally, though, the horses needed a rest.

They called Dan'l back, and stopped in the sparse shade of a stand of withered poplars. Most of the ground was bare of snow, with only occasional patches of it to ride through. In some places there were still drifts, but the party avoided them. The temperature was comfortable, but it was clear it was no longer fall.

They did not cook during the brief rest they took. They built a quick fire, though, put some coffee down, and ate some hardtack. Despite the chest of gold in the wagon, a solemnity had settled over the group. They kept seeing that look of hatred in Eye of Hawk's face as he shook his fist at them before riding off.

Spencer sent Hawkins down to a small creek not far away to get some fresh water in a couple of casks, and Dan'l decided to go with him. Dan'l wanted to splash some water on his face, and drink directly from the stream.

The other three remained back at the wagon.

When Hawkins had filled the casks, Dan'l took one of them from him to carry back. Hawkins stopped him before he could walk away.

"Dan'l," he said.

Dan'l turned to him and set the cask down. "What is it, Hawkins?"

"I been meaning to talk to you. Just you and me."

Dan'l frowned curiously. "Yeah?"

Hawkins hesitated, looked at the ground. He shot a look toward the wagon to make sure they were alone.

"Raven told me something he heard about Spencer."

Dan'l held the ex-soldier's look. "Go ahead."

"Raven overheard Cassidy talking to Logan, when Logan was still alive, before that first attack. According to Raven, Cassidy was telling Logan that Spencer is wanted for murder and robbery in New Orleans."

Dan'l gazed past Hawkins toward the wagon.

"He killed two men, according to Raven. Raven was afraid of him."

Dan'l nodded. "I knew it. I could see it in his eyes. He's a killer."

"He killed the colonel, didn't he?" Hawkins said.

"That would be my guess. And maybe Munro, too."

"That poor little bastard."

"The trouble is, there ain't no proof," Dan'l said darkly. "Nothing we know would hold up in a court. He's clever as hell. But I appreciate you telling me, Hawkins."

"I just wanted you to know. In case of trouble with him, I'm with you. I figure you're the real boss of the outfit now."

Dan'l smiled. "We don't need no boss. We just got to get as far away from Sitting Bear as them horses will take us."

"He won't share that gold with us, will he?" Hawkins asked.

"I wouldn't think that's his first choice," Dan'l

said. "Would it bother you if you didn't get any?"

Hawkins touched his bandaged left arm. "I guess all of us dream of riches."

"Well, I guess we better think about getting out of this alive first. We got the Sioux. And we got the winter. Both of them is coming back, probably."

Hawkins nodded. "Maybe we better get back," he offered. "Spencer will be wondering."

They carried the water casks back and Hawkins attached them to the sides of the wagon. Padgett was kicking up the small fire, and Spencer was at the rear of the wagon, talking privately with Cassidy. When he saw Dan'l, he came over to him, with Cassidy following along behind.

"Cassidy and me been talking," Spencer said to Dan'l.

"Yeah?" Dan'l said.

"It's turning colder again this afternoon. The sky ain't looking none too good neither. You was right, this winter is going to be on us. We was thinking maybe we ought to turn south. To get away from it."

Dan'l nodded. "That wouldn't be a bad idea, Spencer. If it wasn't for Sitting Bear."

"What about him?"

"The chances are, he's coming after us. The farther east we get, the more chance there is that he'll give it up. You turn south and you'll play right into his hands. It'll give him more time to find us."

Cassidy made a face. "We know the winter's

coming. The Sioux we don't know about. Sitting Bear might not come at all. Look at the people he just lost."

Dan'l sighed. "If we head right on east, we're going to cover a lot of ground in the next few days. South, it ain't so easy. And I'm not sure we'd be that much better off, south of here. You might be making the journey back a lot longer for nothing."

"Well," Spencer said. "I respect your opinion, hunter. But I think we'll maybe go the southern route. Cassidy and me is getting tired of freezing our butts at night."

Dan'l shook his head. "You can't make that kind of decision for all of us, Spencer. Maybe the colonel could, but not you."

Spencer bristled. "Is that so, Boone? Maybe you're going to start giving the orders around here?"

Padgett and Hawkins had come over now, and were listening closely.

"I don't intend to give nobody no orders," Dan'l said after a moment. "But I ain't changing the route we picked out, going straight east. And I think the others here ought to be able to make their own choices, too."

"I'll ride with Dan'l," Hawkins said after a short silence.

Spencer eyed him darkly.

Then Padgett surprised Dan'l. "Hell, I guess I'd

rather head east, too. That will get us home faster."

Dan'l caught Spencer's eye. "That's a majority, Spencer. Which means the wagon goes with us."

"The hell it does!" Spencer growled. "I'm the wagon master, by Jesus! The wagon goes where I go!"

Dan'l thought about that. "Maybe that would work out. We could split up the provisions. And, of course, the gold."

Spencer's face changed. "We was splitting the treasure when we got back."

"That was when we was going back together," Dan'l replied. "I think you'd have to admit it's only fair we get our three-fifths now, if we're splitting."

"That makes sense to me," Padgett put in.

Hawkins smiled slightly to himself.

Cassidy pulled his revolver and cocked it. "We ain't splitting no gold up now, by God. You can get yours in St. Louis."

"I don't think I'd like that at all," Padgett said. He now wore Dorf's revolver, and he placed his hand on its butt as he spoke.

Cassidy felt like shooting Dan'l right there, but if he did, he would have to kill Hawkins and Padgett, too. And if the Sioux struck again, he and Spencer might need them.

Spencer was thinking the same thing. "All right, Cassidy. Put the gun away. We don't want no shootout over this."

Cassidy hesitated, but holstered the side arm. Dan'l shook his head. "This ain't getting us nowhere."

Young Hawkins stepped forward to become a mediator. "Why don't we compromise? Head south the rest of today, and tomorrow. We won't get into too much hilly country by then. Then we'll turn east again, and ride hard for Missouri."

Dan'l was surprised by Hawkins's initiative. He might have become an officer, if the war had lasted longer. Dan'l went and leaned against the wagon. "We'll be doing just what Sitting Bear would hope for," he said. "And not really getting out of the winter. But I'll still let majority rule."

Spencer thought about all that. He did not want a confrontation with Dan'l. Not now, or ever. He glanced over at Cassidy. "What do you think, Cassidy?"

"All right," Cassidy said bitterly. "Let majority rule." He turned away from them. "But I vote no."

"That's a couple of no's, I reckon," Spencer said, looking at Dan'l.

"I still like the compromise," Hawkins said.

Padgett nodded. "Sounds fine to me."

Spencer caught Dan'l's eye. "What do you say, Boone? Shall we try to keep the party together?"

Dan'l realized it was pointless to hold out for heading east immediately. "Oh, hell. Why not?" he said heavily.

Spencer nodded. "Then we'll go with Hawkins'

idea. South through tomorrow."

In just minutes they were headed out again, but now to the south. Dan'l rode a half mile ahead, and directed Padgett to lag a half mile behind. He suspected it might be a few days until Sitting Bear came after them, but he was taking no chances.

Dan'l's belly wound had a poultice over it, and was healing well. It was rather shallow. The knife wound in the left shoulder was more troublesome, causing him a lot of pain as he rode along on the appaloosa.

Dan'l had persuaded the rest of them that they must ride hard and long that day, particularly because of the detour, so they kept on until dark. The going had been over rougher terrain, though, and they had not averaged as many miles in an hour. When they finally encamped, in a stand of low-growing trees, it was completely dark, and the temperature had fallen below freezing. Coats were buttoned up, hats snugged tightly over heads. A small wind had arisen, and it was cold just sitting beside their small campfire.

"Hell," Padgett complained, sipping hot coffee. "It couldn't been any colder than this if we went east."

Cassidy gave him a blistering look.

Dan'l said nothing. He'd told them that a detour south might not make any substantial difference, but they hadn't listened. All they were doing was giving Sitting Bear more time to catch them.

The five of them decided there was room for all of them to sleep in the wagon, by moving some provisions around. But Dan'l decided to sleep out on the ground again. He preferred the open air, cold as it was, to crowding up against the others, especially Spencer and Cassidy, both of whom he very much disliked at this point. They would not put sentries out, but Dan'l would be out where he might hear anything unusual.

Spencer did not plan to kill Dan'l immediately. He knew there would be time for that after they got out of Sitting Bear's territory and the danger was past. Then Spencer himself would put a gun up behind Dan'l's ear, while he was sleeping, and blow his brains out.

It was something Spencer was looking forward to.

Hawkins, Padgett, and Cassidy were still sipping coffee at the fire, when Dan'l noticed that Spencer had gone into the wagon. Cassidy was hunched into himself, fighting the cold, wishing they were in St. Louis. Padgett was telling Hawkins about an experience he had had at Yorktown, in the fighting. Dan'l got up from his stool, sauntered back to the rear of the wagon, and looked inside, where Spencer had lighted two lanterns, giving the interior a warm glow and some heat. What Dan'l saw surprised him.

Spencer was sitting on the floor of the wagon, with the gold chest open before him, and was examining some of the jewelry closely, his eyes glittering in the soft light.

He looked embarrassed when he saw Dan'l's silhouette, looking in at him.

"Can't keep your hands off it, eh, Spencer?"

Spencer's face went hard. "Is that any of your business, Boone?"

"It is if you're pocketing any of that stuff," Dan'l told him easily. "But I reckon you're too honest for anything like that."

"Don't worry yourself over it," Spencer said. "Remember, you didn't even want to go there. Anything you get out of this will be gratis."

"Does that mean I don't deserve a full share?" Dan'l asked with a grin. He climbed into the wagon and picked up his bearskin coat near Spencer.

"You figure that out for yourself," Spencer said. He put a large ring back into the chest, on top of all the gold.

"And I suppose you should have more, because you wanted to come," Dan'l went on.

"I told you before. I plan to dole out equal shares." He closed the chest and rose to his feet. They both had to duck some, because of the canvas covering.

"If you don't, you'll have trouble on your hands," Dan'l told him, watching his face.

Spencer grinned an ugly grin. "What's the matter, hunter? Don't you trust me?"

"Frankly, no."

"Well. That just makes me feel awful bad," Spencer said sourly.

"I don't know what's in that head of yours, Spencer," Dan'l said, pulling the heavy fur coat on. "But I'm going to be watching you, mister. You can count on that."

Spencer shrugged eloquently. "I guess that's supposed to bother me?"

"Like you said, figure it out for yourself." Then Dan'l turned and climbed back out into the night.

Spencer looked after him. *You're dead, you son of a bitch,* he said in his head.

The night was bitter cold, but it did not snow.

When they got up the next morning, Cassidy was complaining loudly about the temperature.

"I don't get it," he groused. "There's no way it should be this cold already."

They had all been stiff when they woke up, including Dan'l, who'd slept under the wagon in his coat and a thick blanket. Hawkins and Dan'l cooked some porridge to go with the hardtack and coffee, to warm them up inside.

They headed out again just after daybreak, with Dan'l preceding the wagon by a few minutes. They planned to head south all day, as agreed, then make camp just short of some rather high hills. Padgett still rode behind the wagon on a mount, but Cassidy and Spencer decided to ride on the wagon, their horses tethered to the rear of it.

The terrain was rough and undulating, and even with four horses hauling the wagon, it was slow going. There was shallow snow and mud to drive through, and on three occasions they had to put their shoulders to the wagon to shove it out of some rut or other. At one point they ran into a deep snow drift that blocked their path completely, and they were obliged to drive the wagon around it, losing a lot of time.

Dan'l fretted.

He could feel Sitting Bear's hatred on his back.

In mid-afternoon they arrived at the bank of the Republican River. There was light snow on the ground, the temperature was still below freezing, and the river was frozen over in this rather still, wide place. It looked to Dan'l as if it might have been for a week or more.

They all gathered together on its bank, on foot, and stared across the several hundred yards of white ice.

"I don't know," Dan'l said. "I'll go take a look."

He walked out onto the ice, and Hawkins went with him. Hawkins took a small axe, and they chopped a hole in the surface. Then they came back to shore.

"It's several inches thick in most places," Dan'l said. "It will probably hold the wagon. But it might not."

"Hell, we'll make it," Cassidy said. "I been over thinner ice than this."

Spencer rubbed at his chin.

"We can just follow the river," Dan'l said. "And not cross it at all. It heads east and a little south."

"I wanted to get a lot farther south today," Spencer said. "And you agreed to it. Remember?"

"I remember," Dan'l told him. "I'm just telling you the facts. It's up to you. But remember, you got that gold on the wagon."

Spencer thought about that. "Glad you reminded me. Cassidy, let's get that chest out of there. You got a strong horse, let's strap it to your irons, behind your saddle."

Cassidy did not much like that idea. "That'll make me pretty damn heavy," he said.

"Just do it," Spencer told him.

In less than a half hour, Dan'l helped Spencer and Cassidy strap the small chest—just over a foot at its longest measurement—onto the rump of the big chestnut mare that Cassidy rode. Then they were ready.

"Let's move out!" Spencer told them.

Dan'l and Cassidy rode onto the ice first, and it held them without any problem. The horses were skittery, though, on the smooth surface. There was an inch of snow on top of the ice, so it was difficult to see what they were walking on.

Hawkins then slowly drove the wagon onto the ice. They had also unloaded some cargo, and both

Spencer and Padgett carried small boxes in front of their saddles when they followed the wagon out onto the ice. Dan'l and Cassidy were unencumbered, in case they had to come to the aid of the wagon quickly. There were other boxes that Dan'l and the others would ride back for, after the wagon was across.

Hawkins drove the vehicle very slowly, listening for any cracking underneath him. Dan'l and Cassidy dropped back, riding beside the wagon, watching its every movement.

They got halfway across, and then the back left wheel broke the ice. Hawkins heard it in time to whip the team, and the wagon was dragged out of the shallow hole it made, and kept on going. Then, when they were two thirds of the way, there was a loud cracking sound, and the right rear wheel broke completely through the ice.

The wagon lurched and fell down on that side. The team tried to pull it free, but could not.

Dan'l dismounted quickly, and went over to the sunken wheel. Cassidy also got off his horse, but was careful not to release the reins. The treasure chest was his responsibility. Dan'l bent down to look at the hole.

"How bad is it?" Spencer called down from his horse.

"You two better get down here," Dan'l said. "The whole wagon could go in."

"You walk on across with that gold," Spencer

said loudly to Cassidy. "We'll take care of this."

Cassidy nodded, and turned and headed for the far shore, leading his mount.

In a moment Spencer and Padgett were beside Dan'l.

"It's pretty thin here," Dan'l said. "This is probably where the main current runs. This area could all go. We better get the wagon off of this real quick."

They all put their shoulders to the wagon, and Dan'l grabbed the big wheel in his thick hands. He felt his shoulder wound immediately, but he ignored the pain.

"All right, Hawkins!" he called out. "Move the team!"

Hawkins yelled at the horses, brought the reins down onto their backs, and the wagon lurched. Dan'l applied all of his enormous strength to the wheel, while Spencer and Padgett shoved hard on the back of the wagon bed. The wagon started out of the hole. Then the ice cracked under the left rear wheel.

"It's going!" Dan'l yelled. "Move it forward, or it'll be in the river!"

Hawkins whipped the horses and yelled loudly at them, and the three men at the back shoved with all the strength in them. There was more cracking underfoot, and then both wheels rose out of the ice and the wagon jerked forward. Dan'l had almost lifted the right wheel out of the hole himself.

The wagon rolled on shoreward, but in the next moment, there was more cracking under their feet. Spencer lost his footing and fell onto his side. His horse panicked and trotted toward the far shore, following Cassidy, and then Padgett's and Dan'l's horses went, too. Then a chunk of ice caved in right under Padgett, and he went through.

Padgett cried out, as he sank into icy water up to his chest. "Help! Help me!"

Spencer lay on the ice just beside the four-foot hole, and did not move. The current was now pulling Padgett to the downriver edge of the hole, trying to pull him under and carry him away under the ice. Dan'l knew that once he went under that barrier, they would never see him again.

"God, help me!" Padgett choked out, only his head above water, at the downriver edge of the hole.

"You can't get to him!" Spencer called out to Dan'l. He himself edged further away from the hole and Padgett. "He's gone!"

But Dan'l was crawling on his knees to the hole's edge, where Padgett was going under. The current was strong, and pulling him hard. In a moment, Padgett would disappear under the ice and be carried downstream underwater.

"Reach out to me!" Dan'l yelled. He held his hand out. He heard some slight cracking under him. "Come on, there's no time!"

They could all hear the terrible current in their ears, just beneath the ice.

"I—can't!" Padgett said desperately, flailing his arms about, grabbing at the ice.

Dan'l crawled even closer and grabbed at a waving arm. Finally he caught it in an iron grip.

"Hold onto me!" Dan'l ordered. "Spencer, get to hell away from here! It might go any minute!"

Spencer was already crawling away toward the far shore. Dan'l got a better grip on Padgett, and began backing away from the hole. An inch at a time. The ice did some more cracking, and Dan'l held his breath. The hole widened some; then Padgett's shoulders rose out of the icy water, and then his chest. Dan'l kept pulling and backing away, and suddenly Padgett was back on the surface of the ice.

He was gasping and choking, and looked frozen. Dan'l got onto his feet, as Spencer had also done, and started pulling Padgett farther and farther from the hole and off the weak ice. In a couple of minutes, he had pulled him near the far shore.

"Spencer!" he called out.

Spencer was on thick ice now. He gave Dan'l a sour look, then came back and helped Dan'l carry Padgett toward the shore.

When they arrived, the wagon was already safely ashore, as was Cassidy and his mount with the gold, and also the horses the men had been riding.

They laid Padgett down in the mud and snow. He was shivering uncontrollably, his lips blue, his skin pale. He looked like a suddenly revived corpse.

"Well," Spencer said unenthusiastically. "Looks like you saved him."

Dan'l stood there slumped into himself. Weary, hurting, and cold. All because Spencer had to move on south, against Dan'l's better judgment. He looked down at Padgett and shook his head, wondering if he would really make it.

"Let's get him into the wagon," he said heavily.

Chapter Nine

They drove the wagon away from the muddy riverbank and up onto higher ground, then loaded Padgett aboard and piled thick blankets on top of him, after toweling him down. Spencer wanted to start off immediately, but Dan'l insisted that they get Padgett's temperature up first. Hawkins agreed. Cassidy kept silent.

Padgett shivered violently for a half hour under the blankets. Hawkins finally lay down next to him to give him extra body heat, and that turned the tide for Padgett. He stopped shivering, and his skin turned back to its natural color. All the while, Dan'l kept pouring hot coffee into him.

"You saved my life, Boone," he said quietly, lying there.

"You would've done it for me," Dan'l told him.

Padgett wondered if that was true.

"I won't forget it," he said.

Spencer stuck his head into the wagon. "Well?"

Dan'l looked up at him. "All right, we can move out. But I'll stay in here with Padgett for a while. Cassidy can ride out ahead till I relieve him."

Spencer shook his head. "Oh, hell. All right."

They traveled hard and fast the rest of that day, with Spencer wanting to get as far south as possible before they turned to the east. In late afternoon Padgett was sitting up and moving about, and had managed to eat some hardtack, so Dan'l rode up with Cassidy for several hours, watching for signs of trouble. None came. Spencer insisted they keep going well after sunset, to make as many miles south as they possibly could. They quit well past dark, after traveling a ways by moonlight.

Padgett was up and clothed again by then, and helped prepare the camp. He had been humbled by falling in the river. Despite the riches resting in the small chest at the front of the wagon, he rather wished they had returned directly home, as Dan'l had suggested. He was afraid of the winter now, and of Sitting Bear.

Dan'l's shoulder felt a little better, but the episode with the wagon, and with Padgett, had slowed its healing. Hawkins still carried his left arm in a sling, and it ached all the time.

They all sat around the campfire that night in their coats and tried not to think about the mounting wind that felt so icy on their faces. They were still almost as far from home as they had been at the ravine, and Spencer realized now that the weather was not really different from what it had been farther north. With every day that passed it would get colder and more wintry, and they were a long, long way from Missouri. Their food was low, too, and that could be dangerous. Maybe as dangerous as the Sioux.

It was Dan'l who voiced their problems to the group.

"I hope you ain't got no more objections to heading east tomorrow morning early," he said to Spencer. " 'Cause I ain't in no mood to hear about any more detours."

Spencer grinned. "I said we'd head east tomorrow," he said. "And I'm a man of my word, Boone." Actually, he could not wait to make that move now. But he did not want to seem eager to Dan'l.

"I'm past ready to get to hell out of this country," Hawkins said with a scowl. He was cold all the time, his arm ached badly, and his stomach was churning inside him. He just wanted to get home.

"Likewise," Padgett said.

"You still worried over them Sioux, Boone?" Cassidy asked.

Dan'l despised the combination of stupidity and arrogance that Cassidy sometimes seemed to embody. "Didn't you learn nothing at that ravine, Cassidy? Sitting Bear wants us dead."

Cassidy shrugged. "A lot of folks is wanted me dead. But here I am. Just like I didn't give a goddamn."

"Maybe they'll give up on us now, Boone," Spencer put in, trying to mitigate the impact of Cassidy's rudeness. He did not want any more trouble with Dan'l just yet.

"We ain't hardly any farther from Sitting Bear than we was when we left the ravine," Dan'l pointed out. "Thanks to this second detour. Now let me ask you. You think that'll make any difference to Sitting Bear?"

Hawkins saw his point. "It'll encourage him to come for us," he said heavily.

"That was my thinking," Dan'l agreed.

Padgett and Hawkins exchanged a glance, and both wished they had argued harder to go east earlier.

"Well, let him come," Cassidy said. "We'll kill his other son this time, and he'll go slinking home with his tail between his legs."

Even Spencer looked at Cassidy at that.

"Wouldn't that be nice," Dan'l said, shaking his head. "Look, the facts are, we're down to five guns now, and we ain't got the cover we had before. You can't hardly hide behind one wagon."

Cassidy's face changed slightly, and Dan'l could see he had not even thought of that.

"Also, if we don't find some game pretty soon, we'll be in trouble. That buffalo meat didn't keep, and the good stuff is almost gone. Cassidy and me better try to bring something down tomorrow. The colder it gets, the more meat we'll need."

"That makes sense, Spencer," Padgett told him.

Spencer nodded. "We'll take as much time as we have to, to get some table meat in."

"Hunting will get hard, if the snow gets deep," Dan'l added as an afterthought.

They all sat around and thought about that. Suddenly the gold in the wagon did not seem quite all that important.

Dan'l slept outside again that night, because he did not expect any snow. But it got so cold that he had to pile blankets over his bear coat to keep warm.

He had been right.

Winter was upon them.

The next morning they got an early start in the darkness. They had an hour on the trail before there was real light in the sky. Nothing was as important now as making good time with the wagon.

Cassidy and Dan'l rode out a mile ahead of the wagon, looking for animal spoor, wandering off the main route to seek out game.

For the first couple of hours, there was none.

Then it began to snow.

By late morning the ground all around them was covered, and they had to ride around the drifts.

"Son of a bitch!" Cassidy complained.

He did not want Dan'l to be right. He had hoped they would be spared any trouble with the weather, for more than one reason.

"At least we can track better," Dan'l told him as they rode along the bank of a tiny creek bed, watching for spoor.

Dan'l rode slightly ahead of Cassidy, a tacit admission by Cassidy that Dan'l was a better tracker than he was. When Dan'l had just about given it up, and thought they would have to report back to the wagon for a midday meal, he finally spotted fresh tracks in the snow.

It was antelope, and there were a half dozen of them.

Dan'l did not speak to Cassidy. He merely pointed at the tracks, and waved Cassidy on. They rode on ahead warily, watching for the small herd as they went. When they rounded a bend in the creek, they found them.

The herd was standing in a tight bunch, right out in the open, on a flat plain across the creek, grazing through the shallow snow.

Both men dismounted and tethered their horses to a nearby bush. They slid their long rifles out of their saddle scabbards and crept up to the creek bank.

The water gurgled at their feet. Ice formed near the bank. It was just ten feet across, and clear as glass. It bubbled and tinkled in their ears. The big male antelope snorted and looked right at them. Boone and Cassidy froze in position. The antelope went back to grazing.

They were loaded and primed now. Dan'l nodded to Cassidy, and they both got down onto one knee, aimed the long guns, and cocked them quietly.

The guns erupted at the same moment, kicking in the hands of the hunters, and two of the largest antelope went down as if their legs had been pulled out from under them. The rest scattered across the snowy plain, and were gone before there was any chance to re-load.

Cassidy laughed gutterally. "I got mine right behind the right foreleg. Right into the heart. Can you match that, Boone?"

Dan'l nodded. "I caught mine under the left ear. Brain shot. Didn't spoil no meat that way."

Cassidy stared hard at him for a moment. A head shot was almost impossible at that distance. "Oh," he said.

"Let's go get them," Dan'l said.

But Cassidy stopped him. "Wait. Look over there."

There was a stand of trees off to their left, across the creek, and a half-dozen wolves were standing there, looking at the antelope on the ground, and the hunters. They had been attracted by the noise.

"Oh, oh," Dan'l said. He had had wolves take shot game away from him back east. They did that when they were especially hungry, as these appeared to be.

"Never mind the horses," Dan'l said. "Let's get to them antelope now. Claim our kills."

Cassidy nodded, and they waded the stream, splashing noisily through the water, then hurried to the place in the shallow snow where the antelope lay.

They were both breathless when they arrived. They re-loaded the big guns, but also primed the revolvers at their waists.

"They wasn't scared off by the guns when we took these down," Dan'l said. "They look pretty damn bold."

"Maybe they need a little lesson in firearms," Cassidy said, raising the muzzle of his long gun.

"No, wait," Dan'l said. "Let's see what they decide to do."

The wolves were big, lean, and dangerous looking. Antelope were their natural prey, and they smelled the blood at that moment, and were being driven beyond reason by it.

The wolves started out of the tree line toward the antelope, one at a time. It did not impress them that the men had taken possession of the kills. They came to within fifty yards, then thirty.

"They'll try to back us off," Dan'l said. "Now might be a good time to try to change their minds."

Once again they raised the long rifles. One of the

smaller wolves turned and ran back a few steps. Dan'l and Cassidy aimed at the two big ones in the front of the pack.

Just as they were about to fire, though, the wolves all began acting differently. They began scenting the air, and turning away from Dan'l and Cassidy.

"Hold it," Dan'l said quietly to Cassidy.

They lowered the guns and watched. One of the big wolves made a whining sound in his throat, looked back toward the antelope, then headed back into the woods, away from them. The others hesitated, then followed.

"What the hell?" Cassidy wondered.

"There's something out there," Dan'l told him. He strained his hawk-like eyes, but saw nothing for a moment. Then he spotted the specks on the horizon.

"There!" he said.

Cassidy looked where Dan'l pointed, and saw them. Four riders, coming hard.

"I'll be damned," Cassidy mumbled.

"It's Indians," Dan'l said.

"Sitting Bear?"

Dan'l shook his head. "I don't think so."

"Maybe we better get to hell out of here," Cassidy said.

"No. It's too late," Dan'l replied. "Just hold steady."

In just moments the four Indians reined their

ponies in fifty yards away. Dan'l looked them over. "They're Ogallala Sioux," he said.

"What the hell are they doing up here?" Cassidy asked.

"They're renegades," Dan'l concluded. "And it looks like they want our antelope, too."

The biggest Indian, who wore a feathered headdress, scanned the terrain behind Dan'l and Cassidy to make sure they were alone. He carried some kind of musket, loaded and cocked, and the rider beside him did also. The other two were armed only with bows. But it was clear they had done some trading with—or killing of—other white men.

They kept their distance. The big one raised his long gun into the air. "You violate Sioux hunting ground!" he called out in his own language.

"What did he say?" Cassidy said in a low voice.

"I don't know," Dan'l answered.

"You may avoid punishment. Give us your guns, and you may leave in peace."

"I think he's pointing at our guns," Dan'l said. "Probably asking for them in tribute. We can't give them up."

"He can have mine up his frigging nose!" Cassidy said.

Dan'l nodded. He pointed at his own gun, so the Sioux could see. Then he shook his head. "No. We keep our guns."

The Sioux talked among themselves, and Dan'l

saw the big one check his musket to make sure it was ready to fire.

"They're coming," he said to Cassidy. "We can't wait."

As they both raised the big guns at the same moment, the Sioux reacted, but late. The guns fired again, with Dan'l's just ahead of Cassidy's. Dan'l hit the big Sioux in the chest, and he was blown backwards off the pony, making the horse behind him rear and buck. Cassidy's lead struck the man beside the big one, in the high chest. The horse galloped off with the Indian still on it.

The two others, looking suddenly like angry demons, and thinking the white men were shot out for the moment, now yelled bloodcurdling cries and attacked.

"Here they come!" Dan'l yelled.

Both long guns were thrown into the snow, and both men drew the Annely revolvers on their belts. The Sioux were twenty yards away, coming at a breakneck gallop, arrows fixed on bows. Dan'l carefully cocked his revolver, and raised it to fire just as his target released an arrow.

His shot struck the Sioux in the nose and exploded into his brain, knocking him off his mount. The arrow ripped at Dan'l's rawhides at his side, but did not touch his flesh. But the pony crashed headlong into Dan'l, and he hit the snowy ground.

Cassidy had gotten his gun up and ready, but did not get a shot off before the other Sioux hurled a lance at him. He ducked down just in time, and the weapon grazed his upper arm and buried itself in the ground behind him. At the same moment, he grabbed at the reins of the horse, and yanked as the rider raced past. The pony turned, and the Sioux went flying, as Cassidy also hit the ground.

Now, though, Dan'l was on his feet again and priming the Annely. The last Sioux got onto one knee, armed with a tomahawk, and was about to hurl himself onto Cassidy. Dan'l cocked, aimed, and fired a last time. The Sioux fell right on top of Cassidy, a hole in his torso, front to back, that he could have thrust his hand into.

There was a lot of blood on the snow where the two Indians lay dead. Cassidy shoved the Sioux off him, growling an obscenity. But when he got up onto one knee, and saw what Dan'l had done, his mood changed.

"I like that last shot of yours," he admitted with a wry grin.

Dan'l caught his eye. It was the most you could ever expect from a man like Cassidy. Dan'l nodded to him. "It's all in a day's work out here, Cassidy," he said offhandedly.

Then he turned and headed back toward their mounts as if none of it had happened.

Chapter Ten

Cassidy realized, after that death struggle with the renegade Sioux, that he would not want to be the one to try to kill Dan'l Boone. First of all, he was beginning to think the Kentuckian was unkillable. But secondly, Boone had saved Cassidy's life. He could not kill a man who had done that. If Spencer still intended to do it, Cassidy would not interfere. But he would not help Spencer, and he would be willing to tell him that.

Back in camp, Dan'l and Cassidy skinned and gutted the antelope carcasses, then hung the meat on the side of the wagon to drain. They had cut off a few choice cuts for the midday meal.

Things were looking up. They had meat to last a while, and there was still no sign of Sitting Bear. They went through an area in the afternoon where there was almost no snow, and Spencer was beginning to think they would outrun the Sioux and the winter.

Then, in late afternoon, it began snowing again.

Out in front of the wagon a half mile, Dan'l reined in when the first flakes came down, and studied the sky behind them. It was very dark. He was afraid they were in for another blow.

By the time they camped for the night, it appeared he was right. A cold wind had blown up, driving snow along with it.

They were in for it again.

"We don't have the protection we had last time," Dan'l told Spencer. They were camped out on rather flat ground, with no real hills in sight. "It's going to hit us hard."

That was an understatement. By the time they had finished eating, they were in the middle of a blizzard. The wind was blowing the snow straight sideways, and it pelted their faces and hands like gravel.

They could hardly hear their own voices.

"Make sure the animals are secure!" Spencer yelled at Padgett, who was completely recovered now from the dunking in the river.

Hawkins had already climbed into the wagon, and Cassidy now joined him there. They began fastening covers over the open ends of the canvas to keep the wind and snow out. The horses were picketed to some thin trees beside the wagon.

Dan'l brought several old blankets and fastened them over the horses' rumps, but he knew that would not help a lot. Already the temperature was way below freezing.

"It's going to be hard on the animals," Padgett said above the wind.

Dan'l nodded. "There ain't nothing we can do about it."

Spencer had climbed inside the wagon, too, and Dan'l and Padgett soon followed. Dan'l had given up on sleeping in the open on a night like this. They all made their beds inside, and it was fairly crowded. Cassidy and Hawkins had attached blankets to the wagon ends, and that kept the wind out pretty well. Outside in the blackness, the wind howled and snow pelted the sides of the wagon.

"It'll get down to zero in this," Dan'l said, propped on his bed. "Maybe lower."

"Son of a bitch," Spencer said. He cast a quick look at the small chest in the front of the wagon, with its treasure cache. It did not seem quite so wonderful now as it had earlier.

The two oil lanterns flickered in the occasional blast of air that came inside. Cassidy sat against the wagon bulkhead, chewing on a piece of hardtack. "I hope this don't keep on like this. We got a long way home."

He had voiced the feelings of every man in the wagon, so nobody else spoke for a long while. Then, finally, Hawkins spoke. But it was not to the others. He was talking to himself.

"I wish to hell we'd never heard of that gold," he said quietly, lying on his bed.

Spencer cast a quick, hard look at him.

"I'd trade my share for five hundred miles of prairie right now, no questions asked," Padgett put in. "Just to get us away from all this."

"What the hell is the matter with all of you?" Spencer fumed. "You going to let a little snow scare you? In another couple days we'll leave all of this behind us. Sitting Bear. Most of this weather. And we'll still have the gold."

Dan'l shook his head. He was propped against the side of the wagon across from Cassidy. "Forget the gold. We made our decision on that, for better or worse. We got what we got, and we better deal with it. As soon as this storm passes, I say we start traveling as fast as we can move. And maybe we'll have to go at dark on both ends of the day."

"If we can dig out of this," Hawkins said.

They all looked at him, and felt his fear. *If* they could dig out. *If* they could move the wagon. They all knew that if the snow got too deep too quickly, they were stuck. Maybe until spring. With no way to feed themselves except sparse hunting.

"Hell, it might not matter, anyway," Padgett offered. "If Sitting Bear catches us."

That was as much as anyone wanted to hear. They turned the lanterns down and tried to go to sleep. The five of them huddled together against the fury of nature outside the wagon. The wind kept howling in their ears. And every time one of them woke up, the howling was still as fierce.

Then, Dan'l awoke again, and it was quiet outside. He carried no watch, but a clock inside his head told him it was an hour or so before dawn.

Dan'l got up and, stepping over Hawkins, made his way to the rear of the wagon. The blanket there had come loose at the bottom, and there was a smattering of snow on the wagon floor. He unfastened the blanket and squinted to see outside.

Everything was white.

"Is it over?" Spencer asked sleepily.

"It looks like it," Dan'l said.

With the bearskin coat on, he stepped down to a wooden step, and then onto the ground outside. He sank into the snow knee-deep.

"Damn!" he muttered.

"How bad is it?" Spencer asked.

"Bad," Dan'l told him.

He waded through the snow, and saw that it had drifted up onto the side of the wagon waist-high. It was still numbing cold, and he rubbed his hands together to get circulation into them. He pulled a pair of gloves out of the coat, and put them on. Then he went over to the horses.

They were stiff and unmoving. One saw him and made a small sound in its throat. He looked closer, and saw one of the team was on the ground, as was Padgett's mount. He bent down to look, and saw they were frozen stiff. A third horse, Spencer's mount, looked bad, but was at least standing up. It would never recover enough to leave with them, though.

Dan'l rubbed the coats of the other animals down with his hands, and they responded to him. There might be some frostbite among them, but they looked all right to travel.

Spencer came up behind him.

"Oh, shit," he said, looking at the downed animals.

"Yours is ready to go down, too," Dan'l said. "We'll have to shoot it."

Spencer looked at it. "It's dead on its feet," he agreed. "Goddamn it."

He took the Annely out of its holster, and primed and cocked it. He aimed at the horse's head and squeezed the trigger. The explosion startled the other animals, and brought them out of their stupor. Spencer's mount hit the ground beside the other dead horses.

"Now what?" Spencer said.

Cassidy came out of the wagon, clutching at himself against the cold. "What happened?"

"You can ride on the buckboard with Hawkins," Dan'l said to Spencer. "We can even use Cassidy's mount in harness. Padgett and him can stay on the wagon, too. But I don't know if we can get it out of this."

Cassidy came up beside them. "Holy Jesus!" he exclaimed.

"What a goddamn mess," Spencer said.

"You shouldn't went down for the gold," Dan'l said. There was no accusation in his voice. He was just stating a hard fact.

"Like you said, let's forget the gold for now," Spencer said testily. "Let's try to dig the wagon out."

"It won't do no good if it's all this deep," Dan'l told him. "You can't drive no wagon through this. I'll just go take a look out there where it's flat."

"I'll get the others up," Spencer said, blowing on his hands.

Dan'l walked out onto the prairie, away from the wagon. As he walked, the snow became less deep, and finally, on the open areas, it was just a few inches in depth.

Back at the wagon, they were having trouble getting Hawkins up. His feet had been exposed part of the night, and were stiff and numb. Padgett thought he might have light frostbite. Hawkins finally got up, but found it difficult to walk and could not get his boots on.

Padgett was working on getting some circulation into Hawkins's feet when Dan'l returned. Spencer and Cassidy were out shoveling snow away from the wheels of the wagon.

"If we can get through this drift, I think we'll be able to move the wagon," Dan'l told the others.

"But we got to get some feed into them horses."

"Hawkins can't walk yet," Cassidy said. "He won't be no good to us for a while."

Dan'l went inside the wagon, and saw Padgett massaging Hawkins's feet.

"I'm sorry, Dan'l," Hawkins said.

Dan'l examined the stockinged feet. "Go get some snow outside," he told Padgett.

"Huh?"

"Just get it," Dan'l said.

Padgett brought a big pail of snow in and Dan'l placed Hawkins's feet in it. Hawkins had been feeling some excruciating pain, but now that was relieved somewhat.

"Keep doing that till the swelling's gone," Dan'l said. "By noon maybe you can wear your boots, and start walking around."

"Thanks, Dan'l," Hawkins said.

"You tend him this morning," Dan'l said to Padgett. "We don't need you outside."

Dan'l went to help Spencer and Cassidy clear the wagon of deep snow, and get the horses fed and harnessed up. It was daylight by then, and it promised to be an overcast, very cold day. But the storm had passed.

"Could we get more snow?" Spencer wondered.

"Not right away," Dan'l said. "Let's see if we can get this wagon moving."

They did not eat that morning. They just had coffee, then got under way. Spencer grumbled some about Padgett "wasting" his time with Hawkins, but did not cause any trouble about it.

It was difficult for the new team of four horses to get the wagon moving ahead. Dan'l, Cassidy, and Spencer all put their shoulders to the wheels, and finally it moved. For the first hundred yards, it would lurch to a stop in deeper snow, and they would have to push again. But then they were up onto flat ground, with only two or three inches of snow in most places. They would come to an occasional drift, and Dan'l would guide them around it.

They made fairly good time, but not what Dan'l had hoped before the storm.

In late morning they entered very different terrain, with undulating hills, and there was not as much snow. The horses were finally able to move the wagon with little difficulty, and they made much better time. They stopped just once to rest the horses, and the men managed to cook up some antelope meat over a hastily made fire. At that stop, Spencer got Cassidy aside.

Cassidy was still chewing on a chunk of meat when Spencer glanced over his shoulder furtively, then spoke.

"I'm going to do it tonight," he said.

"What?"

"Boone. It's tonight. I made up my mind."

Cassidy suddenly found it difficult to swallow the piece of meat. "Jesus. Is this really necessary?"

Spencer eyed him suspiciously. "You ain't going soft on me, are you, partner?"

Cassidy shrugged, remembering the shot that had killed the renegade Sioux, just when Cassidy had been in fear for his life. "Hell, no."

"Do you want to share the gold equally with everybody here?" Spencer suggested. "Would you rather have twenty percent or fifty percent?"

Cassidy wiped his hands on his heavy wool coat. "I reckon you know the answer to that." When he spoke, his breath came out in spurts of white fog.

"Well, Boone is the only thing that stands in our way," Spencer told him. "Not only that, he just might decide to tell the authorities back east what he thinks about Davison's death. And Munro's."

"That ain't no business of mine, Spencer. I'll be leaving St. Louis just as soon as we split that gold. I don't care what he tells the folks back there."

"You forgetting you killed Munro?" Spencer said levelly. "They can come after you, you know."

Cassidy was irritated by all this. He knew he should not have let Spencer bully him into smothering Munro. "You ain't getting no help from me on Boone," he said at last. "He's a dangerous son of a bitch."

"I'll take care of Boone. It'll be a real pleasure. You just keep out of the way."

"I thought you wanted him alive till we was sure that Sitting Bear wasn't going to run us down."

"Sitting Bear?" Spencer grunted. "He'd've been

here if he was coming, wouldn't he? Every mile we cover puts us farther from that Sioux. Anyway, look around you. You think he wants to chase us toward Missouri through this snow? He's probably holed up for the winter already."

"I don't know," Cassidy said. "I get this feeling on the back of my neck. I just hope you ain't jumping the gun. If we get into Indian trouble, that Kentuckian could make the difference."

Spencer sighed. "Hell, I thought you had some guts, Cassidy. You're starting to sound like Boone."

Cassidy held his tough look. "It was Boone that said the Sioux would attack us at the ravine. And it was Boone that told us winter was coming early. Now he tells us that Sitting Bear's got a score to settle. Maybe we better start listening to him."

"It was one thing to attack us at their sacred site," Spencer argued. "Right in their hunting ground. But we're way out of Sitting Bear's territory now. If it was summer, he might come. But not in this."

"I hope to hell you're right," Cassidy said.

Spencer clapped him on the shoulder. "Tonight," he repeated quietly. "Just keep out of my way, that's all you got to do. Then you and me will really be in charge of this expedition."

Cassidy nodded heavily. "All right," he said.

* * *

Back at Sitting Bear's village, the storm had not hit quite so hard, and the snow was not as deep as where the Davison party had camped the previous night. Sitting Bear had assembled his warriors. At the same moment that Spencer was telling Cassidy of his plan to kill Dan'l, Sitting Bear stood before his grand lodge, looking over his troops. They had all just mounted their fastest ponies, and were awaiting his order to ride out. They were armed with bows, lances, and war hatchets. Their faces were covered with war paint, and many wore a wolf's head over their own. They were pledged to kill the entire Davison party before it got out of their reach. Pale Coyote, the one who had been saved from Dorf and Cassidy, was in their midst.

"Our horses are ready, Father," Eye of Hawk said, standing beside the chief.

Sitting Bear turned to him. Not far from the village, in the tribe's current burial ground, Iron Knife's body was decaying on a high platform built off the ground, in the Sioux tradition, where vultures picked at it and the weather ravaged it.

"I have given this much thought, my son," Sitting Bear said to Eye of Hawk. "You may not ride with us to take our revenge on your brother."

Eye of Hawk could not believe his ears. "What? Do you know what you are saying, Father? It is my sacred duty to seek vengeance! My brother lies dead!"

Sitting Bear nodded. "I will represent our family

in this. I am chief. I am his father. You must remain behind to protect the village and to take leadership, if I should fall in this encounter."

"The village does not require my protection!" Eye of Hawk protested angrily. "I will go, Father! I will shed the blood of these defilers, these murderers of royalty!"

"You will stay!" Sitting Bear ordered firmly. Nearby, two warriors looked toward him. "I command you! You will do what needs to be done. More courage is needed to stay here and keep the family line intact than to go and fight again. You are important to the tribe and to the family line. I am sorry, but you stay."

Eye of Hawk looked for a brief moment as if he would strike his father. But then his face changed and settled into hard lines of dark resolution.

"Very well. You deprive me of my greatest glory. But you are chief. I will not fight you on this."

"That is well," Sitting Bear said. "You do me honor. You do the tribe honor."

Eye of Hawk turned, bristling, and walked away.

"You do not wish us well?" Sitting Bear called after him.

Eye of Hawk stopped and turned back slowly. "Yes," he said.

Sitting Bear walked over to him. "I could not live with two sons dead. Do you understand?"

Eye of Hawk hesitated. "Yes."

"You make me proud," Sitting Bear said.

A few minutes later, Sitting Bear was mounted on his white pony and was leading the fifty-odd warriors out of the village.

The trek that day for the Davison party was a laborious one. They were in and out of snow all day, and some even came down in mid-afternoon, making visibility bad. Fortunately, the new fall did not add much to that already on the ground.

There were times when Dan'l had a hard time making a decision about their route. Ordinarily he would have guided them around the steeper terrain, but often now the lower places held the deepest snow. But they were stuck only once more, and just briefly, and they managed to make some good miles because they kept going well past dark again.

By the time they finally stopped, the cold had enveloped them once more. There was little wind by then, but their breath came out in white mist, and their nostrils caked with ice.

"It ain't even December yet," Spencer complained at the campfire. "What will it be like out here later?"

"You don't want to be here, I can tell you that," Dan'l said.

They had found a windswept hillock to camp on, with almost no snow on it. Dan'l figured it might be colder for them, but at least there was less chance of the wagon getting snowed in if it began to snow again.

They roasted some antelope meat over a bright fire, and kept warm at the same time, sitting around it on camp stools. Padgett kept stamping his feet on the ground irregularly, irritating Cassidy. Hawkins's own feet had recovered from the cold, although there was still some dark-looking flesh on a couple of toes, indicating a light frostbite.

The meat crackled and sizzled on the small spit they made from an aspen branch, and its odor was pleasant. They all wore head protection now. Cassidy had found a coonskin cap with heavy fur, while Padgett and Hawkins tied wool kerchiefs across their hats and under their chins. Spencer had donned a heavy wool cap, and Dan'l just tied his wide-brim Quaker hat down over his ears with a short length of hemp.

They were five heavy-looking, dark blobs of humanity squatting around that yellow fire, with the black-and-white ground stretching off in all directions, into the blackness. It reminded Dan'l of similar camps he had made in the wilds of Kentucky, when it was still virginal.

"I think the animals will be all right tonight," Dan'l said, poking the fire with a stick. "It won't get all that cold."

Spencer looked at him. This was his chance to make something happen. "Maybe one of us should sleep out here," he suggested. "Since there won't be no snow, probably. You and Cassidy did run onto them Ogallala."

Dan'l had been thinking of that, anyway. He hated sleeping in with the rest of them, all crowded up inside. "I can do that," he said. "I'll sleep by the fire, and maybe be better off than the rest of you."

They all knew that was not true. "Well," Spencer said, "one of us could take a turn at it."

Dan'l looked into his face and knew he did not mean it. "No problem, Spencer. I'm used to it."

Spencer relaxed. He did not want to do what he had planned inside the wagon. It would be too obvious to the rest of them that way. "It's settled, then," he said.

Hawkins gave him a dark look. He did not trust Spencer at all. Any time Spencer suggested something, Hawkins figured there was an ulterior motive. He took his arm out of the sling, and moved it about, making a face.

"Maybe I can use this arm tomorrow," he said.

"It's about time," Cassidy told him, getting up and walking over to the horses picketed nearby. Hawkins looked after him soberly.

"Don't let him bother you," Dan'l said. "We're all a little out of sorts by now."

They ate leisurely, enjoying the warmth of the fire. Cassidy was finished first, and went into the wagon. He was very tense about this night. Spencer followed, then Hawkins. Padgett stuck a stick into the fire, and bright sparks floated upward into the darkness.

"I hear it was like this at Valley Forge," Padgett said to Dan'l when they sat there alone. "Except some of them didn't even have shoes to wear, or proper coats. Hawkins and me just missed that."

"Hawkins says you was a good soldier," Dan'l said.

Padgett arched his brows. "He said that? Hell, it was him. He got a medal, you know. Charged right into the British muskets. It's a miracle he ain't dead."

"I couldn't figure what all the fuss was about, at first," Dan'l said, remembering. "I fought with the British against the French. Had some friends among them. Damn fine soldiers. I hated to finally take up the gun against them."

"We had to do it," Padgett said.

Dan'l nodded. "I know."

"Well, I guess I'll get some sleep."

"See you in the morning, Padgett."

Padgett paused before leaving. "Be careful out here, Kentucky man."

Dan'l grinned at that. "You can count on it."

An hour later, they were all on their blanket beds, four of them in the wagon, and Dan'l out by the fire, with the wagon at his back. The fire was guttering out, and he watched the last coals glow in the dark. For some reason unknown to him, he felt uneasy about falling asleep that night.

Inside the wagon, Spencer waited. He could not fall asleep, or it might not get done. Another hour passed, and the others were snoring around him.

He still waited. He lay there thinking of what he would say to them when it was over. He would drag Boone's body out to the horses, and say he had mistaken him for an intruder in the dark. He did not really care whether Hawkins and Padgett believed it. They would not challenge him. Later, he would tell them he had decided not to share the gold. Give them a few coins apiece, maybe, but nothing more. If they gave him trouble, they would go the way of Boone.

Maybe they would anyway.

Of course, Cassidy might object to that much killing.

Spencer lay there thinking it out. Maybe he did not need to convince Cassidy of anything. Or confront the other two. Maybe the best thing was just to sneak out of camp some night, after Boone was taken care of, and take the chest with him. He could travel twice as fast as the wagon. If Cassidy came after him, he could handle him. He would not even go to St. Louis. He would take the gold and head for New Orleans. Where a rich man could enjoy himself.

Finally, he took a cheap watch from a pocket and looked at the time. It was almost three a.m. The hunter was surely asleep.

He got off his bed and moved past Cassidy and Hawkins to the rear of the wagon. Cassidy woke and tensed. Hawkins mumbled something in his sleep. Then Spencer climbed out into the night.

A small breeze chilled him immediately. When he came around the corner of the wagon, he squinted and saw Dan'l on the ground beside the fire.

At his side Spencer carried the Annely revolver that was always with him. He was good with it. He knew guns well, and was acquainted with their good and bad points. The Annely would occasionally misfire, so he had done an extra good job of priming. He was ready.

He walked carefully over to the still figure on the ground. His pulse pummeled his ears, and he was angry at himself for having fear. It was only a sleeping man lying there, not some goddamn ancient god, as the Apaches believed of Dan'l. It would require only one shot to the back of the head.

He took one last step forward, and came to within five feet of Dan'l. His shoe crushed some stiff grass near the fire.

Suddenly Dan'l whirled around onto his back, looking right down the muzzle of Spencer's gun.

But Dan'l's hand held his revolver, too, primed and cocked, and it was pointing at Spencer's heart.

"What the hell is going on, damn you!" Dan'l spat out.

Spencer almost squeezed the trigger, but then thought better of it. He quickly lowered the muzzle of his side arm. "Hell, I didn't mean to scare you, Boone. I heard something out here. I went to look at the horses, then come over here to make sure you was all right."

Dan'l eyed him warily for a long moment, then lowered his gun. "You sure you was looking at horses?" he said in a hard, low voice.

Spencer put on a hurt look. "For God's sake, Boone. What do you think? I ain't got nothing against you. You're jumpy as a goddamn cat. That imagination of yours is acting up again."

"You come sneaking around me at night like that, you might end up breathing out a new hole in you," Dan'l said, studying Spencer's face.

"Is that a threat?" Spencer said innocently.

"Take it how you like," Dan'l told him. "Now, I recommend you get back inside the goddamn wagon, where you belong. I'll take care of what's going on out here."

Spencer shook his head and holstered the gun. "Jumpy as a goddamn cat," he said to himself. Then he turned and walked back to the rear of the wagon, and climbed inside.

Once inside, he stood at the entrance for a long moment, and found that he was shaking slightly. It had been close. If he had pulled that trigger, Boone would have killed him, too.

Now he had accomplished nothing.

And he had put the Kentuckian on his guard.

Out on the ground, Dan'l lay there and stared into the black sky and wondered if Spencer had been going to blow a hole in the back of his head. Once again, there was no proof.

But the suspicions were mounting against him.

After that incident, Dan'l slept like a log. He knew that if Spencer had murderous intentions, there would be no further trouble on that dark night.

Spencer was not dumb enough, or brave enough, to make a second try.

Things were strained between Dan'l and Spencer the next day. Dan'l did not speak to him all through the morning meal or during the preparations to leave. Then he rode out ahead of the wagon, to keep clear of the others for as long as possible.

It it had not been for Hawkins and Padgett, Dan'l would have abandoned Spencer and Cassidy to their fate, whatever it might be, and ridden east by himself. But without him, the party might not make it back. Even if Sitting Bear did not come.

The terrain was flat again in the morning, and the wagon moved along without much difficulty. But after the midday break, the sky clouded up, and the temperature rose some, and a heavy, rather wet snow started coming down.

By mid-afternoon, there was a lot of it on the ground.

Dan'l took them up into higher ground, in the hope of getting out of any deep snow, but there was plenty there, too. The wagon plowed through rocky areas, and up and down a couple of high hills. In late afternoon, Dan'l came across a snowed-over crevasse that appeared quite deep, and rode back just in time to prevent the wagon from being driven into it.

"Whoa! Hold it up!" he yelled from the far side of the split in the earth. The crevasse was not visible, because of all the snow. "There's a long hole in the ground under this drift. We'll have to go around. Head south for a hundred yards."

Hawkins was driving, and waved across at Dan'l. "I wouldn't have seen it," he called back.

Cassidy rode up beside the wagon. Since they were making better time in the shallower snow, he had taken his mount back from the team, so now the wagon was pulled by three horses. "Can I jump it?" he said to Dan'l.

"I wouldn't try it," Dan'l told him. "The appaloosa just made it."

Cassidy nodded, and headed toward the end of the crevasse, ahead of the wagon. Hawkins whipped the three-horse team, and the wagon lurched drunkenly ahead. Spencer watched gloomily over his shoulder.

When they reached the far end of the crevasse,

Dan'l stopped them again, and dismounted to test the edge of the hole. It was twelve feet across in places, but narrow where he was. Padgett had gotten out of the wagon to probe on his side. Remembering his rather awkward fall into the river earlier, Dan'l began to stop him.

"I got the edge of it!" he said to Dan'l before Dan'l could speak. He was poking with a shovel handle. "It follows right along—"

A large chunk of crusted snow broke away at his feet, exposing a precipitous drop-off, and suddenly Padgett was sliding down into it.

"Hey!" he yelled.

Then he was gone.

"Son of a bitch!" Dan'l swore from across the narrow hole.

Snow floated upward into the air from the hole, and then it was very quiet. Dan'l went carefully to the edge and looked down. It was all rock and snow, with no sign of Padgett.

Cassidy had dismounted, and now was peering down, too. "He's buried under that stuff!" he said.

Hawkins and Spencer got off the wagon and came over to the crevasse. Hawkins looked very worried.

"Padgett!" he yelled down.

Spencer was shaking his head. "That hole could be bottomless. He ain't got a chance under all that."

"That's the goddamn truth," Cassidy said.

"We can't just leave him down there," Hawkins blurted out. "He could be alive."

Spencer looked down. It was a fifty-foot drop, just to the snow. And that was not the bottom of the pit.

"You want to jump in there after him, maybe?" Spencer suggested wryly.

Hawkins hesitated.

"I'll go down," Dan'l said.

They all looked at him. "Are you out of your mind?" Spencer said.

But Cassidy took a hundred-foot coil of rope off his mount. He came over to the edge with it. "Will this help?" he called over.

Spencer turned and looked at him as if he had gone crazy.

Dan'l nodded. "Just throw it over. I'll do it from here. With the appaloosa."

Cassidy nodded, and hurled the rope across the six-foot gap, and Dan'l caught it. "Come on around," Dan'l said.

Cassidy cast a quick look at Spencer, and followed Dan'l's request. He went far around the end, to be safe, while Dan'l uncoiled the rope and tied it to the appaloosa's saddlehorn. Then he dropped the length of it into the hole. It hit the snow pile on the bottom.

Cassidy was now walking toward him, on his side of the hole. Dan'l said to him, "The appaloosa is pretty good at this. But you better steady him."

Cassidy nodded. "Glad to." He had been secretly glad that Spencer had failed to murder Dan'l, and Spencer had noticed that relief. But Cassidy did not care.

Dan'l shed the big coat and gloves, and began shinnying down the rope to the bottom of the hole. Across the way, Hawkins and Spencer watched him go down. Cassidy steadied the horse as Dan'l's weight strained on the rope.

Then he was on the snow, and sinking into it. He looked up fifty feet and saw their faces up there, watching him. He looked around. "Padgett?" he called out.

Nothing.

"Padgett?"

It looked hopeless.

Then he heard a muffled voice. "Boone!"

"He's alive!" Dan'l yelled up.

He began digging into the snow near him with one hand, hanging onto the rope with the other. He saw a hand emerge, digging up toward him.

"Padgett!" Dan'l said.

In another moment, Padgett's face was partially visible, snow-smeared and icy. Dan'l grabbed Padgett's outstretched hand.

"Hold on!" he commanded Padgett.

Padgett nodded. Dan'l looked up toward Cassidy. "Guide the appaloosa away from the hole!"

Cassidy nodded, and the horse began backing away from the crevasse. Dan'l began rising on the rope, and then Padgett was pulled free of the snow, and was being hauled to the surface, hanging onto Dan'l for dear life. In just moments they reached the brink, and Dan'l climbed out of the hole, bringing Padgett with him.

They lay on the snow at the top for a moment, Dan'l breathing hard. It was the second time he had had to save Padgett from death in a few days.

"Can't you keep out of trouble, for God's sake?" he said crossly to Padgett as they lay there together.

Padgett was brushing heavy snow off him. For the second time, Dan'l was the one willing and able to pull him to safety. He focused on Dan'l now, looking pale. "I was always the clumsy one of the family," he said, trying a small grin.

Dan'l sat up and returned the smile. "Come on, you little bastard. We got miles to make."

Chapter Eleven

Early winter had set in for good now.

As they moved on through the high country that day, there were very few areas that were not completely snow-covered. And each day some new snow came down. As Dan'l had suspected, it was going to be a long, hard winter on the Great Plains.

He hoped they would not be out there when the worst came. There had been a westward expedition the previous year that had been caught for the winter. They had run out of food entirely, and had begun boiling rawhide and leather for what remained of food value, and chewed dead grass that lanced through the heavy snow. Then, when things got really bad, they had drawn straws and chosen one of them to quit feeding. When that individual had finally frozen to death, they had all cut chunks off him and consumed human flesh. Just one of them had survived to tell the tale, their hunter-guide. And he was not the same man. He had begun stopping people on the streets of St. Louis, to relate the horror story to them. Complete strangers. And of course no one wanted to hear such things. Just before the Davison party had left for the West, last summer, he had been thrown into a lunatic asylum, and Dan'l figured he would never come out.

That was what winter on the prairie could do to people.

Padgett had been badly bruised by his fall, and badly scared. Even more so than at the river. He rode the wagon all the rest of the day, recovering once again from near-tragedy. He acted differently now, too. He was very quiet, and when he spoke, it was generally about getting back, and what he would do when they got to St. Louis.

He treated Dan'l with something akin to reverence now. When they finally quit for the day, finding another windswept rise of ground with little snow, Padgett came out of the wagon and helped set up camp, brought Dan'l the first cut of roasted meat, and poured his coffee for him.

Dan'l finally gave him a sour look. "What the hell you think you're doing, boy?"

Padgett shrugged. Nearby, Hawkins grinned to himself. "Just trying to help out," Padgett said innocently.

"Well, go help somebody else," Dan'l told him irritably.

"You can get me some coffee," Hawkins suggested with a smirk.

Padgett gave him a look. "Right."

Later, at a moment when Spencer and Cassidy were over making sure the animals were secure, Padgett came over to where Dan'l was coaxing up the fire.

He crouched beside Dan'l, at the fire, looking rather small and thin next to Dan'l. He rubbed at his hawk nose for a moment, squatting there. Dan'l finally looked over at him curiously.

"What is it, Padgett?"

"I was just wondering," Padgett said. "About Spencer."

"Yeah?"

"I don't think he really wants to share that gold with us."

Dan'l grunted. "Did you just figure that out?"

"Hawkins and me, we couldn't cause him much trouble about that. But he knows you would."

Dan'l glanced at him again.

"I think he'd have to get rid of you, before it become an issue," Padgett said. "I just been doing some thinking about that."

Dan'l laughed gutturally. "Better just think about getting home," he said. "Forget the gold, and forget me."

"He might try to kill you, Boone," Padgett whispered conspiratorially.

Before Dan'l could reply, Hawkins came up to them. He had heard the last, despite Padgett's lowered voice.

"He's right, Dan'l," he said quietly, looking over his shoulder. "He killed in New Orleans, and I think he killed the colonel."

Padgett looked up at him. "New Orleans?"

"It's a long story," Hawkins said.

Dan'l stood up, and Padgett did, too. "Look," Dan'l said. "Why don't we just let it go?"

Padgett sighed. "You can't just ignore the danger. Maybe you ought to . . . get to him first."

Dan'l stared at him. "Murder him?"

"Better him than you."

"Dan'l couldn't do that," Hawkins said.

Dan'l agreed. "I ain't turned into no Spencer yet. I hope I never will."

"I owe you," Padgett said. "I think maybe I could do it. Some dark night."

"Nobody owes nobody that big," Dan'l told him. "Forget it, Padgett. You ain't no murderer neither."

Cassidy was now walking toward them, and they all stopped talking when they saw him.

"So," he said. "Any predictions for tonight, Boone?"

* * *

When Dan'l woke the next morning, he knew Sitting Bear was coming.

It was just a feeling in his gut, but he knew with a certainty the Sioux chief was out there on their trail somewhere.

Traveling twice as fast as they could.

"He's on his way," he said, staring out over the white plains.

"Huh?" Cassidy said from nearby.

"Oh. Nothing," Dan'l said.

Cassidy walked over to where Spencer was feeding the horses. "Boone is talking to himself," he said.

Spencer shot a look toward Dan'l. "I had some bad luck the other night. But I'm going to rid myself of that bastard. Even if I have to take him face-to-face."

"Are you serious?"

"I said it, didn't I? I'm fed up with that son of a bitch. Playing hero for these soldier boys, and trying to tell me how to run a goddamn expedition. He's the only thing that stands between me and the rich life."

Cassidy looked at him.

"Well, I meant you and me, of course."

"Did you, Spencer?" Cassidy said slowly.

Spencer held his clouded gaze. "What the hell, Cassidy. You going to get crazy on me now?"

"We're partners, Spencer. Don't forget it."

"I ain't forgetting nothing. Now go get the

wagon ready for hitching."

Cassidy gave him a sober look, then walked away.

They got under way shortly, and the going was slow that day, because of snow on the ground. There was a lot of winding and weaving around the deep places, and the wagon got stuck a couple of times and had to be pushed loose.

Dan'l thought, though, that if they could put another hundred miles or so behind them, the weather might become a little milder, and they could get to St. Louis well before Christmas.

But that would only be possible if Sitting Bear gave up on them.

And Dan'l did not think that would happen.

When they stopped at midday, they had not covered much ground. Dan'l decided to let Cassidy ride out ahead and find the best route for them, while he dropped back of the wagon for a half mile, where he could watch for Sitting Bear. He stopped regularly and stared out behind him over the rolling, white terrain. But he saw nothing.

At the break, in a stand of leafless elder trees, Spencer was very quiet. He was angry over Dan'l's continuing to make decisions for the expedition, taking the initiative away from Spencer himself, who considered himself boss of the party.

They were paralleling a thin, bare woods, and Dan'l wondered if there was any game in it. He was considering taking a look after they headed out again. Hawkins built them a fire, and Padgett put on some coffee. They were breaking out containers of food, and paying little attention to what was going on around them, when Dan'l looked up toward the nearby woods and saw the bear coming at a lope. It was just fifty yards away.

It was a grizzly.

"Bear!" Dan'l shouted.

They all looked, and saw it coming. It was showing no fear of them whatever, which was typical of a grizzly. It came on toward them as if they were just chunks of meat for its next meal.

Cassidy started running toward the wagon to get his long gun, but Dan'l stopped him.

"There ain't no time for the rifles! Get off the ground! Climb onto something!"

The others wasted no time following Dan'l's suggestions. The bear came lumbering toward them, looking very big. It was one of the largest Dan'l had ever seen. A male, alone and hungry.

Hawkins and Padgett both climbed small trees, though Hawkins had trouble with his arm. Spencer climbed atop a snowy, five-foot boulder and hunched down there, drawing his revolver. Cassidy jumped into the wagon, even though it was still hitched to the team. Dan'l ran to the far end of the wagon, ready to climb inside if it became necessary.

Then the bear was there.

It came right into camp, roaring at the treed

men before heading on to the fire, where they had unpacked some dried meat. The bear ate the meat hungrily out of an open box while they all watched. Dan'l remembered a grizzly in Tennessee that had come into a camp of three sleeping men. It had bitten the face off one before the others woke up, and then busied itself with disemboweling him. One of them got up a tree, but before the third one could get away, the bear brought him down and began mauling him, too. It tore his right arm off through his screaming, and then came and broke his neck when the screaming did not stop. The man in the tree could only watch in horror while the bear ate some more of the first fellow, and then wandered back out of camp, its muzzle crimson with blood.

Now this bear was rummaging through crates and boxes, tearing into them, making a mess. The team of horses at the wagon were rearing and plunging, but the bear ignored both them and the out-of-reach men. The two picketed mounts were nearby, whinnying and kicking.

Spencer had primed and cocked his revolver.

"Don't shoot it!" Dan'l warned from the wagon. "You'll only make things worse!"

Suddenly the bear turned toward the two mounts—the horses Dan'l and Cassidy rode—and headed at a run toward the nearest one, Cassidy's horse. Before the horse knew what was happening, the big bear lunged onto it and brought it down.

Dan'l's appaloosa strained and kicked, then finally broke free and ran off. The horse on the ground was struggling with the bear, but it was useless. In moments its throat was torn open, and the bear was ripping the belly to get at its innards.

Cassidy threw Dan'l his Kentucky rifle from the wagon, and Dan'l caught it with one hand. He nodded at Cassidy, and saw that the rifle had already been loaded and primed.

Dan'l peered around the corner of the wagon, cocking the long, heavy gun. The bear had not seen him. At the moment, it was ravaging the horse. There was a lot of snorting and grunting from the grizzly. They all watched silently, from their hiding places. The three horses in harness had stopped rearing, but were spouting fountains of steam from their wet nostrils, wide-eyed and terrorized.

The bear finally got off the mauled and partially eaten corpse of Cassidy's mount, and ambled back toward the low fire, red-muzzled. It suddenly spotted Spencer for the first time, squatting atop the boulder, and made a charge that almost made Spencer drop the gun he held in his hand. The bear reared up and threw itself against the boulder, but could not make it to the top because of the slippery snow. Dan'l had the rifle to his shoulder, but did not fire. The bear turned away from the boulder and Spencer just as quickly as it had charged, and looked right at Dan'l.

It reared up again onto its hind feet, standing seven feet high, and roared so loudly that Dan'l could feel the sound of it in his chest. Dan'l knew he was dead unless he could fire a fatal shot with one try. He put the front sight on the bear's chest, and squeezed the trigger.

The hot lead hit the grizzly's heart dead center, exploded it like a ripe melon, and fractured the animal's spine on its exit through its body.

That did not stop the bear. It still charged at Dan'l, even with its heart torn apart and its back broken. It roared to within fifteen feet, then ten.

Its legs collapsed under it, and it fell onto its face.

It struggled to its feet, growled fiercely at Dan'l, and collapsed again.

It was finally dead.

"Jesus Christ!" Spencer said from the boulder.

Dan'l went up to the animal and touched its head with the muzzle of his rifle. It did not move. Dan'l let out a long breath. His father, Squire, had told him when he was a boy that a bear is not dead until you have it skinned. Dan'l was always cautious with a shot one, no matter how many bullets it had taken.

"It's all right!" he called to the others.

It took several minutes for them to gather from their "safe" places. Hawkins and Padgett were wide-eyed when they looked down at the bear, and at the horse it had killed.

"Damn!" Padgett murmured.

"That was one goddamn ugly bear," Cassidy said.

Spencer eyed Dan'l sideways. "I notice you didn't try to kill it till it come for you."

"Oh, Christ, Spencer!" Hawkins said.

Dan'l regarded him impassively. "He couldn't climb that boulder, he was too heavy. He didn't threaten nobody but me."

"You might've thought it was a threat if *you* was on that boulder," Spencer countered.

Dan'l did not respond. He put the rifle back into the wagon, and Cassidy caught his eye. It had been his quick action that had gotten Dan'l the rifle in time to kill the bear.

"Nice shooting, Boone," he said quietly.

Dan'l nodded. "He give me a good target."

Spencer stared hard at Cassidy, realizing the Kentuckian was winning him over, and in that moment he made up his mind definitely to exclude Cassidy from any share of the gold.

"I got to go find the appaloosa," Dan'l said to them. "I'll take the lead team horse. Maybe a couple of you could get busy on that bear."

"What?" Spencer said.

Dan'l sighed. It was always an argument with Spencer, no matter what Dan'l said. It was getting worse between them. "The bear's got to be skinned and butchered. We're going to need that meat, if we get through this. It could make the difference between life and death."

"To hell with that," Spencer barked. "Leave that goddamn bear alone. It would take hours to butcher it. Boone and Cassidy can find lots of game as we move. Let's get to hell out of here. Maybe we can get out of snow country."

Cassidy stared curiously at Spencer. It was obvious Dan'l was right. But Spencer had been on the short end of too many disputes since he killed Davison and took command of the expedition. Now it was a matter of ego.

"Dan'l's got a good point," Hawkins put in, massaging his left arm. His handsome, young face looked rather pale and tired. "That bear could feed us all the way to St. Louis."

Spencer was furious, and it showed in his face. "In the first place, bear meat ain't fitting to eat! It tastes like shit! And in the second place, I'm giving you a goddamn order as head of this expedition! Forget the goddamn bear and get that third horse free of harness. Cassidy will need it to ride."

Dan'l turned to face Spencer. "This ain't really up to you, Spencer. Remember, we been through this before?"

Spencer felt an anger in his chest that had been building up inside him ever since Dan'l first challenged him. Suddenly his Annely revolver was in his hand, primed and cocked.

Everybody reacted with surprise.

"All right, you son of a bitch!" Spencer gritted out. He was not going to wait to catch Dan'l asleep. He was tired of waiting. His anger overrode his patience. "I had enough of you. You're a goddamn menace to this whole expedition. Now the talking to you is over. You got to go so we can survive."

"Don't be a jackass, Spencer," Dan'l warned him.

"Spencer, for God's sake!" Hawkins cried out.

But Spencer knew there would never be a better chance to do it. He had caught Dan'l completely off guard. His finger whitened over the trigger.

"Wait!" Padgett suddenly yelled. And in the next instant, as Dan'l fell into a crouch and went for the skinning knife on his lower leg, Padgett impulsively threw himself at Spencer, grabbing for the gun.

Dan'l had saved his life twice. Now it was his turn to re-pay the enormous debt.

Padgett reached the gun, but it went off anyway and hit him in the side. He fell to the ground at Spencer's feet, and Spencer almost fell with him.

"Goddamn you!" Dan'l spat out. He lunged at Spencer as Spencer frantically tried to re-prime his weapon. Dan'l hit him hard before Spencer could complete the operation, and they both hit the muddy ground beside the bear. Spencer used the revolver as a club and struck Dan'l alongside the head with its barrel.

It was a blow that would have knocked many men down for good, but Dan'l just shook it off, rolled once with Spencer, and pinned him to the ground with the knife up under his chin.

The point of the blade broke the skin on Spencer's throat. Dan'l held it there.

"Don't kill me," Spencer said, breathless. "I was just going to wound you. To teach you a lesson."

"The hell you was!" Dan'l said.

"Kill him!" Padgett said from the ground beside them. He had just been grazed, and was not losing much blood.

Dan'l heard the plea just as he was about to shove the knife into Spencer's brainpan. He paused, hearing the words tumble around in his head. They were the only words that could have stopped him.

He withdrew the blade.

Spencer let out a long breath. He said nothing.

Dan'l climbed off him, and slid the knife back into its sheath. "Get up, you son of a bitch," he said.

Spencer rose slowly, shooting a look toward Cassidy. He made a mental note that Cassidy had made no move to help him. He rubbed a thick hand across his broken nose.

"All right. Now what?" he said, not looking at Dan'l.

Dan'l helped Padgett to his feet, and saw that his wound was a shallow one. He shook his head.

"What the hell is the matter with you?"

"I owed you," Padgett said.

"You damn near got yourself killed," Dan'l told him.

"The kid ain't hurt," Spencer said.

"You bastard," Dan'l said. "If there's a menace to this expedition, it's you. I ought to killed you."

"I told you. I wouldn't've killed you."

"Like hell," Padgett said, holding his side.

"Maybe we ought to just leave you here," Dan'l suggested. "With some food and water. You ain't fit to travel with civilized folks."

"Oh, you want to steal my gold?" Spencer said tightly.

Dan'l shook his head. "No, I'd give you your share of the cache. A fifth, that is."

"Sounds like a damn good idea to me," Padgett said. "Why don't we vote on it?"

Spencer gave him a brittle look.

Cassidy rubbed at his thick beard, and remembered that he might get more of the gold if Spencer survived. "That would be the same as putting a bullet in his head," he said evenly.

Spencer regarded him icily. It was a weak defense, but it was better than nothing.

Now Hawkins spoke up. "It probably would," he agreed.

Dan'l shrugged. "Then I guess he stays. But things ain't going on the same, Spencer. You ain't telling the rest of us what to do. You ain't fit for that."

Spencer was relieved that Hawkins had said something. But he had not found much humility. "Maybe that makes you the boss?" he said to Dan'l.

"There ain't going to be no boss," Dan'l replied. "All our lives is at stake. We all ought to be able to speak our mind."

"Damn right," Padgett said.

"Absolutely," Hawkins agreed.

Cassidy hesitated. "I can live with that," he finally said.

"Hell, all right," Spencer finally said. "It don't matter that much to me."

Dan'l grunted softly. "Now get to skinning that bear, why don't you?" he said to them.

When he headed for the team horse to throw a saddle on it, he brushed past Spencer and almost knocked him down.

Spencer stared hard after him, wondering what had gone wrong.

Wishing Dan'l was dead.

Chapter Twelve

It took two hours to butcher the bear. Dan'l found the appaloosa in half that time, and towed it back to camp. When the bear was finished, Dan'l suggested they also cut some flank meat off the horse, and they did. The meat was all hung in strips to dry along the sides of the wagon. They then moved on out, and because the snow was very light on the ground in that area, they used just two horses to pull the wagon, and kept a saddle on the third one, for Cassidy. At this point, they needed a guide out in front of the wagon, and Dan'l in the rear to watch for trouble.

They passed into some low country that afternoon, where there was little snow on the ground. The temperature was down too, though they still had to try to avoid a lot of deep mud.

The countryside was taking on a different look. They were losing the long vistas and distant horizons, and the terrain was getting more of an eastern look. The prairie was broken up now by patches of trees, small streams, and ridges and low hills in places.

But they were not out of Sioux country.

Unknown to them, Sitting Bear was not far behind. His war party had ridden very hard, found the dead Ogallala Sioux, and were able to estimate that the expedition was only hours ahead of them.

They were getting to the far boundary of their territory, but Sitting Bear was committed. He was going for them.

The wagon ran into some hilly terrain in the afternoon, and even though there was almost no snow, the party was slowed way down. Dan'l began to feel uncomfortable about their progress. Sitting Bear now seemed much more of a problem than the weather. Dan'l could feel him back there, gaining on them.

Spencer was very quiet. He and Hawkins took turns driving the wagon, while Padgett nursed the shallow wound that Spencer had given him. The men were close in the wagon, but almost never spoke.

Things were very tense.

Dan'l had been reluctant to give Spencer a loaded gun when they decided to keep him on, but then he realized that they would need him if and when Sitting Bear caught them. So Spencer still carried the Annely on his hip.

They were all wearing side arms now—they had found an extra one in Davison's gear—so they all had the convenience of both pistols and rifles.

They stopped when late afternoon came. They were heading into more hilly country, and the two-horse team was tired. Dan'l had fallen way back after their midday break, looking for Sitting Bear. But there was nothing back there in sight.

When they settled into their night camp, Spencer and Cassidy fed and tended the horses, while Dan'l and Hawkins prepared the food and got a fire going. Padgett was excused from work generally, because he needed the rest. The wound was healing well, and Dan'l knew how important it was to let it heal, and avoid infection.

Cassidy and Spencer tied feed bags on the horses, picketed to tall, slender elms with bare branches.

"I expected more from you back there," Spencer told the hunter. "You turning on me, boy?"

"I ain't turning on nobody," Cassidy said. "That was a goddamn dumb play, facing Boone down like that."

"If that stupid soldier boy would've kept out of it, I'd've had him," Spencer complained.

"Yeah, you might have put one in him. But then he'd've nailed you with that knife. You'd probably be dead now."

"Is that a vote of confidence?" Spencer snarled.

"It's telling you what is," Cassidy said. "Even then, you're lucky I spoke up. You'd be out there on the prairie by your lonesome. You wouldn't've made it back by yourself."

"I would, by God. If just to get even with that son of a bitch farmer-turned-hunter."

Cassidy gave him a sly look. "You better just let that go."

"Let it go?" Spencer said. "Ain't you forgetting that box of gold and jewels? You want to end up with a goddamn fifth share?"

"Not particularly."

"Well, Boone'll make sure they all get theirs," Spencer reminded him. "As long as that son of a bitch is around, that stuff ain't ours."

"Well, I don't want to challenge him," Cassidy said. "I heard stories about him that make you think. Killing Indians like they was flies. Fighting grizzlies with a knife. I ain't sure he could be killed with just a gun."

Spencer eyed him. "So that's why you're being so cozy with him. You're scared of the Kentuckian."

"Call it what you want. But I like to give him a wide berth."

"If you and me was to draw down on him together, he wouldn't have a chance," Spencer said in a half-whisper. "Ain't it worth the risk? For the gold?"

Cassidy remembered that moment when Dan'l had saved his life, when the Ogallala Sioux was about to kill him. He sighed heavily. "I'll give it some thought," he said.

Over at the fire, Padgett had just put on a big pot of coffee. Hawkins was piling up some wood nearby, and Dan'l was slipping some dried meat on a stick to cook over the fire.

"We didn't make much distance today," Dan'l said to Padgett. "We're still in a lot of danger out here. We're like ducks on a pond."

Padgett had a thick bandage on his side, and it hurt like a toothache. "You think he's coming, don't you?"

"Sitting Bear? I know he's coming."

Hawkins drifted over to listen.

Padgett stared into the crackling fire. "He'll kill us all, won't he?"

Dan'l looked at him. "He'll try to."

"What chance do we have?" Padgett wondered.

Dan'l shrugged. "I don't think about stuff like that." It seemed as if death had always been at Dan'l's elbow as long as he could remember. He had no fear of it now. If it came, it came. He wanted to get back to Rebecca and the children but he knew in advance that might not happen. And Rebecca, pretty Rebecca, knew it, too.

"I just can't help thinking," Hawkins added. "That if the colonel was still alive, none of this would have happened. We'd be long gone from here, and wouldn't have to worry over the weather or the Sioux."

Padgett met his bleak look, and understood. "We all know who we can blame for the colonel's death," he said.

Dan'l poked at the fire. "I been in enough courts of law to know you can't sentence a man to death without hard evidence," he told them. "Otherwise, I'd've killed that son of a bitch back there."

"You should have killed him today," Padgett said.

Hawkins gave his friend a dour look.

"I had to kill a half-breed once, back in Carolina," Dan'l said, deep in thought. "Name of Saucy Jack. A couple of local boys named Nick and Little Red got him all liquored up and told him some lies about me. When he saw me in town the next time, he called me out, and I had to shoot him."

A brief silence fell over the fire.

"Jack waren't no bad fellow. He just got riled by them country boys, and let his liquor do his thinking for him. I hated myself for a while after that shooting. I didn't have no choice about it, of course, but I got down on myself, anyway. Said I'd never shoot a man down without good cause again. I didn't figure I had a real good reason with Spencer."

"He tried to kill you!" Padgett protested. "Maybe he would have."

Dan'l smiled through his thick beard, took the dark Quaker hat off his head, and looked at it for a long moment. "I been meaning to thank you, boy. But you oughtn't did it. It was a fair fight."

"Fair?" Hawkins said.

"As fair as most, I reckon. When I got him on the ground, I could see it in his eyes. He knowed he made a mistake. He had given it up. There ain't no honor in killing a man like that."

"Honor!" Padgett repeated.

Hawkins grinned. "You talk a lot like an Indian, Dan'l."

Dan'l nodded. "I think a lot like them. I was practically raised by them. Whenever Paw got out the trade goods and sat down with the Cherokee, I was right there on the blanket with them. Some was good friends. They taught me things about the woods that's hard to come by."

"The colonel said you were adopted by the Shawnee," Hawkins said.

Dan'l laughed quietly. "Oh, that was old Blackfish. He was smarter than most British officers he was fighting against. It was him that first called me Sheltowee. In them Frenchie wars, the chief finally captured me. But he had heard so much about me, he wouldn't kill me. Adopted me as a son, actually went through a tribal ceremony. I liked the old man.

"Trouble was, he wanted to make me a Shawnee warrior. Never let me leave the tribe. So I had to escape. They chased me for four days before they give up. Then old Blackfish put a death warrant out on me. I was a big disappointment to him."

"Jesus," Padgett said.

"Some folks think I act more Indian than white," Dan'l concluded. "But what that usually means is, I treat Indians just like I would white folks. They don't like that."

Hawkins nodded. Besides Davison, he was the one who had liked Dan'l from the beginning. "I suppose those same people wouldn't like it much that you were made an Apache god," he said with a wide grin.

Dan'l shook his head slowly. "That waren't nothing I put into their heads. I tried to tell them, but not many was listening. Except the chief's son, and he tried to kill me."

Hawkins laughed, but when Dan'l turned a sober look on him, his face went straight. "Sorry, Dan'l."

"He burned my partner over a spit," Dan'l said pensively. "Like a pig. Except he would've killed the pig first."

Hawkins swallowed hard.

"That shows they're different from us, don't it?" Padgett suggested.

Dan'l sighed. "In their world, it ain't immoral to cause physical pain. But they won't play with a man's mind, like we do all the time. It's all how you're raised."

"You wouldn't act the way they did," Padgett said.

"No," Dan'l replied. "But I try to stand by my own code of honor. Just like they do."

Padgett nodded. "I see your point."

Cassidy walked over to them and noticed the talking stopped. "I got to replace a shoe on one of them team horses. You know where that box of iron is?" he asked Dan'l.

"I'll get it," Dan'l said, rising.

Before he followed Dan'l, Cassidy gave the two ex-soldiers a long, studious look.

Almost five miles to the west, Sitting Bear and his small army were encamped on a stream bank that ran to within a few hundred yards of where the Davison party had stopped. They were well out of sight of the wagon, but they knew from the freshness of the wheel tracks in the scattered snow that they were very close now. Sitting Bear planned to close the distance between them the following day, and then attack on the next morning.

A quiet resolve permeated his camp.

They all knew that the barking sticks would kill some of them in the attack before they destroyed the expedition. But then the Place of Sleeping, and Iron Knife, would be avenged.

The entire war party slept out in the cold, under the heavy-looking sky, wearing bearskins and buffalo robes, except for Sitting Bear, who had a lean-to built for himself. Not for his comfort, but as a symbol of his authority. The Indians built a couple of very low fires, only after it was determined that they could not be seen from the east. Gruel was consumed, and dried fish, and individual warriors chanted quietly to their gods for a successful battle.

In mid-evening, Sitting Bear called Pale Coyote to his lean-to.

Pale Coyote was perhaps Sitting Bear's most decorated warrior on this trek, since Eye of Hawk had been left behind. He had received elk's-tooth necklaces and exquisitely made headgear previously for his heroic deeds in battle against the Ojibwa and the Teton Sioux. He was a high-ranking *akicita* and was a leader of his local Strong hearts, the elite warrior society. Because he was related to Sitting Bear by blood, he was treated like royalty by the tribe.

When Pale Coyote joined him, Sitting Bear was seated cross-legged on a fancy blanket, smoking a long, ornamented pipe. A bodyguard stood beside the lean-to, looking fierce in his war paint, which would never come off until the party returned to their winter village.

Pale Coyote asked permission, then sat down beside his chief, looking strong and muscular beside the older man. Both men were draped in soft cow-buffalo robes.

"I can see them in my mind's eye," Sitting Bear said when Pale Coyote had seated himself, facing out toward the low fires and the groups of huddled warriors. "They must think we have forgotten them. Forgiven them for their evil deeds."

"They may not think of us at all," Pale Coyote suggested. "When gold blinds the eyes of the white face, it clouds his memory also."

"There is one who remembers," the chief said. "The one called Sheltowee. The one who killed my son."

Pale Coyote looked over at him. "Yes."

"A great wrong will be avenged soon," Sitting Bear went on. "But it becomes clear now. Others like them will come. Many others."

"It would seem so."

"If they come in numbers, we cannot fight them with our traditional weapons. We must have the barking sticks."

"The Apaches are already using them," Pale Coyote said. "Against the Spaniards."

"When we have killed these men," Sitting Bear said, "we will take their guns. Later, we will capture a white face and make him show us how these weapons work. But all of these must die immediately."

Pale Coyote made no comment, but again he was thinking of Dan'l Boone, the one called Sheltowee, the hunter named Ancient Bear by the Apaches, and held in reverence by them. He was different from the others. He acted more like a Sioux than a paleface. And he had saved Pale Coyote's life.

"Must we kill Sheltowee?" he finally said very quietly to his chief.

Sitting Bear regarded him curiously. "The white Shawnee? He is the man who killed my son, your cousin."

"He defended his own life, my uncle. In battle."

"He was at the Place of Sleeping!"

Pale Coyote nodded. He knew that Dan'l had not wanted to go after the gold. But Sitting Bear was not listening to reason at the moment.

Sitting Bear looked into his eyes. "They must all die, nephew. We have no choice."

Pale Coyote looked at his feet.

"It is likely it was your white Shawnee who murdered our cousins we found out on the high plain. He is a much feared warrior. We will be sure he dies honorably, in battle."

Again, no response.

"The Buffalo Dreamers have guaranteed us a great victory," Sitting Bear said more softly. "We must not demean their prophecy with talk of mercy for these whites. Any of them."

Out in the cold wind, they could hear the low chanting of several warriors, praying to their gods for the white man's blood.

* * *

The Davison party was up in the dark the next morning, and under way before dawn. They had resolved to put a lot of miles behind them that day, because Dan'l was absolutely convinced that Sitting Bear was back there, gaining on them with every hour that passed.

Cassidy rode out ahead of the two-horse wagon again, and Dan'l brought up the rear.

In mid-morning, Dan'l spotted a mule deer off to the south several hundred yards. Realizing how much better deer meat was than bear or horse, he decided to go after it.

He could not get close, though, because the deer saw him at a distance, and headed back west of the wagon. Dan'l followed it, in case he got a better shot. He rode slowly, watching for the animal ahead of him, heading away from the wagon all the time. Finally, just as he was about to give up, he saw something on the summit of a small rise of ground, moving toward him about a mile away.

But it was not the deer.

It was a Sioux warrior.

"Son of a bitch!" he muttered.

Sitting Bear was very close behind, he knew now. This was a scout sent to find the Davison party's exact location. There was only one way to buy them a little time. He had to end the Indian's mission.

The wagon trail that the Indian was following

came right past a stand of box elder trees on Dan'l's left. So he quickly rode into the trees, knowing the warrior had to come very close past him.

When he got there, he dismounted quietly. The Sioux had not seen him yet. He was riding slowly toward the trees, watching the ground, reading spoor.

Dan'l slid the rifle from its scabbard, but realized he had no time to load and prime. The Sioux was too close. Dan'l picketed the appaloosa well into the trees, in some dense, dead brush, then hurried over to the edge of the clearing. The Indian was only fifty yards away.

Dan'l primed the revolver on his belt quickly. The Sioux was coming right past him. Dan'l stepped out from the trees, aimed at the Indian's heart, and squeezed the trigger.

There was no explosion of gunpowder, just a dull fizzing sound. The hammer had fallen onto a dud cartridge.

In the same instant, the Sioux yelled out in surprise. He had been at the ravine, and knew who he was looking at. Sudden fear filled his face.

"Sheltowee!" he breathed.

While Dan'l was trying to extract the cartridge, the Indian gouged his heels into the side of his pony, and charged directly at him in desperation.

Dan'l had sworn softly when the gun misfired. Now he looked up to see the horse pounding down on him. He took a side step and grabbed at the Sioux's rabbit coat as he thundered past. The Sioux was pulled off his saddle and went down with Dan'l, in his iron grip.

They hit the ground hard, and the horse ran off. They rolled there, grunting and straining, the Indian with a knife in his hand.

Dan'l held the knife away from his throat, smelling the Indian as they rolled on the ground. The Indian was strong, and young, and his head was now filled with possibilities. He was actually in a death fight with the great Sheltowee, god-son of the Shawnee, ancient god of the terrible Apache. If he managed to kill him, he would be a tribal hero. His name would go down with the legends of the past, and old men would tell his story for generations to come at village fires.

The blade came within two inches of Dan'l's throat, then an inch. Their arms trembled with the exertion, and Dan'l thought he had never seen a more powerful Indian. Unknown to Dan'l, the warrior was a close friend of Pale Coyote, and Pale Coyote had told him astounding tales of this white face.

Dan'l felt the tip of the blade break the skin of his throat. He gathered all of his energy, twisted his gun hand loose, and swung the barrel of the Annely against the Sioux's head.

It cracked hard and the warrior fell off him. Dan'l got the cylinder free and raised the gun just as the Indian was ready to thrust the knife at his chest. He squeezed the trigger again, and the gun fired loudly. The Indian was hit in the forehead. A blue hole appeared there, and blood and matter sprayed out behind him. He just stared at Dan'l for a long moment, the knife still in hand, then collapsed onto his face at Dan'l's knees.

Dan'l was breathing hard, and a trickle of crimson inched its way down his throat from the shallow stab wound.

"Damn!" he said, gasping for breath. "That was one damn fine soldier."

He got up unsteadily, and looked around for the Indian's pony. It was nowhere in sight. Dan'l could only hope it did not know its way back to Sitting Bear's camp.

He unpicketed the nervous appaloosa and rode hard back to the wagon.

Chapter Thirteen

The wagon had just been pulled to a stop for a midday break when Dan'l rode up in a gallop and jumped off his mount onto muddy ground.

"Where the hell have you been, Boone?" Spencer said from the front of the wagon. "Cassidy thought we'd lost you, for Christ's sake!"

"Sitting Bear's here," Dan'l said loudly, walking his horse to the wagon. "I just killed one of his scouts. There might be more. We got to make tracks. Now!"

Cassidy stood beside the wagon, a canteen in hand. He just stared dumbly at Dan'l. "Holy Jesus!"

"Are you sure he was from Sitting Bear?" Spencer said.

Hawkins and Padgett had gathered around Dan'l, wide-eyed.

"How sure do I have to be?" Dan'l barked. "There ain't no reason to think some other tribe is out here tracking us like goddamn bloodhounds! We ain't got time to argue this! Get aboard that wagon and let's move!"

"I don't believe it!" Spencer muttered. "I thought that old bastard had surely give up on us."

"I didn't think he would," Hawkins said to himself.

"Damn it!" Padgett swore, throwing a coffee cup to the ground.

"Boone's right," Cassidy said after a moment. "We got to move. Fast."

It took them just minutes to get ready and leave. They put Cassidy's horse back on the wagon, for extra speed, and he rode in the rear of the wagon with a cocked rifle across his knees. Dan'l trailed behind on the appaloosa, hoping to head off any sneak attack from behind.

It was a hectic several hours. Dan'l realized there was little hope of outrunning Sitting Bear and his mounted warriors, but at least they might find a better defensive position to fight from, if they kept moving.

In late afternoon, they came across such a site.

They came to the bank of the Smoky Hill River.

The river was rather wide at that point, and very deep. On the far side, it was iced over.

Dan'l arrived at the river just after the wagon. They all climbed down and stood on the bank together.

"It's running way too fast here," Spencer said. "We'll have to follow downstream to a good crossing place. We want to put this between us and the Sioux."

"Trouble is," Hawkins said, "if we find an easy place, they'll follow us right to it."

"I'd still like to have the river between us," Padgett said. "At least for a while."

Cassidy shook his head. "With the time that's left today, the most we can do is find a crossing place and try to get to the far side. They'll probably be on us tomorrow morning."

"Well, then, at least they'll have to attack across the river," Spencer argued, irritated that Cassidy was opposing him again.

"It's pretty clear this is the deep side," Cassidy kept on. "It ain't just impassable for the wagon. It could pull a mount's feet out from under it. On the other side, it's sand bars and easy riding."

"You making a point?" Spencer said impatiently.

"I think he's making a good one," Dan'l said, standing there holding the reins of the appaloosa.

They all turned toward him.

"If we make our stand here, we can pull the wagon up parallel to the riverbank, just a few feet from the water, and fight from behind it. The

Sioux won't be able to get behind us because of the river."

Cassidy nodded. "If we cross over, where it's shallow, they'll be able to ride around us just like we was out in the open prairie. There won't be no place for us to hide."

"By Jesus, that's right!" Hawkins commented. "Some of us had that situation in the war. With the deep water behind us, the Sioux won't dare enter the water. It'll be like having our backs to a canyon wall. We can keep them all in front of us, where we can pick them off."

Padgett scratched his head. "Maybe you got something there."

"Well, maybe so," Spencer acknowledged. "But if you stop here, you might have them on us tonight."

Dan'l shook his head. "They won't start something at the end of the day. They'll want to be fresh. And they'll want to make a last appeal to their gods tonight."

Spencer shrugged. "Oh, hell. Let's do it, then."

It did not take long to make their arrangements. They pulled the wagon along the bank a short distance, until they had a small stand of trees shielding them at thirty yards, and a small rise of ground between them and the trees. They placed the wagon right by the bank, with just ten muddy feet of ground between it and the rushing, brown water. Then Dan'l and Hawkins walked the four horses downstream another two hundred yards, well away from the wagon, and out of sight in a thicket of trees and underbrush. They picketed the animals securely there, and fed them, and then returned to the wagon. The other three had the rifles out and ready, and stacked ammunition on the ground behind the wagon, both for the rifles and the revolvers.

While the others were outside preparing a meal, Spencer found himself alone inside the wagon, and decided to act on an idea that had been tumbling inside his head ever since Dan'l had ridden into camp at noontime with his news of the Sioux. He decided there was no reason for him to be there when the Sioux arrived tomorrow. He would take his chances alone, on a saddled horse. The weather would be better as he headed on east now, and he was certain he could make it to one of the forts in the Missouri territory.

Of course, he would not leave without the gold.

He recalled that, besides Cassidy, there was another member of the party who placed high value on that chest of treasure. Padgett talked every once in a while about what he would be doing with his share, and was always keeping an eye on the small chest at the rear of the wagon.

Dan'l would suspect Cassidy if Spencer used him in his little plan. So he would use Padgett.

"Hey, Padgett!" he called out of the wagon. "Want to give me a hand with this box of primers?"

Padgett was doing nothing special at that moment, so he climbed aboard the wagon, and helped Spencer move the box to the end of the wagon bed. Then Spencer turned to Padgett.

"Don't stumble over that gold when you turn around."

Padgett looked down at it. "I wonder if we'll ever get a chance to enjoy it."

"If them Sioux burn this wagon like they did the other one, it'll be gone, too. Just like the silver was."

Padgett forgot for a moment how he had come to distrust Spencer. "I see what you mean."

"Too bad there ain't a better place for it," Spencer said casually, acting like he was looking for another box.

That set Padgett to thinking. "Hell, we could take it out of the wagon. Hide it somewhere."

Turned away from Padgett, Spencer let a smile curl the corner of his mouth. When he turned back, it was gone.

"You think that might work?" Spencer asked.

"Well, if we should survive them Sioux, it would be a shame if that gold was ruined. And all that valuable jewelry."

"Well, that's true," Spencer said. "I just don't know where we might hide it. It's all pretty open along here, till you get down by the horses." He glanced sideways at Padgett.

"Hell," Padgett said. "Let's just take it down

there. Hide it in the bushes right there. Then if the wagon goes, we still got it."

Spencer arched his brows. "That ain't a bad idea of yours, boy. Maybe you ought to mention it to the others."

"I will," Padgett nodded.

Everything worked out perfectly for Spencer from that moment on. Padgett went to Hawkins first, and Hawkins thought it was a good idea. When they went to Cassidy and Dan'l with it, Cassidy thought little of it since these two were raising the issue, and made no objection. Dan'l was so busy with checking ammo boxes, he hardly paid any attention. The gold was the least of his worries.

So, with Spencer otherwise occupied and acting unconcerned about their doings, engaging Cassidy in conversation about the amount of ammunition they had, Padgett and Hawkins loaded the gold and jewelry into two saddlebags—Spencer had conveniently set the bags on top of the chest to give them the idea—because the bags were easier to seclude in the underbrush. Then they carried the saddlebags down to the stand of trees, and hid them in with the horses.

Some of the gold coins were left behind in the chest, but that did not dismay Spencer when he looked later. Over eighty percent of the wealth of the chest was now ready to be ridden away with.

Now the next phase of his plan had to go right.

There was a lot of talk over the evening meal of how they would meet the attack, if it came in the morning. Their voices were quiet and sober. Cassidy was the only one who now gave any thought to the removal of the gold from the wagon, but even he did not seriously worry about Spencer. It had obviously been the two ex-soldiers who had concocted the idea of hiding it, and where. Anyway, Cassidy's mind was now on the Indians. To be realistic about it, their chances of survival in an all-out attack were slim, indeed.

It was Dan'l who did most of the talking about Sitting Bear.

"He might come before light," Dan'l told them as they huddled around a low fire, still sipping chicory coffee from tin cups. "Hoping we won't be awake."

"We'll have to kill as many of them at long range as we can get a bead on," Spencer said from across the fire. He seemed particularly amiable to Dan'l.

"We won't get in more than a couple shots apiece with the rifles," Padgett said. He was becoming very tense, and wondered how he had been able to even think about the gold, just an hour ago.

"That's why that Annely ammunition is so important," Cassidy said. "We want it all within easy reach."

"Sitting Bear won't quit this time," Dan'l said.

A silence fell over them like a blanket.

"He lost a son to us. I doubt the other one will even be with him. He'll fight to his own death, if necessary."

"What if we kill him?" Hawkins asked.

"That could make some difference in the way they fight," Dan'l guessed. "But I think they'll be geared to a complete massacre, no matter who goes down."

"We're going to need sentries," Spencer said.

Dan'l nodded. "Absolutely. I'll take the two-to-six shift." He knew that was the most important one. And the most dangerous.

Spencer spoke up quickly. "Fine. I'll go to two."

Cassidy looked over at him.

"I could take some of that," Hawkins offered.

"No," Spencer said. "I can't sleep, anyway. You boys try to get some rest for the fighting."

"They might not come tomorrow," Cassidy said.

"They might not come at all," Padgett suggested.

Dan'l shook his head. "They're coming, all right. That scout I killed was wearing Sitting Bear's emblems on his bow. They're right behind us, I'd guess no more than two or three miles. Close enough to get here real quick. I'd guess there ain't no good reason for them to delay anymore. They'll be primed to kill about now."

"They'll want to kill us all, I guess," Padgett said, looking scared.

"Maybe not right away," Dan'l replied. "They'd

probably prefer to take a couple of us alive."

Once again, they fell silent, thinking about that. Hawkins pulled the collar of his coat up close around his chin, against a chill breeze that was moving through the camp.

"It's going to get cold tonight," Hawkins said. "Maybe we'll all freeze to death before they can kill us. Wouldn't that make old Sitting Bear mad as hell?"

They all looked at him seriously, and he stifled the low laugh that had begun in his throat.

"There ain't nobody freezing here this night," Dan'l said. "Our blood is boiling too hard."

They dropped the subject, and Cassidy started talking about St. Louis, and the women there, and Spencer and Padgett joined in to pass the time. Finally, as the fire guttered out, they drifted off to the wagon, one at a time. Dan'l decided to sleep inside with the others until his turn came at sentry, because he would rest better, and he would need to be alert when he took over from Spencer.

Just before ten p.m. Spencer found himself alone in the camp, which was just the way he wanted it. He sat on a stool beside the fire, which he had punched up a bit, listened to the sounds of the others' low voices inside, and watched silhouettes made by the oil lanterns and the canvas cover. Then the lights went out, and the voices died off.

It was very quiet out on the prairie in the middle

of a winter night. There were no crickets or tree frogs to liven the night with their nocturnal music, and even the coyotes were holed up and silent. The only sound that came to Spencer's ears was the rushing water behind the wagon, as the river flowed past in the darkness.

Spencer waited two full hours before he made his move. He rose from the camp stool, walked quietly to the far end of the wagon, and looked inside. Everybody appeared to be asleep.

He had been lucky. Dan'l Boone had been so preoccupied with what was coming that he had not considered the consequences of the re-positioning of the gold.

Spencer filled a canteen with water and hooked it onto his belt. Then he went to a stash of dried meat hanging on the side of the wagon, and stuffed some into his shirt, under his coat. Lastly, he pulled Cassidy's saddle out from under the wagon, slowly, and carried it off away from the wagon.

He looked back at the wagon. He was ready. It had been a big decision, but he knew it was the right one. There might be danger to him out there on the plains, but not as much as when Sitting Bear arrived. And this way he would have the gold. No arguments. No confrontations.

Spencer crept away, the big saddle over his shoulder, and moved quietly downstream to where the horses were picketed. A couple of them guffered nervously at his approach, but he quieted them down.

He threw the saddle down. He had no idea exactly where the two ex-soldiers had hidden the gold, so he began systematically scouring the underbrush nearest the animals, back and forth in the dark, looking and feeling with his hands. It was cold and muddy, and brambles pulled at his clothing. He was just beginning to panic slightly when he spotted the saddlebags. They had been well hidden.

When he tried to pick them up, he was surprised by their weight. It was a struggle to get them over to the horses. He was breathing hard with the effort.

He had a choice of mounts. But whereas Dan'l's appaloosa was a swift riding horse, the team animal Cassidy had been riding was stockier and sturdier, and could bear the extra weight better, over a long ride. So he threw the bags and the saddle over that horse, and fixed it all into place.

He led the mount out of the trees, and into the open. It guffered quietly again. He looked back, and could not even see the wagon in the darkness.

They were still sleeping.

It had worked.

He patted one of the saddlebags, smiled to himself, and climbed aboard the horse. What a bunch of goddamn fools they were. They deserved exactly what he had given them. Cassidy included.

He rode off into the night, downriver.

He would wait to cross at the very best place. By the time Sitting Bear swooped down on the wagon at dawn, he would be fifty or sixty miles gone.

That pleased him very much.

Dan'l woke an hour before the time he was to relieve Spencer, and just out of curiosity, moved to the front of the wagon and peered outside into the cold and blackness.

He squinted and rubbed his eyes.

He did not see Spencer.

Coming fully awake, he climbed to the ground, and walked over to the fire. The camp stool still sat there. Empty. He looked around.

"Spencer?"

No reply. He walked over to the rise of ground before the wagon, and peered out into the night.

"Spencer?"

He turned and stared at the wagon. When he walked back to it, he saw water spilled onto the ground under the water container. Then he looked quickly under the wagon, and saw that Cassidy's saddle was missing.

"I'll be damned." he said quietly.

He went to the front of the wagon and looked in. "Cassidy!"

Cassidy awoke bleary-eyed. "What is it?"

"He's gone," Dan'l said.

Hawkins and Padgett both were awakening, too. "What's the matter?" Padgett asked.

"Spencer?" Cassidy said.

"That's right," Dan'l told him.

Cassidy uttered an obscenity, sat up, and pulled on a big, woolly coat. He jumped down off the wagon, and stood beside Dan'l. "That son of a bitch. Are you sure?"

"I'm sure," Dan'l said. "He took your saddle."

"Son of a *bitch!*" Cassidy swore.

"Is it Spencer?" Hawkins was asking.

"He's gone," Dan'l told them. "Come on, Cassidy. Let's go look at the horses."

They both had the revolvers strapped on. They strode down the riverbank together, side by side, saying nothing until they arrived at the stand of trees.

When they got there, the animals were still acting nervous. Dan'l quieted the appaloosa, and looked around the area. There was light snow on the ground in the trees, and there were obvious tracks of Cassidy's mount, leading away to the east.

Dan'l glanced around in the bushes. "Ain't this where the boys brung the gold?"

Cassidy had already been thinking about the gold. "Yeah. Ten to one it's gone."

Before Dan'l could respond, Hawkins and Padgett came up behind them. Padgett went right to where they had hidden the saddlebags. "It is gone," Padgett said with anger in his voice.

"Son of a bitch," he went on. "I remember now. It was Spencer that got me to worrying over the gold, and thought it should be hid. That bastard!"

"You should've knowed better!" Cassidy said darkly.

"We told you what we were doing," Hawkins reminded him.

Dan'l pointed at the tracks leading away. "You can tell he's got extra weight aboard. See how deep the prints are?"

"He wasn't going to share it, anyway," Cassidy said. "Not from the beginning."

They all stared at him.

"All right, yeah. He told me. Said I would get my cut. But I expected this, I guess."

"Why the hell didn't you tell somebody?" Hawkins said.

Cassidy just looked away. "I'm riding after that goddamn gold!" He jerked a thumb toward the appaloosa. "I'll take the appaloosa. He's faster than the others."

Dan'l turned to him.

"I know it's your mount," Cassidy said. "But I'm doing this for all of us. I'll bring the stuff back here, and we'll split it up."

"Yeah," Padgett said with sarcasm. "And the moon is made of green cheese."

Cassidy got a hard look on his square, bearded face. "I don't give a goddamn what you think, soldier boy. Somebody's got to go stop Spencer, and I elect myself." He went to the appaloosa, and began unpicketing it. "I'll just take the appaloosa to the wagon and throw a saddle on it."

"Hold it," Dan said behind him.

Cassidy turned. The last person in the world he wanted to have a fight with was the Kentuckian. But he was desperate to go after Spencer.

"Yeah?"

"You ain't taking that appaloosa," Dan'l said.

Cassidy looked nettled. "Come on, Boone. I'll pay you fifty dollars for it, if that's what you want. Then you can buy it back when I return here."

"I ain't selling," Dan'l told him.

Tension crackled suddenly in the air between them.

"Damn it, all right! I'll take a team horse, and still catch him!"

Dan'l shook his head. "You couldn't catch Spencer tonight, and probably not tomorrow. He's got too good a start on you. And the farther you track him, the less likely it is you'll want to come clear back here to see whether any of us survived the Sioux."

"So what are you saying?"

"I'm saying we need you right here. And we could need the animals. Going after Spencer is a wild-goose chase. Unless you don't plan on coming back."

Cassidy frowned heavily. "You calling me a liar?"

Dan'l hesitated. "I'm telling you the truth. Whatever your intentions are."

"Well, by God, you don't own this wagon train!" Cassidy blurted out. "I'm taking a horse and going after Spencer!"

He turned to untie the picket rope of the leanest team horse. But Dan'l came up to him, grabbed him by the shoulder, and spun him around.

"Don't make us get into it, Cassidy."

Cassidy was very emotional, though, and had lost some of his reason. Without thinking, he swung hard at Dan'l's chin and connected.

Dan'l went down hard on his back. Cassidy reached for the Annely, but he couldn't get at it. Now Dan'l had his feet under him, and launched himself bodily at Cassidy.

"Jesus!" Hawkins murmured.

Padgett stumbled away from the action.

Dan'l hit Cassidy with his full body weight. They went flying against the nearest team horse and pushed it into a thicket, and it whinnied in panic. The two men fell under its hooves for a moment, and Dan'l was kicked in the side, but just a glancing blow. Cassidy punched wildly at Dan'l's face, and some of the blows landed. They rolled away from the horses, and all three animals were rearing and guffering now, trampling the underbrush.

Dan'l threw a right fist into Cassidy's face and

broke his nose. His own face was bloody, cut at the mouth and also under his left eye. Cassidy's nose was streaming blood now, as they rolled and punched. Finally Dan'l broke free, grabbed Cassidy by his dark wool coat, and pulled him to his feet. Cassidy was wearing out, and already wished he had not started the fight.

Dan'l held Cassidy up close to him, his fist poised again to deliver a final blow. Cassidy was weak in the legs.

"You killed Munro, didn't you, you bastard?"

Cassidy looked into Dan'l's eyes. "You tell me. You got it all figured out, ain't you?"

"You son of a bitch!" Hawkins breathed.

Dan'l threw a last punch into Cassidy's face, and Cassidy went down again. He scrabbled there in the mud, trying to get up, but could not.

"Kill him," Padgett said breathlessly.

"He made me do it," Cassidy said in a thick voice, from the ground. "He would have killed me."

"Goddamn you!" Hawkins said.

"Munro wouldn't have lasted another week, anyway. I wouldn't done it, otherwise."

"That makes it right, you bastard?" Padgett growled.

"Spencer killed the colonel, didn't he?" Dan'l said. His black hat had fallen off, his thick hair was wild, and he looked very dangerous, standing there over Cassidy. Cassidy eyed him fearfully, knowing Dan'l could kill him with his bare hands, if he so chose.

Cassidy nodded. "I had nothing to do with it. But he admitted it to me. Later."

Dan'l shook his shaggy head. "This has been a goddamn nightmare."

"I'll deny what I said about Munro," Cassidy said, sitting up. His face was very bloody.

"Let's kill the son of a bitch now," Padgett said.

Dan'l shook his head. "No. We need him now more than ever. Get on your feet, damn you."

Cassidy struggled to his feet and wiped a hand across his face, smearing the blood. He eyed Dan'l fearfully.

"Now get back to the wagon," Dan'l told him. "It's only a little while till first light, and they might come before that. We got to get ready."

Cassidy made no further protest.

He'd had quite enough of the Kentuckian for one night.

The next couple of hours passed very slowly. They all knew Sitting Bear was coming, and they wanted it to be over with. Stomachs tightened up, and nerves were taut. When Hawkins began considering what the odds were of his survival, he wanted to be on one of those horses just like Cassidy had planned, riding away from there as fast as the animal could carry him. He wished he was in St. Louis, all of this behind him, and he was safe to live out his young life like everybody else. Or better yet, in Boston. Anywhere but here.

Padgett was so scared that his hands had begun shaking slightly as he moved boxes of ammo to where they would be right at hand.

Cassidy and Dan'l tried to keep their minds off it. Cassidy washed his face. His nose was swollen out to his cheeks, but he did not notice much now. Dan'l had swelling at his mouth and under his eye, but forgot completely about those small injuries. In the last hour before dawn, he busied himself with positioning all of them around the wagon, with their backs to the river, and making certain all the guns were in good working order.

The first light on the horizon did not show Sitting Bear's little army, but suddenly it was there, upstream, waiting for the wagon to be silhouetted by the rising sun.

It was Dan'l who spotted them first.

He could hardly make them out, off to the west. But as light continued to flood the sky, the Sioux became visible, stretching along the horizon from the river's edge out about a hundred yards. All mounted. Ready to kill.

"There they are!" Dan'l announced.

They looked past the side of the wagon and regarded their enemy silently. It was clear that there were over fifty of them, all Sitting Bear's best warriors, all devoted to deadly revenge.

Padgett's heart skipped in his chest, and his

palms became sweaty. It was a cold sweat.

"Damn!" Hawkins said softly, his handsome young face grim with tension.

"There's too many," Cassidy said stoically to nobody in particular.

Dan'l glanced over at him. "We ain't dead yet," he said. "So let's not by-God act like it."

"Kind of ironic, ain't it, Boone?" Cassidy responded. "None of what went before means shit now, does it? I mean, it's just us and them Indians now."

Dan'l grunted. "Don't scare the boys, Cassidy."

"Let him talk," Padgett said. "He just makes me mad, and then I can fight better."

"Look," Hawkins said flatly. "They're coming."

Several hundred yards away, a short distance from the river, Sitting Bear was unleashing the first wave of his mounted warriors.

"Death to the defilers!" the grim-faced chief yelled loudly, brandishing a long, decorated lance in the air. "Death to the white face!"

Pale Coyote came up beside him. He was in charge of the second wave. "We will go now, Uncle!"

"May the old gods ride with you!" Sitting Bear replied.

Pale Coyote raised his own lance, and dropped it, and the second wave of warriors rode off with Pale Coyote leading them, yelling and whooping.

Sitting Bear kicked his mount in its sides, and galloped off after them.

As the first warriors arrived at the wagon, the defenders fired their long guns. Each of the four men had hit at least one warrior in the first minute or so of the fighting, and Dan'l had killed three of them in rapid succession, re-loading and priming faster even than Cassidy.

The noise was deafening: the yelling of the attackers, the rapid gunfire blasts, the arrows whining around them, thumping into the wagon and hissing into the muddy river.

The sky was light now, and the defenders were easily visible to their attackers. The Sioux were a bit dismayed to find the wagon so well situated that they could not get behind it and circle it in the way they liked. Not only did the positioning protect the defenders from back-shooting, but it aborted a smooth flow of the attack. Indians would race past the wagon, shoot off a couple of arrows, then have to wheel their mounts around and head back in the opposite direction, over and over again. In doing so, they ran into each other, and a couple of collisions unseated the warriors from their rawhide saddles, leaving them easy targets on the muddy ground. A few rode in a big circle before the wagon, heading out toward the trees, and coming back around again to resume the attack. Some of Sitting Bear's sharpshooters reined in and held a position out by the trees, readying flaming arrows to shoot at the wagon.

"Keep firing!" Dan'l yelled at the others. He was standing at one end of the wagon, and Cassidy at the other. Hawkins and Padgett had taken up positions inside the wagon, behind stacks of boxes and crates, and were firing out of each end of the vehicle.

"I got another one!" Padgett yelled in the melee. "Damn, look at them go down!"

"Shut up, damn it, and keep shooting!" Dan'l ordered. "Hawkins, see if you can hit some of them sharpshooters!"

They were all shooting with the side arms now, because of the proximity of their targets and the guns' fast-firing capability. A lot of Indians were going down, and not one defender had been hit.

A red-painted warrior tried to ride in behind the wagon, past Cassidy, and was shot full in the face. He somersaulted backwards off the horse, falling at Cassidy's feet, and the horse galloped on past the wagon, almost knocking Dan'l over at the other end of it.

Hawkins had picked up a rifle again, and picked off a firebrand shooter at the perimeter of the battle. But two flaming arrows had already hit the wagon, and had set it afire. The wagon blazed brightly, as the battle continued.

Frustrated by the excellent defensive position Dan'l had created for the defenders, two mounted warriors rode recklessly into the river to get behind them. One was caught in the swift, deep water immediately, and both he and his mount were carried away by the roaring current. The second one aimed an arrow at Dan'l's back, but before he could release it, he was also knocked off his horse as the mount went under. Both disappeared from view in the river.

The Indians' numbers had now been reduced by a third, and corpses were scattered before the wagon, the ground rich with spilled blood.

"By Jesus!" Padgett yelled from one end of the wagon. "We're beating them! By God, we're winning!"

An arrow hissed into the wagon and smacked into Padgett's thigh, knocking him onto his back.

"Oh. Oh, damn." He gritted his teeth against the terrible pain. "Hawkins!"

Hawkins looked toward him, and in the next instant, an arrow exploded into the back of his head, behind his left ear, and thrust out through his right eye.

Hawkins rose to his feet, his jaw working, looking with his one eye right at Padgett. He was pointing, as if trying to respond to Padgett.

"Oh, holy God!" Padgett exclaimed dully.

Hawkins took a step forward, then fell onto his face among the crates and boxes in the wagon.

Flames were crackling all around him. Outside, Cassidy brought another Sioux down, then an arrow caught him in the side, below the ribs.

"I'm hit!" he yelled.

"Shit!" Dan'l muttered. "Keep firing if you can!"

Cassidy tried to ignore the arrow sticking through him, and re-primed his Annely. Dan'l felt an arrow graze his right arm and splash into the river behind him.

Padgett saw the flames closing in on him. He dragged himself to the back gate of the wagon, hauled himself up onto it, and then over. He fell onto the ground at the right rear wheel, and Dan'l dragged him to the back side of the wagon, out of sight of the whooping warriors. He then fired his Annely again, knocking another Sioux off his horse.

Dan'l saw that Cassidy had not fired again. He was leaning against the burning wagon, out of the action, trying to remain conscious. Dan'l turned back to the battle, and was hit in the head by an arrow.

The arrow was deflected off his skull, putting a crease in his scalp, but Dan'l went down and out.

It took just moments for the attackers to realize there was no more shooting coming from the wagon. Sitting Bear, looking grim on his white mount just fifty yards away, gave another signal, and his warriors closed in.

The warriors swarmed in, yelping and shouting. They could not board the wagon, because it was burning so hotly. They came in on the defenders from both ends of the wagon, though, and when they saw that all were disabled, they began dismounting with their knives and tomahawks.

Pale Coyote was among them. He had been shot in the right arm, but not badly. One of their seasoned warriors bent over Padgett, who was disabled but wide-eyed now, and took a razor-sharp war knife to Padgett's scalp. Padgett could not fight back. His screams were heard above the celebration of the Sioux. The warrior cut the entire scalp off, ripping it free at the end, and Padgett's eyes saucered even wider, and his cry split the cold air. He no longer resembled the soldier Dan'l had ridden with. The warrior held the scalp aloft, with its dark, slightly curly hair, and let out a loud war whoop.

Cassidy was still conscious, and two warriors were dragging him out in front of the burning wagon to work on him slowly. Another one stood over the scalped Padgett and, seeing he was losing consciousness, drove a lance through Padgett's heart.

Padgett's body jumped when the cold steel entered it, and then lay lifeless.

Another warrior had dragged Dan'l's unconscious form out in front of the wagon, too, but then realized that Dan'l was not conscious. He straddled Dan'l fiercely, looking down into the bearded, rugged face.

"Sheltowee!" he mumbled.

He raised the tomahawk above his head, intent on splitting Dan'l's skull wide open.

Chapter Fourteen

In that moment when the warrior held the tomahawk high above Dan'l's head, visions of greatness flooded through his brain. He would be the one who killed Sheltowee. He would carry the scalp in his belt, and it would later decorate his lodge. Just as he had dreamed, earlier.

He gripped the war hatchet tightly, preparing to bring it down savagely onto Dan'l's face.

"Wait!"

The voice came from over his shoulder. He paused and looked. Pale Coyote was standing there.

"What?" the warrior said in frustration.

"It is Sheltowee. And he is still alive. I saw him move."

Dan'l's eyelids fluttered open, but he could not

focus on what was happening.

"I know that! His scalp is mine!"

Pale Coyote stood face-to-face with him. Nose-to-nose. He was as tall as the warrior, and just as fierce-looking.

"You will not kill him."

"I will kill him! He is my captive! It is the tribal law!"

Suddenly Sitting Bear rode up and dismounted. He looked at the two warriors, then down at Dan'l.

"It is Sheltowee," he said.

"Yes, and he is my prisoner, Great Chief!" the tall warrior said angrily.

"He deserves special consideration, my uncle," Pale Coyote said unemotionally. "I merely ask that we discuss the matter."

Sitting Bear hesitated. "Very well. I see he is coming to life. We will allow him to view the results of the white face's trespass."

Pale Coyote let out a small breath. The other warrior turned and walked away, very frustrated. On the ground, Dan'l focused now on Sitting Bear, then Pale Coyote.

Dan'l sat up unsteadily. He looked around at the carnage, the burning wagon. Then he turned back to the two Sioux. "Looks like we lost one."

Sitting Bear turned to Pale Coyote for translation.

"Sheltowee praises the brave Sitting Bear and his warriors for their great victory."

Sitting Bear narrowed his eyes on his nephew, then looked down at Dan'l. He nodded to Dan'l. "Deal with the other one first. Then you may discuss him."

"Thank you, my chief."

Cassidy had regained consciousness completely. Two warriors were stripping his clothing off as he lay supine on the muddy ground. One of them hurled an obscenity at Cassidy, and Cassidy weakly spat at him.

Pale Coyote held a lance above Dan'l.

"They will kill your comrade. Do nothing. Say nothing. If you do, I must kill you."

Dan'l felt the blood in his hair, and looked up at Pale Coyote. He was very weak and dizzy.

"Do not even move," Pale Coyote said tightly.

The two warriors over Cassidy grabbed his hands and held them out away from his body, and two others came and held his feet, until he was spread-eagled on the ground. Standing nearby, Sitting Bear directed a fifth warrior to go to Cassidy and begin.

Dan'l remembered getting a glimpse of head-shot Hawkins, burning up in the wagon. And he had heard, through his semi-conscious state, the death cries of Padgett.

The fifth warrior stood over Cassidy and stabbed carefully into Cassidy's eyeballs with a long knife. Cassidy shrieked with each wound. Dan'l turned and saw the eyeball fluid running onto Cassidy's cheeks. He had been blinded in just seconds.

Cassidy struggled in their grasp. "You bastards! You goddamn cowards!"

The same warrior grabbed Cassidy's tongue, lopped half of it off, and held it up for the others to see, grinning broadly. Blood ran freely over Cassidy's face, and he was spitting and coughing.

"Damn!" Dan'l murmured. He had seen this kind of thing many times before, but it never failed to disgust him.

"Keep silent!" Pale Coyote hissed at him.

Now another warrior came up to Cassidy. Others had gathered around to watch the killing. Sitting Bear stood off at a short distance, watching, glad that his people had this opportunity to vent their anger.

This second warrior now took a sharp knife and sank its point into Cassidy's hairy chest just below his throat, and then drew it down forcefully toward his groin, opening him up from chin to belly.

Cassidy screamed out in agony as the warrior ripped the flesh aside and dug into Cassidy's innards with his bare hands, pulling out his entrails and spilling them into the mud.

Cassidy's screaming stopped, and he went into shock. His body quivered. Then he lost consciousness. The warrior reached up into his chest cavity, pulled out Cassidy's still-pulsing heart, and held it high.

There was a lot of yelling. The warrior took a bite out of the heart, and smeared his face with its blood. Some of the Sioux began dancing around the new corpse, singing in a monotone.

"Nice friends you got," Dan'l grated out, turning his head away.

Pale Coyote scowled fiercely at him.

Several warriors were gathering around Dan'l, and looking toward Sitting Bear curiously. Dan'l sat there, very sober.

"Get up," Pale Coyote told him.

Dan'l regarded him without expression. Then he climbed awkwardly to his feet. He looked terrible.

"There were five of you," Pale Coyote said. "Where is the fifth man?"

"He run off last night," Dan'l said. "With the gold."

Pale Coyote smiled slightly. "There is no loyalty when the fever strikes."

Dan'l sighed. "Spencer never had none," he said.

Now Sitting Bear came over and spoke to his nephew in their own language. "I remember this man saved your life. But he also violated the Place of Sleeping."

"Yes!" a warrior cried out. "He must die!"

Pale Coyote paused a moment before he spoke. "Sheltowee did not wish to go to the Place of Sleeping. It was the man called Spencer. He has fled with the gold. He has betrayed Sheltowee and the others."

Sitting Bear looked over at Dan'l. He wished he could speak some English. But he had never been good with languages.

"When did this Spencer leave?"

"Last night, in the darkness," Pale Coyote replied. "He will be many hunting grounds to the east, by now. On a riding horse. We would not catch him."

Sitting Bear sighed heavily.

"This man is a great warrior," Pale Coyote argued. "He does not deserve to die like that." He jerked his hand toward Cassidy. "He is a son of Blackfish, the great Shawnee."

Sitting Bear looked over at him. "You suggest we spare him? After what he has done?"

The warrior who had first stood over Dan'l with the tomahawk stepped up, his face filled with anger. "Pale Coyote would violate tribal custom! This captive is mine, to do with as I will!"

Pale Coyote met his dark look. "That is a petty custom. I am speaking of important things, things we must live with forever!"

Dan'l came forward to confront Sitting Bear. "Ask him if he would rather have me or Spencer," Dan'l said to Pale Coyote.

"Keep your silence!" Pale Coyote commanded him.

"Ask him," Dan'l insisted.

Pale Coyote turned to Sitting Bear and repeated the question. Sitting Bear and the entire assemblage of warriors stood silent for a long moment.

"How may I make the suggested trade?" Sitting Bear said to his nephew.

Pale Coyote translated, and Dan'l nodded. His head pounded with raw pain, and he felt as if he might collapse at any moment. "If I live, I will go after the man named Spencer. The man who killed two of our own party, and stole from them. The man who took us to the Place of Sleeping, against my advice. I will go after him and kill him."

Pale Coyote stared long at Dan'l, then turned to his uncle and repeated the summary in Siouan. Sitting Bear listened patiently. But before he could respond to Dan'l, the big warrior came between them.

"These are all lies! He just wants to save his miserable white skin! I will kill him! It is my right!"

Pale Coyote felt a great debt of gratitude to Dan'l. He cast a diamond-hard look at the other warrior. "You will do as you are told!"

Another warrior came up behind the tall one, war hatchet raised to strike. Mere *akicita* soldiers did not speak to noble personages like Pale Coyote in this manner, and live to brag about it.

But Sitting Bear waved him off.

"If you wish to defend this man, do so," the chief said expressionlessly to Pale Coyote.

Pale Coyote gave him a sober look, then turned to the tall warrior. "Very well. Take your prisoner if you can."

The tall warrior now hesitated. He did not want a fight with the chief's nephew. But he raised the tomahawk dramatically.

"I accept the challenge!" he said.

Pale Coyote was armed only with a war knife, and he was still healing from the wounds he had received at the first battle. But he was a clever fighter, and all present knew it.

The tall man struck out with the hatchet. Pale Coyote stepped aside fluidly, and the blade grazed his arm.

"Hell, don't do this!" Dan'l grunted.

But nobody paid any attention. Pale Coyote stabbed forward with the knife, and it cut a shallow wound into the other man's side. There were some mutterings among those watching. All were there, except for some warriors who were now looting the burnt wagon, and a few others who were out looking for the horses.

The tall Sioux brought the tomahawk down toward Pale Coyote's head in a fierce swing. Pale Coyote caught the hand with the weapon and neatly stabbed under it. The knife sank to its hilt in the tall warrior's belly.

The warrior grabbed at himself as if snakebitten, his eyes widening, and then he fell to his knees in the mud, crimson seeping between his fingers over the deep and fatal wound. With his last strength, he hurled the hatchet at Dan'l. It sailed wildly past Dan'l's head, and hit the ground well beyond him.

The warrior fell onto his face at Pale Coyote's feet.

"Christ," Dan'l muttered.

"What did he say?" Sitting Bear asked Pale Coyote.

Pale Coyote's arm was bleeding, but not badly. He did not seem to notice it. He was breathing shallowly.

"He said, Uncle, that he regrets our brother's death," Pale Coyote said quietly.

Sitting Bear narrowed his dark eyes on Dan'l. "Why did you come here, Sheltowee?"

After a translation by Pale Coyote, Dan'l replied. "We came to make maps of the Great Plains. And to see whether farming could be done here."

"This is Sioux hunting ground," Sitting Bear countered, after the translation.

"We hoped the Sioux and white man could live together in this wide land," Dan'l finally told him.

"We do not believe the Apache legend," the chief said.

"Nor do I," Dan'l assured him.

"We do not think you are an ancient god."

"You're very right."

Sitting Bear waited a long time after that translated exchange, with Pale Coyote watching his face after each reply. Dan'l waited now, too.

"You will kill the man Spencer?" Sitting Bear finally asked him.

Pale Coyote repeated. Dan'l nodded. "If I catch him, I will. He crossed a line. There ain't no going back for him. And there ain't nobody to do it but me."

"What would you do with the gold?"

Dan'l thought that one over for a long moment. "There won't be nobody to give it to. And it don't mean much to you. I guess I'd give some to these boys' relatives. Maybe keep a little myself."

Sitting Bear liked the honesty of the answer. He found himself smiling a wan smile.

"You have heart, Sheltowee."

"Very little, beside the great Sitting Bear," Dan'l said.

"Where are your horses?" the chief asked.

When Pale Coyote translated, Dan'l sighed. "They're down the river in that bunch of trees."

The chief, Pale Coyote, and several warriors looked in that direction.

"There are three animals. I'd need the appaloosa," Dan'l said.

"He will require the spotted horse," Pale Coyote told the chief. "We may have the other two."

Sitting Bear nodded. "You may live, Sheltowee. I will trade your life for the hope of your killing the man Spencer."

"I'm much obliged," Dan'l said humbly.

"You may have your guns also."

There was a lot of muttering among the warriors, and a couple of them walked away to show their disappointment. Pale Coyote let out a long breath. He knew they had done the honorable thing.

"Let me ask you a question, Sheltowee," the chief added, after a moment.

Pale Coyote translated, and watched Dan'l nod.

"Is it true you are the adopted son of Chief Blackfish, and that he made you his own to replace the thousand Shawnee of his tribe you had killed bravely in battle?"

Dan'l listened with interest to the English version, and then shook his head slowly. "Stories become greater than reality, Chief Sitting Bear. I have killed Shawnee, but not so many. And I did not accept Blackfish as my father. He kept me as a prisoner, and I escaped only because of his trust in me that I would not leave him. But I had to return to my own people."

"You are an honest man, Sheltowee. And a great warrior. Go and find the defiler, and avenge our humiliation."

"I will do my best, Great Chief."

Sitting Bear returned to his warriors, and gave them instructions about riding back to their village. Dan'l and Pale Coyote found Dan'l's saddle under the wagon, charred but usable. The Kentucky rifle was also intact, and he located the Annely revolver where he had dropped it. Pale Coyote helped him with all of that, and some ammunition, and they walked to the trees downriver. Pale Coyote took possession of the two team horses while Dan'l saddled the appaloosa and slid the rifle into its saddle scabbard.

He was ready to ride. He was no longer seeing double, and his aches and pains were bearable. He was a lot better off than poor Cassidy, or the two ex-soldiers.

Dan'l climbed aboard the appaloosa and looked down at Pale Coyote.

"You saved my life. I won't never forget it."

Pale Coyote nodded to him. "Ride to the east, Sheltowee. Be among your own people. If you return to Sioux territory, I cannot guarantee your safety."

Dan'l secured the flat black hat onto his tousled head, and even that hurt. "I understand."

"Good-bye, Sheltowee. May the gods ride with you."

Dan'l grinned stiffly. "I couldn't ask for more than that," he said.

Then he rode off downriver.

Chapter Fifteen

The next morning was bitter cold.

Spencer had camped late after a long first day out from the wagon, and now rose groggy and tired.

But nobody had come after him, he figured. He had made excellent time and had ridden long hours, so he reckoned he had made it. His little plan had worked, and he alone had the Spanish gold.

He had no way of knowing that everyone at the wagon was dead, except for Dan'l, whose life had been spared only so he might track Spencer down. Spencer did not care whether the Sioux had attacked, or who had lived or died. If the Sioux killed everybody, that was better for him. If they had not, the expedition would never catch him, anyway. He would head for St. Louis first, he had decided, but stay there only long enough to buy supplies. Then he would head on down the Mississippi to New Orleans, where there were people he could sell the gold and jewelry to. There were a lot of ways to spend money in New Orleans. He would find all of them.

Spencer decided that Dan'l Boone was the only one of the expedition he had to concern himself with, in the event he somehow survived the Sioux. If Dan'l got back to St. Louis, he might try to find Spencer there. But he would never think of traveling to other towns to look for him.

The Kentuckian was not Sitting Bear.

He had other things to do with his life.

Spencer donned his wool coat that cold morning, saddled up, and headed out early, just before light broke in the east. He could not be absolutely sure that Dan'l was not back there somewhere, tracking him like a Comanche. So he would continue to ride hard for the next couple of days until he got into Missouri territory. He would be safe then.

The heavy saddlebags were once again decorating the big stallion's flanks, and they were very heavy, so the horse was still tired from the previous day's hard ride. Spencer did not concern himself much with horses, though. He figured the animal could do whatever he asked of it, if he forced it.

Spencer had had only hardtack and coffee for his light breakfast, but he was not hungry, anyway. Hunger was not a factor at that point. And he felt no fatigue, because he was so determined to put distance between himself and the Davison wagon.

He rode into some hills on that second day. There had been a snowfall in the night, so the ground was covered with the white stuff. The roan stallion plowed through some rather heavy drifts in the early morning, and that tired it some more, so the going was slow. Spencer spurred the animal relentlessly, and the horse responded.

In late morning, he saw a snowshoe rabbit, and slid the long rifle from its irons, but by the time he was primed and ready to shoot, the rabbit had disappeared.

"Damn the luck," he mumbled to himself. He had begun talking out loud to himself, just to hear a human voice. Sometimes, out there, a man lost faith in the notion that there was anybody else out there in the whole world besides himself.

It was a lonely feeling.

"Come on, horse. We got to keep moving."

At midday he came to a deep stream.

It was not frozen over, and the water was swift. It was thirty yards across, and there appeared to be no easy place to ford it.

"Well, we'll do it here," he told the horse, his breath fogging with each word.

The mount guffered in response, nervous about the water.

Spencer sat on the horse and recalled all he had had to do to get this far. It had all started with Davison. If he had not killed Davison, none of this could have happened. The colonel would not have gone to the ravine. His stupidity had almost spoiled it from the beginning. But now Spencer was almost home free. Only patience was required.

He spurred the horse forward, and it walked into the icy water. Spencer felt the water on his feet, and then his lower legs. There was no way to see exactly how deep the stream was at its deepest point.

The horse stopped, more nervous with the cold water rushing against its belly.

"Come on, you goddamn baby!" Spencer shouted at his mount. "You afraid of the cold?"

The horse made a small blustering sound, and plowed on. Five feet further. Ten. The middle of the stream was just within reach.

The current pulled the horse slightly sideways, and its legs suddenly buckled under the pressure and the weight on its back. It lost its footing, slipped in deeper, and suddenly was swimming downstream, flailing in the water.

"Son of a bitch!" Spencer yelled.

The horse tipped over in the water, and Spencer

slipped off the saddle and went in, still holding the reins.

Spencer grabbed at the saddle, sputtering obscenities, trying to keep his head above water. The saddlebag beside him slid downward, and that panicked Spencer. He grabbed it tightly with one hand, the other clutching at the saddle.

"You idiot animal!" Spencer gasped.

The horse started swimming for the far bank, and was making some headway slowly. Spencer held on for dear life, and finally saw the shore ahead of them. The horse came out of the deep water, and was walking awkwardly again. A few moments later it emerged from shallow water, eyes bulging, still scared, dragging Spencer with it.

Spencer released his hold on the saddle and slumped to the ground in light snow. The horse walked a few steps away, shook itself off, and stood there looking miserable.

Spencer saw the saddlebags were hanging very low on his side of the horse, and had almost fallen into the river. He lay there soaking wet, icy cold despite the wool coat, and shook his head slowly.

"I should've took the appaloosa, you goddamn weasel!"

The horse turned to look at him pitifully.

Spencer sat up weakly, breathing hard. He pulled his Annely from his belt, and aimed it at the horse's head. "I ought to blow that goddamn pea brain out of your head!"

The horse turned away, shivering.

Spencer got to his feet, walked to the horse, and slugged it across its nose. It whinnied and ran away a few steps, looking back at him.

"Goddamn you!" Spencer yelled.

He stood there assessing the situation. He would have to undress and wring the water out of his clothing. The sun was coming out now, so maybe he could get them mostly dry by just wearing them. But all of that would take time, as would re-adjusting the saddlery. It was after noon now, and it was clear that he had lost the rest of the day for travel.

He had lost valuable time.

Well, he thought, he had saved the gold. And himself. And he still had the goddamn horse. So maybe it was not so bad, after all. He would build a good fire, get warmed up, and try to get a good rest.

It was his only choice.

It was unlikely there was anybody back there, anyway.

He would not even think about it.

Dan'l had found it easy to track Spencer on that first day. But the snowfall that night had obliterated Spencer's trail, and it had become very difficult to pick up spoor.

Now, on the second day, the going was difficult,

and it was late afternoon when Dan'l finally picked up the tracks in the fresh snow, starting at Spencer's last encampment. He gained some time then, riding several hours more, until dark.

When he stopped, he figured he was only a couple of hours behind Spencer. The tracks were fairly fresh.

Dan'l came to a steep hill, and when he inspected it closely, he saw a cave at its base, almost head-high at the entrance. A cold wind had come up again, and Dan'l decided that this would be a good place to get out of it. He picketed the appaloosa close to the entrance, in some bare trees, hanging its irons on a stiff branch. Then he took his rifle and crawled into the cave.

It was a good twenty feet deep, with boulders on its floor, dark, hulking shapes in the dark. There was a musky smell of animals. But Dan'l could see or hear nothing to concern him.

He found a flat place near the entrance, put a bedroll down, and laid his head on it. It was much warmer in there than it would have been out in the wind. Dan'l fell asleep in his bearskin coat.

It was a good sleep that night. He dreamed he was back in Kentucky, in Boonesborough, in bed with Rebecca, and his children were sleeping in the next room, and all was right with the world. He said Rebecca's name a couple of times in his sleep.

The night passed uneventfully.

Then came morning.

When Dan'l woke, the bear was standing over him.

Smelling him curiously.

Its face was inches from Dan'l's.

"Damn!" he cried out, still half-asleep. His right hand went automatically to the rifle at his side, which was loaded and primed.

This bear had been in the cave all night with him. It had been one of the dark forms in the night that he had thought was just another boulder. Because of the wind at the entrance, Dan'l had not heard the bear breathing.

The bear reared on its hind legs, and its head touched the ceiling of the cave. It was as shocked as Dan'l to find a living man in the cave with it. It roared loudly in his face, the sound reverberating in the cave.

Dan'l scrambled away a few feet, and got the muzzle of the gun between him and the bear. There was some light from outside, and the bear looked mountainous, but Dan'l realized immediately that he had had some luck. It was not a grizzly, like the one that had attacked the wagon camp earlier. This was a brown bear, and much less ferocious than its cousin.

But it stood exactly between Dan'l and the cave entrance.

This bear was not as big as the grizzly, nor as aggressive. If it had been a grizzly, Dan'l figured he would have been dead. But this bear was big enough and deadly enough to kill him in a moment, if it decided to.

Dan'l rose slowly to his feet, taking the rifle with him. He did not want to shoot. That would bring the bear down on him, and it could inflict severe wounds or kill him, even with a dead center hit in its chest.

Dan'l opened his mouth and let out a roar of his own, but a lesser one than the bear's. It came rolling out of his throat like a loud growl, and the bear listened silently, still in an attack position.

Dan'l lowered himself onto one knee, the rifle ready to fire, showing the bear he was prepared to fight, but was not inviting a battle.

The bear growled menacingly, but dropped down to all fours. It kicked dirt at Dan'l, and Dan'l held his ground. Dan'l got off his knee, and edged around to his right. The bear took the cue, and moved warily to its right, away from Dan'l, edging back into its den, letting Dan'l move carefully toward the entrance.

The bear growled fiercely, moved to the rear of the cave, and faced Dan'l again. Dan'l sidled on to the entrance, and backed out of the cave, into early sunlight.

Dan'l lowered the rifle and found that sweat had broken out on his face, despite the cold. He could feel a trickle of it run down from under his right arm, under his clothing.

"Damn," he muttered as he backed away from the cave.

He had slept all night, he figured, with the bear. When morning came, because Dan'l was wearing a bearskin coat, the bear had been confused when it found him there.

He had been extremely lucky.

He walked over to the small trees, and the horse was still there, very nervous. He was lucky again.

It took just moments to saddle up and get out of there. He did not want to wait for the bear to change its mind.

Dan'l found Spencer's trail easily again, and rode hard for a while, expecting to catch up with the killer within hours. When he did, he knew it would be him or Spencer. One of them would not walk away from the confrontation. There was too much at stake on both sides.

The trail became fresher as the sun rose in the sky, melting off a lot of snow. When Dan'l had begun his ride, every branch of every tree was laden with a fluffy white trim, sparkling pristine in the morning sun, giving a fairyland look to the hilly countryside. The snow underfoot had crusted, and it reflected like glass in the early hours, making him squint hard against its glare. But now it was melting away, and the muddy ground was showing in places.

Dan'l pushed the appaloosa hard. He knew that Spencer would be doing the same with the other stallion, and Dan'l had to catch up with him, not just keep pace. When he came to bare ground, he would spur the appaloosa into an easy gallop until he ran into deeper snow again.

In mid-morning Spencer's tracks became very fresh, with snow melting into them. Dan'l realized that he was just behind Spencer, and tensed up inside. When Spencer found out Dan'l was back here, he would surely try to kill him, knowing that when he did he would have no other opposition to his well-laid plans. He could tell whatever story he pleased in St. Louis, and there would be nobody to contradict him. He could say that Dan'l had killed Davison and Munro. Or anything.

Dan'l slid the rifle from its moorings as he saw that he was heading into high, rocky terrain for a while. A perfect terrain for an ambush by Spencer.

It was just a half hour later that Spencer spurred his mount up onto a high crest, with snowcapped boulders all around him, and turned to examine his own trail.

His face changed dramatically.

"Goddamn it!" he swore.

There was a black dot back there, against the snow. It was a horse and rider, coming on fast.

Spencer could tell by the way the rider moved the horse forward that it was the Kentuckian.

Spencer had convinced himself that nobody would be coming after him, so he had taken his time in leaving his camp, warming up by his fire, trying to get the chill off from the river dunking, making sure his clothing was dry.

Spencer guided the horse behind a boulder, then dismounted and looked again on foot. Yes, it was Dan'l Boone, all right. But he apparently had not spotted Spencer yet.

"All right, you son of a bitch," Spencer said aloud. "If this is the way you want it. You can ride into my gun. Then that'll be the end of it. For good."

He slid his Heinrich rifle from its case, and loaded and primed it. Now Dan'l was just a half mile away, and coming on hard. Watching the ground. Spencer laid the rifle on the boulder before him, after knocking the snow away. He would have just one surprise shot, so he could not miss. He would wait until Dan'l was close. He would aim for center chest. Then it would be over. Spencer figured the others of the Davison party had been killed by the Sioux; otherwise Cassidy would be with Dan'l.

The Kentuckian was the last of them.

And he was in Spencer's sights.

Back on Spencer's trail, a quarter mile downhill from the boulder Spencer hid behind, Dan'l reined in. He thought he had heard a horse up there in the rocks. It was a sound that most men would have missed. But Dan'l was accustomed to listening for faint sounds, and seeing things other men did not see. That was how he had stayed alive so long.

He studied the rocks and snow, and saw nothing. But Spencer's trail led right into the boulders. He was up there ahead somewhere, and Dan'l figured he was not far away. He readied his Kentucky rifle. He could feel Spencer's eyes on him, but could not see him.

Dan'l spurred the appaloosa forward, holding the long gun across his saddle. The mount stepped into deep snow, and reacted in fright, throwing its head upward. Dan'l heard hot lead crack into the animal's forehead instead of his chest, and then the loud explosion of the Heinrich.

The appaloosa dropped under Dan'l like a chunk of stone, and fell partially onto Dan'l's legs.

Dan'l swore softly, pinned momentarily by the weight of his mount. The horse was dead, and had been so before it hit the ground. Dan'l looked toward the big boulder, and saw Spencer move out from behind it, trying to see whether he had hit Dan'l. Spencer was frantically re-loading now, and his gold-laden mount had wandered out from behind the boulder. Dan'l shook snow off his rifle, and raised its muzzle with one hand. Spencer was cocking and aiming his own long gun, but before he could fire, Dan'l squeezed off a round.

Up on the hill, Spencer yelled and grabbed at his side. The round ball had struck him under his left arm, but had not penetrated. It had cracked a rib and ricocheted off. Spencer fell to the snow, holding his side. He looked at the wound, and saw it was not bad. But in that same moment, his frightened horse ran off into the rocks.

"Come back here, you dumb sack of shit!" Spencer yelled after it.

But the horse disappeared from sight, up beyond a rock outcropping.

Spencer realized he was suddenly on foot.

Down the hill, Dan'l finally wriggled loose from the fallen appaloosa. His legs were bruised, but no bones were broken. He rose to his feet and realized that he would be dead, or dying, if that hot lead had hit him.

Spencer was on his feet, too, and holding his side. He cupped his hands to his mouth, and yelled at Dan'l.

"Let it go, Boone! While you still can!"

Dan'l shook his shaggy head. "I'm coming, Spencer! Make your peace with yourself!"

Spencer was ready to fire again. He raised the muzzle of the Heinrich to get off a second shot. Dan'l dived for the appaloosa's corpse, and hit the ground just as Spencer fired. The lead thumped into the horse's rump harmlessly.

"I'm warning you, Boone!"

Spencer headed farther up into the rocky terrain, on foot, going after his horse. He knew that if he could find it before Dan'l caught up with him, it would all be over. He could either kill Dan'l from a distance or leave him out there to starve to death. Either way, the hunter would never be a threat to him again.

Dan'l re-loaded the rifle as he watched Spencer disappear into the rocks; then he checked his ammo pouch to make sure he was not out. A moment later he moved on uphill.

Spencer quickly learned that his horse had run so far ahead that it would not be a factor in the confrontation with Dan'l, so he steeled himself to having a shootout on foot with perhaps the best shot he had ever met. That meant he had to be smart to survive. Cunning.

He had to outwit the Kentuckian.

Dan'l came into the rocks slowly, watching every rock and shrub. The snow was three to four inches deep there, and Spencer's tracks were obvious. Dan'l carried the rifle at ready. He had been known to drop deer and antelope by just quickly raising the muzzle and firing, without ever getting the stock to his shoulder. With a careful aim, he had hit targets as small as a silver dollar at a hundred yards.

Spencer knew all that. The one man he had not wanted after him was Dan'l Boone. But now he had to deal with that fact, and immediately. Still up ahead of Dan'l by two hundred yards, he decided on a plan. He came to a wide opening in the rocks that extended for fifty yards ahead of him.

Instead of heading right through it, he turned off to his right, making obvious tracks. Then, he would go up farther and cross the opening beyond Dan'l's sight.

In just minutes, Dan'l arrived. As he saw Spencer's trail turn right abruptly, his brow furrowed. He looked in the direction of the tracks, then up ahead, at the clearing with no tracks in it. And in that moment, he knew he was in Spencer's sights.

The sun was out, and just as he threw himself to his left and rock cover, he caught the glint of gunmetal up ahead. The long gun exploded loudly and reverberated in the boulders, and Dan'l felt a stinging at the side of his neck, and knew he had been grazed. He had hit the rocks hard, and was further bruised by them. He felt blood trickling down his neck, and swore under his breath.

"Sorry, Spencer! You missed, you bastard!"

Spencer was furious with himself. He had had a clear shot, but had waited too long, wanting to be sure of a kill. If it had been Padgett in his sights, or even Cassidy, he would have done it right, he knew, and that made him even angrier. His fear of the Kentuckian had prevented his killing him.

Spencer scrambled away awkwardly between boulders, in deeper snow, trying to put some distance between himself and Dan'l. He had forgotten his mount for the moment. All he wanted now was to survive the next half hour.

Dan'l came out into the open when he heard the

noise of Spencer's leaving, and got a glimpse of him running back into the clearing. Dan'l took aim, but Spencer was hidden from view by the rise of ground.

Dan'l slogged through the snow after him, watching all around himself. His head was still throbbing with pain from the wound at the wagon, and he still had dizzy spells. But he ignored all of that, and his stiff shoulder, and an arm wound, and now the blood at his neck. He plowed ahead like a bull, knowing in his head that he could outlast Spencer, if he just did not let Spencer kill him in an unguarded moment.

Dan'l gained on Spencer as they charged through the rocky area and crested it a half mile farther along. Spencer's legs had gone weak now, and as he entered a deep-snow area, they started giving out on him. He finally fell on his face into the snow, and his rifle was momentarily buried in a deep drift. Then he heard the sound behind him.

He turned quickly, breathless, and saw Dan'l standing just thirty feet away, the long gun in hand and ready to fire.

Spencer frantically reached for his rifle, and as he did so, he saw Dan'l raise the level of the Kentucky gun.

Spencer froze in place.

"Wait!"

Dan'l just stood there, stone-faced. "What for, you son of a bitch?"

Spencer thought fast. "I—know where the stallion run off to. It has the gold on its irons."

"So?"

"You don't want to go back empty-handed, do you?"

Dan'l stared hard at the thickset figure in the snow, with its broken nose, balding pate, and evil eyes. He wondered why Davison had ever hired him.

"I don't care about the goddamn gold," Dan'l growled at him. He raised the muzzle again.

"We can be partners!" Spencer said quickly. "An even split! But you won't know where to find the animal!"

Dan'l's finger tightened over the trigger.

Spencer threw the long gun away from him. "Look! I'm unarmed! You going to shoot me down in cold blood?"

"You got some other way in mind?" Dan'l said.

"We'll find the horse together. You can have all the gold. I mean it. You can truss me up and take me into St. Louis for trial. That's fair, ain't it?"

Dan'l sighed. He had never shot a man like this in his life. And Spencer was right. He could take him to the law without much trouble.

He lowered the muzzle of the gun.

"You goddamn whimpering coward. Get on your feet."

Something released its hold on Spencer, deep

inside him. He tried a grin, and rose clumsily from the snow.

"You won't be sorry about this, Boone. You'll be rich."

"We need that mount to get clear of here," Dan'l said. "Now, where did it go?"

Spencer pointed to the south. "It run off in that direction. We can find it in an hour or two, I'm sure."

Dan'l shook his head slowly. "All right. You stand right there."

Spencer nodded, and Dan'l turned to retrieve Spencer's rifle, a few feet away in the snow. As soon as he turned, he heard Spencer go for the Annely at his side. The weapon was primed and ready. As Dan'l heard the cocking sound, he turned and saw the side arm aimed at his face.

Dan'l pulled off a round without aiming, and the explosion pounded in their ears. The hot ball of lead punched Spencer in center chest, popped his heart, and shattered a posterior rib on exiting his back. Spencer's gun also went off, and blew a small hole in Dan'l's hat, but did not touch him.

Spencer had been blown off his feet, and dropped like a potato sack in the snow, arms and legs apart, eyes bugging out as he realized what had happened to him. His jaw worked silently twice, and he died there, the look of surprise still on his hard face.

"You stupid bastard," Dan'l said, standing over

him. "You could've lived. Till they put a rope around your neck in St. Louis."

Spencer's eyes were glazing over. He had gambled with Dan'l and lost, and he had paid the ultimate price.

Dan'l let out a long sigh and looked around. There was no sign of the stallion. If it had run south, as Spencer had said, it would pass over a lot of rock, and be almost impossible to track. And it could be miles away by now.

The fact was, Dan'l had to accept the idea that he was once again on foot in the wilderness. But this time he was perhaps a hundred miles or more from the nearest settlement. In the beginning of winter.

It did not look good.

Dan'l took the ammo pouches off Spencer's belt, and stuffed Spencer's Annely into his own belt. There was nothing else Dan'l could use. He turned without another glance at Davison's killer, and headed to the crest of the rocky hill, through untrodden snow.

When he got up there, he got a pleasant surprise.

Just a hundred yards away stood the stallion. Fully equipped, and with the saddlebags filled with Spanish treasure on its irons.

"Damn!" Dan'l said quietly.

The horse guffered at him and just stood there.

Dan'l made some low whistling sounds, and

walked slowly toward the animal. It shied away for a few steps, then held its ground. In another few minutes, Dan'l had its reins in his hand.

"Now ain't this nice," he said to it. "Looks like them Sioux gods is smiling on both of us today."

The horse threw its head toward him gently, showing its acceptance of him. It smelled his familiar smell, and that of the appaloosa, and felt assured that all was well.

Dan'l stuffed his rifle into the scabbard on its irons and boarded the animal. He patted it on its neck, then looked down at the saddlebags, stuffed with riches.

"Well, let's get on back to St. Louis," he told it quietly. "We got us some living to do."